EMERGENCE

First published in Australia by Harbour Publishing House 2018
This edition published in Australia by Marita Smith 2022

Text Copyright © Marita Smith

www.maritasmithauthor.com

The moral rights of the writer have been asserted.

This is a work of fiction.

Graphic Design by Design For Days

Cataloguing-in-Publication entry is available from the National Library of Australia
catalogue.nla.gov.au

Author: Marita Smith
Book Title: Emergence
Series: Kindred Ties
Number: Book Two
ISBN: 978-0-6456821-2-0
Subject: Science Fiction

KINDRED TIES
BOOK TWO

EMERGENCE

MARITA SMITH

"If you want to find the secrets of the universe, think in terms of energy, frequency and vibration."

— Nikola Tesla

To my dear friend Ayumi, who read every draft.

1

Shock Tactics

Ariana pulled at her restraints, metal biting into her wrists as she struggled for breath. The electrodes plastered to her chest and scalp burned, each one like a red-hot poker. Head pounding, she lifted her gaze to the reinforced glass wall. Robyn and the earthship felt like a once familiar dream beginning to fade. Even memories of her brother's face were starting to blur, leaving a sickening feeling in the pit of her stomach.

Fang and Derek stood watching her, surrounded by a retinue of scientists and glinting machines. Derek leaned forward and pressed the intercom. It crackled in the eerie stillness of the chamber. "Once more."

Ariana shook her head. "Derek, please –"

Current flooded her body. The pain locked her jaw, sending her muscles into fiery spasms. Her entire body felt on fire, every nerve ending pushed to breaking point. Blood pounded in her ears, a scream ricocheting through her skull. A tiny bronze-speckled salamander writhed in a small cage beside her. The sight of him sent fat tears streaking down her cheeks.

Jericho, she thought.

Blue light skimmed across her limbs, brightening as it encased her body in a vibrant electric sphere. The pain dulled as the spirit energy washed through her. Ariana closed her eyes and let it fill her mind and body. Calm descended on her in a wave.

I am here. The salamander's voice caressed her mind.

I don't know how much more I can take.

They want to understand your aura, little one. They want to use its power.

Ariana opened her eyes. Derek and Fang stood rooted to the spot, staring at her as the blue light flickered outward, tendrils raking the walls. Fang raised the receiver and the blue light halted, rushing back towards Ariana. The chip at the base of her skull throbbed as it interrupted the flow of energy. She felt nothing; riding out the pain as if she were outside her body. Ariana catalogued the red gashes on her wrists and ankles, the burns left by the electrodes, as Jericho twitched then lay still.

It lasted only a heartbeat.

The electrodes pulsed again and Ariana jerked, gasping for breath and rattling her restraints. Sparks jumped from her skin into the air. When she looked up again, Derek was watching her, a momentary flicker of pain on his face.

The heavy door swung open to reveal three scientists. As they wheeled Jericho away, Ariana reached out for the touch of the salamander's mind but felt nothing. She heard the familiar snap as the wheelchair was unfolded behind her, then slumped into it as her restraints clicked open. Eyes glazed and head pounding, she tried desperately to take note of her surroundings, looking for anything she could use to escape, but the room was bare. Ariana clung to the wheelchair as she was trundled through the door into the clinical corridor. The harsh fluorescent lights blurred as her vision clouded. She tried to keep her eyes open, but darkness claimed her.

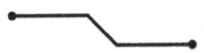

Fang leaned over the monitor looking at the zigzag lines on the screen. "Her heart shouldn't be able to handle such a strong electrical current. Yet that's precisely what triggers the energy response."

"Her aura," Derek clarified. "And she can produce it without stimulus."

Fang glanced over her shoulder at Derek, eyes like daggers. "Co-operation was not forthcoming. We tried saying *please*. The inducement is necessary." Fang flicked to another readout. "Her heart actually stopped for a moment today. Interesting."

"What?" Derek scrambled forwards to read the data over Fang's shoulder. Ariana's cries seared into his memory. *Derek, please.* His legs trembled as he replayed the betrayal in her eyes. *She doesn't understand how important this is*, he told himself.

Fang clicked her fingers and two scientists turned. "Compare today's session against the last two weeks. I want a breakdown of incremental gains on my desk by tomorrow." She turned back to Derek. "Life endangerment triggers the activation of her energy response. She seems to gather energy from thin air. It's unbelievable."

"We've talked about this. She doesn't just conjure it up from nowhere – it comes from a parallel world, a place she and the other walkers call the *spirit world*." Derek rubbed his temples. He remembered the first time he met Fletcher the earth walker and his bear, Eva, when he too was stunned by the walker's supernatural powers. Robyn, Terence and Catherine had readily believed in the existence of the spirit world and had never probed to discover the limits of the walkers' powers. He'd always thought that was a mistake.

Fang waved a hand in dismissal. "Miranda clung to superstitions, too. Every observable phenomenon has a scientific explanation. We just haven't found it yet."

"I'm not saying the spirit world exists," Derek retorted. "But Fletcher, Ariana and Eli – they draw on some strange energy source. You keep reactivating the chip too soon." Derek turned away from Fang as he spoke, eyeing the empty shock chamber. He wanted to find a rational scientific explanation. *Even if it comes at the cost of torturing an innocent sixteen year old girl?* He closed his eyes, pushing Ariana's pain out of his mind. The only time the walkers had been able to summon a vast amount of energy, they'd been in mortal danger. *This is the only way.*

Fang leaned over and touched his shoulder as if she'd read his thoughts. Derek almost flinched at the sudden tenderness. "Derek, I've seen what the girl can do. I'm not about to give her free rein of this power, or she could rip even this specially designed chamber apart. I'm not going to risk it, Derek, and that's final."

Derek nodded and turned on his heel. "I'll be in the command centre if you need me." He didn't want to stay in the shock chamber a moment longer than necessary. Fang seemed determined to ignore his input. He should have known Fang wouldn't listen to him, even though he'd spent countless hours observing the walkers. He thought of Fletcher shimmering with green energy, Eva wreathed in it by his side. Eli the air walker's aura was red, the colour of an ageing supergiant star. The energy they summoned was tangible, measurable. There had to be a way to figure out how they did it. Fang's icy calm as she dismissed his ideas made him want to reach out and shake her.

Fang turned back to the monitor. Faint sparks still arced through the chamber beyond the glass. Ariana's chromatograms were exactly the same as Fletcher's and Eli's. Irritation rippled through her at Derek's presumptuous criticism. There were times she questioned the decision to allow Derek to join them at the new MRI base in Bulgaria. His time among Robyn and the others gave her a niggling doubt as to his loyalty.

She wondered whether Miranda would approve of his presence and their experiments. Not that it mattered. Vulcan was now in charge, and he wanted results, so results he would get. *I'm no closer to figuring out those strange compounds*, Fang thought. *This is the only way to understand the source of their power.* She pushed Ariana's terrified face out of her mind.

It's the only way.

2

Equilibrium

"There are riots in Moscow, Belgium, the Netherlands. The authorities claim a mutant influenza strain was accidentally incorporated into the vaccine. Millions are dead. There's talk of bioterrorism."

"You know very well that there has to be external pressure for a system to evolve. Better designs prevail; obsolete ones perish and are swept away."

"They can barely burn the bodies fast enough, Miranda. They think it's contagious."

"I'm not the one who allowed a highly experimental genetic activator into general circulation."

"You knew what Vulcan would do. Is being an accomplice any better?"

"I think you'll find there's a lovely death certificate

in the Chinese system with my name on it. Hard to be an accomplice from the grave."

"You are insufferable, you know that? To top it all off, Vulcan's extraction units are sweeping through the terrified masses, plucking convergers as they appear."

"And Robyn?"

"Robyn's still unaccounted for."

"You're worried about her."

"Of course I'm worried about her. Forgive me for experiencing a human emotion. She's the one, I'm sure of it. I wish the deception wasn't necessary. If I could have prepared her, perhaps this would have played out differently."

"Now we have the girl, she'll come to you."

"Vulcan has the girl, Miranda, not me. The man has wrested the institute in a terrifying direction. I warned you."

"We were running out of time and it worked, didn't it? The program turned out to be a complete success. All three walkers exist. We stand at the dawn of a new era. Trust me, Robyn will come to us."

"Your definition of success leaves a lot to be

desired. This isn't a game anymore. Vulcan's made sure of that."

"Oh, survival is always a game. Evolution is just a game, one I intend to win."

Robyn ran, legs pumping, arms scissoring through the air. Branches whipped past her face and arms as she pushed deeper into the forest. She didn't dare turn around. The suffocating weight grew closer and closer, building to a roar in her ears. Energy tingled up her legs with each impact, as if the earth itself was feeding her life force. Every few steps, energy coiled downward, dissipating between her bare toes. A dizzying combination of push and pull. Her skin crawled as she registered footfalls behind her, someone crashing through the undergrowth. Sweat dribbled down her spine, sticking her singlet to her body as she leapt onto the goat track of a path at the top of the ridge.

"Coming in hot," Sara called as she sprinted past, her leopard, Ming, loping beside her. Robyn skittered to a stop on the cliff edge, heart pounding, as the sinewy leopard deftly navigated the hairpin turn. Fletcher and Eli appeared a second later. The full weight of their auras descended on Robyn as if she'd suddenly donned two winter coats. Her skin felt too tight, her limbs jumpy. The feeling hadn't equilibrated in the two weeks since she'd had the injection to activate the convergence sequence in her mitochondria. It was beyond her control. Whatever was changing inside her was happening at a cellular level.

Eli grinned and broke away in pursuit of Sara, his osprey Una shadowing him above the canopy. Fletcher joined her at the cliff edge, Eva barrelling to a stop behind him. The earth walker flicked his hair from his eyes, looking at the tiny dot of the earthship below, the hazy disc of smoke from the chimney trapped within the valley. Robyn followed his gaze as she caught her breath.

It felt like a potter had picked up Robyn's family farm and recast it. Proportionally, it was the same; the vegetable garden in the same spot, the wood stove that spluttered when first cranked. The difference was the sheen of brightness that brought every object into stunning clarity, heartbeats chorusing in trapped chests around her, whispers on the breeze only she could hear. The forest itself was a swirl of colour and light, crisper and sharper than she remembered. Each individual trunk defined, every sound magnified into a symphony.

If only it was enough to fix everything. All their work had played right into the MRI's plans, and now Fang had Ariana.

And Derek.

Eva wailed at Fletcher's side, her breath condensing in the cool air.

"We can't just hide here, Robyn. Ariana needs us," said Fletcher.

Robyn heard the thinly veiled anger in the earth walker's voice but also the unspoken censure, *why aren't you doing anything?* They'd had this argument over a dozen times. As always, the righteousness in Fletcher's eyes made her heart ache. "We need information. The twins are working on it. We can't just set off on some half-baked rescue attempt." Robyn couldn't risk losing anyone else. Not now, when the walkers and convergers felt like the siblings she never had. Her parents were good Catholics in all ways but one. Light skittered across her eyelids as her birthmark burned. The green light Fletcher had triggered in the spirit world had been visible in both hemispheres for two long minutes.

Long enough for thousands of grainy smartphone videos and a handful of observatory photos. An aurora in broad daylight. Unheard of. It had sent the scientific community into a tizz.

"The world will find out about us sooner or later," Fletcher spat. "We need to warn people about Nyx and the sun song."

I know. Robyn had run through scenario after scenario in her head, but every one involved revealing the existence of the convergers, who'd be shuttled away by government scientists before they could figure out how to stop Nyx. They'd take her, too. There was too much at stake. Fletcher should know that. "You're right. And we will. When the time is right."

"That's bullshit." Fletcher turned away. "I'm heading back." Eva pivoted and nearly knocked Robyn over, sending an apologetic wail over her flank as she followed Fletcher through the trees.

Robyn sank down onto a rock, uncertainty washing over her and dispelling the flow of endorphins and dopamine in her system. She hated being pulled in so many directions at once. There was so much that needed to be done and not enough time to do it in. She hated thinking about what Fang was doing with the activation vector. What twisted experiments was she conducting on Ariana? What new scheme was she cooking up to snare the people whose DNA held the convergence sequence? It was all too much. Fletcher was right to be angry. *I'm supposed to be protecting them, helping them, only I have no answers to give them*, Robyn thought. She jumped as her phone vibrated in her pocket. A dinner summons. Robyn sighed and turned back, noticing the tiredness of the sunlight slipping between the trees. Energy swirled through her spine, slowing her worrying mind, and she gave in to the rhythm of her feet. She caught up with Jacob on the return leg just as Sara and Eli raced past her.

"What's the hurry?" Jacob called out, his face beet red.

"Catherine's made burritos," Sara yelled over her shoulder, her words already Doppler-skewed.

Robyn coasted downhill next to Jacob. His bee, Poppy, clung to his earlobe like a punk accessory.

A bubble of conversation hit Robyn the moment she crossed the threshold. The woodstove roared in the corner of the living room as Catherine orchestrated a frenzy of movement in the kitchen. Fletcher refused to meet her eyes – apparently carrying a plate stacked with spelt tortillas required complete concentration.

Sara guzzled water straight from the tap, wiping her mouth on her sleeve as she straightened. "Good run. I love that hill, the view's amazing."

"It's too steep." Jacob looked pained as he followed Robyn inside. "And it goes forever."

The table lapsed into silence as burritos were wrapped and consumed. Robyn inhaled two, savouring the nutty tortillas and paprika-laced beans. Catherine rose to refill the crock of hummus and Robyn watched her. They were still sharing a wardrobe; Catherine wore a long chunky jumper Robyn had knitted when she was fifteen. It looked good on her, though that was hardly saying anything. Catherine could make a hessian sack look couture.

"Crap." Kara used her elbow to wipe a splodge of sauce from her laptop.

"I did say no electronics at the table." Catherine put down the hummus, and Sara and Jacob's hands collided in midair in their rush to claim it.

"Sorry, Mum," Kara pouted.

"Don't call me that!" Catherine sank into her chair with a sigh. "How many times do I have to tell you?"

"Don't send me to bed early, please." Kara raised her hands in a prayer position against her lips.

Catherine cast her eyes skyward. "Anybody, feel free to step in."

Sara cleared her throat and carried her plate to the sink. "Thanks for dinner –"

"Don't you say it," Catherine threatened.

"– Mum," Sara finished.

Catherine raised her arms in defeat and Robyn stifled a giggle. It all felt so … normal. Jacob laughing. Sara standing with her arms crossed behind him. *Bah-bum. Bah-bum. Baaah-buuum.* Robyn felt the weight of their heartbeats, the breath from their lungs, swirls of energy in the air.

Until Kara swivelled her laptop and the joking atmosphere evaporated.

Robyn stared at the list of names onscreen. More than half were crossed out. *Our list*, Robyn realised. *The names of potential convergers we identified.*

"We've been tracking them down. Fang's moving faster than I imagined, rounding them up," Kara said, her eyes grim.

"It's only been two weeks," Catherine said, looking horrified.

Two weeks since Robyn and Terence had volunteered to be guinea pigs for the activation dose they'd created. She'd survived but Terence hadn't. Robyn gripped the edge of the table in growing horror. A fifty percent survival rate was hardly a success. People would die.

"And the activation dose isn't safe," Robyn blurted out. Derek knew that. Surely, he wouldn't allow Fang to activate the names on the list. Except – this was exactly what Derek wanted, casualties be damned. Her dinner rose in the back of her throat as she thought of innocent kids being rounded up and exposed to the activation dose she'd helped create. Down the table, Catherine's face had grown pale. The other convergers sat frozen, giving Kara their full attention.

Bah-bum. Bah-bum.

"The MRI has around sixty so far." Kara clicked on a grainy photograph of an industrial lot. Rugged mountains loomed behind what looked like a disused warehouse. "This is where they are now. A compound in Bulgaria."

"This is where they have Ariana, you mean." Fletcher gripped a spoon so hard Robyn worried it would snap. Her chest tightened and her head roared with sound, thickening the air around her. *Bah-bum.* Robyn pushed her chair backwards and stumbled toward the door. Catherine called her name, but the deafening vibrations swallowed it up. *Bah-bum. Bah-bum.*

It's my fault, Robyn thought, the accusation on Fletcher's face etched into her mind. *It's all my fault.*

Robyn followed the winding track down to the stream, the rush of sound dissipating as her bare feet bounced on the damp leaves, zinging with the contact. There was a hint of frost in the air, icy pinpricks reaching her lungs.

In the clearing, soft moonlight bathed the cairn of rocks above Terence's grave. Robyn knelt in front of it, curling her feet beneath her like a pilgrim seeking wisdom in ages past. The energy in her system calmed, slowing the feedback loop of fear and uncertainty in her mind.

The ground felt *loud*, as if her mind was suddenly

more receptive to the comings and goings of life on a smaller scale. She'd spent a chunk of her childhood here, following her mother as she picked plants, dug up invasive introduced weeds and whispered to the trees. Now the trees seemed to whisper back. Robyn breathed in the rich humus swelling around her. Mist rose from the decomposing material. Organisms worked at every level, seen and unseen, unicellular to complex multicellular organisms. Each a part of the whole, each surviving, contributing.

Except humans. A legacy of taking, not giving.

She placed a hand on the nearest rock, smoothing her thumb over the eroded ridges and valleys. Given time, everything changes. Every system evolves, but disequilibrium is the natural order. Disorder is the natural order. Is it possible to reach equilibrium in such a complex system? Or is disorder all we can really hope for as a species? The convergers represented a connectedness with the natural world long forgotten, an evolutionary jump. A way to restore equilibrium. She had to believe it. But now Fang had the emerging convergers in her grasp. And if Robyn was sure of anything, it was that Fang's interests were not in balance or equilibrium.

Only power.

Tears threatened at the corners of her eyes. She didn't feel strong or capable enough to deal with any of this. She was terrified. For Ariana, for the people who had no idea they carried the convergence sequence in their mitochondria. For Eli and Fletcher, Sara and Jacob. Maybe her body would reject the changes to her genome and shut down entirely. Maybe she'd join Terence here in the clearing before long. Maybe, maybe, maybe.

With an effort, Robyn pushed her fears away. *I can't give in to anger or fear. I have to look forward.* Closing her eyes, she listened to the gentle sounds around her. High above branches swayed, their leaves rustling in an eternal dance. Blood pounded in her ears as she focused on her breathing. The rustling faded and her shoulders grew heavy. She felt the white light swallow her as Terence's voice surged through the ground to whisper in her ear.

You will save them.

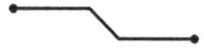

The glade was still, the trees closest to the clearing dancing along a vivid spectrum of light brightening the gloom. Robyn pressed her palms into the grass and counted to ten before she tentatively stood, pleased to find the earth didn't sway beneath her feet. She searched for the orange-robed boy she had met two weeks ago, but no-one emerged from the darkness. Energy buzzed through her system. She hadn't tried crossing over since the day Derek left. It sounded better that way – left, instead of abandoned.

She stood in the clearing for several minutes, watching the lights. Beyond their comforting glow was total darkness. The ground thrummed with energy, the air thick and viscous with it. Robyn blinked in surprise as she found herself in the midst of the trees. She hadn't consciously made the decision to step into the forest, but now she pushed deeper into the thick avenues of swaying trunks. The trees bore silent witness, releasing lights that hopped from trunk to trunk like spectres, reminding her of the fairytales her mother read to her as a child. Sprites and goblins. Light shouldn't travel like that, as if it was a living creature instead of a collection of electric and magnetic fields, a stream of excitable photons. As she watched, the lights following her coalesced into glowing orbs, detaching from the trees to orbit her with brightness. Not lanterns but hovering quivery spheres hemming her in. The ground vibrated beneath her feet and a wave of sound enveloped her, the vibrations clarifying into single frequencies as if someone had plucked a series of strings on a cosmic harp. Robyn's mind eased. Three notes rang through the trees, sending a cascade of lights dancing from trunk to trunk.

She stood very still, the combination of sound and light tugging at the core of her being. The ring of orbs flashed green as one frequency sounded, pulling on her skull and lifting her onto her tiptoes. Anger, longing, all tinged with desperation. Fletcher. She felt the walker as if his mind was tethered to her own, a combination of touch, sight and sound that made her skin crawl. Robyn gasped as she recognised the feeling – the strange pull she had been experiencing in the walkers' presence but visceral, like it was a living part of her. *I'm connected to them, all of the walkers*, Robyn realised. She grasped at the next frequency, higher this time. The orbs flickered red. Robyn closed her eyes, feeling for the brush with Eli's mind. She found threads of fear mixed with determination as she skimmed across his consciousness. Tears slid down her cheeks at the beauty of the connection.

Only one more frequency. Robyn concentrated as the orbs flared blue. Whiteness blinded her. She saw bunched sheets, a bare sink and toilet. The lingering feeling of Ariana's fear brought a choked sob to her lips.

The orbs hovered a moment longer before disappearing back into the trees, melding into the bark. Robyn sank to her knees, clutching at the threads in her mind. Red, green, blue.

Around her, the forest kept whispering.

3

Metabolism

The temple is unique among other examples of ancient Laotian architecture. Higher beams, elaborate mosaic work that should not have penetrated this far up the Mekong for another thousand years. Although the city now crowds the mountain on each side, it is tempting to posit that the original temple was situated far from any village. There is no trace of animal husbandry or agriculture in the surrounding hillside prior to the last several thousand years. The temple is very much a lone outpost, which makes it all the more intriguing. What did they do here, and why?

Miranda Collins, Working Notes.

Catherine sat at the tiny desk wedged beside the ancient chromatograph. She'd already run today's blood samples, yet she lingered. *Derek is out there hurting people. Hurting kids.* Part of her still refused to accept that after everything they'd accomplished together, he had betrayed them. People would die because of it. *Because of my work.* Catherine brought a fist down onto the desk, the searing pain vibrating through her wrist almost a relief. It's what Terence's absence felt like – a jarring break that refused to heal, impossible to forget.

"I don't know if there's anything else we can do," Catherine whispered to the computer screen. She rubbed her eyes and pulled up the graph again. Every morning she'd been taking blood samples from the convergers Fang had activated in Beijing, Sara and Jacob. Unlike the walkers, the convergence sequence on their mitochondrial genome was stable, and it was possible to analyse their cellular energy levels. Using the original lab results as a baseline, she'd plotted the daily change in adenosine triphosphate levels. For two weeks, the graph continued to ascend, much higher than any recorded human level of cellular energy production. The conclusion was inevitable. *They were getting stronger.*

A knock sounded on the door. "Catherine? Is that banana bread ready to come out of the oven?" Sara asked.

Catherine cleared her throat. "Yeah. Could you –?"

"On it."

Catherine waited as the printer stirred to life. For now, she could keep everyone here safe. It wasn't much, but it was enough.

When she emerged from the lab, Sara and Jacob were already sitting at the table with steaming slices of banana bread. Eli was rummaging through the fridge. He stopped when he saw her. "Ricotta?"

"Back shelf. Somewhere behind the miso."

"Ahah!" Eli held the jar aloft.

"Fletcher?" Catherine asked as she poured herself a cup of tea.

"Went back to bed," Sara said through her mouthful.

"He hasn't been sleeping much," added Jacob. Poppy crawled through his hair.

"And Robyn?" Sara asked.

"She didn't come back last night." The camp bed had lain empty beside Catherine, blankets neatly folded. "It was a shock for all of us."

"Not really." Sara shrugged as Eli passed her the

ricotta, pausing to slather it on her breakfast. "It was only a matter of time after Derek gave the MRI the names."

Catherine froze at the counter, stunned by Sara's frank assessment of the situation. *They're not kids anymore*, she reminded herself. *It's possible they're stronger than all of us.* She joined the others at the table, her mind on the new data.

"I feel guilty for hiding out, but I know it's the only option we have right now," Eli said, sending a kind smile Catherine's way. "You and Ariana were lucky in Beijing when you rescued us. The MRI won't let their guard down again. If they're collecting convergers – if this is really happening – then it's serious. We have to work together to figure out what to do."

"Someone should give Fletcher that memo," Jacob said, dolloping honey on his banana bread as Poppy twirled around his head.

Sara stopped chewing. "And it still doesn't make it suck any less."

"No, it doesn't." Catherine sighed. She finished her tea and stood up, pulling a blanket from the lounge.

"Where are you going?" Sara asked.

"I'm going to find Robyn."

Robyn opened her eyes against the brightness, momentarily confused. She picked at a stone under her hip and sat up. The cairn of rocks glistened with dew.

Catherine stood above her with a blanket. "Did you sleep out here all night?"

"I didn't mean to." Robyn smoothed the leaves from her hair, wincing as she realised she probably looked like a troll. Catherine didn't flinch, which was a good sign. Maybe she only looked half as terrible as she imagined. It shouldn't matter, but it did. Robyn wouldn't care if Kara saw her covered in dirt, but Catherine – it was different. Robyn turned to face the cairn of rocks. It had been different for a while now, but she still couldn't answer the little voice in her mind saying *why not?* And God, it didn't help when Catherine stood there looking concerned and stunning all at once. Robyn ducked her head and spread a palm against the soil. She imagined Terence's body deep below her, his face calm as if asleep. It pushed all thought of Catherine out of her mind in a guilty rush. If she'd been a better scientist, a better friend, then none of this would have happened. *I'm sorry,*

Terence. Sorry that you died and I lived, that your sister is a prisoner of the MRI. I'll make this right somehow, I promise. Vibrations reverberated from the earth, trickling energy into her fingertips.

Catherine draped the blanket around her shoulders and took a hasty step backwards, as if sensing Robyn's thoughts. Now without anything to hold, Catherine wrapped her arms around herself. "Well, come on in before you get sick."

Robyn nodded, turning back to the cairn. She stayed with Terence for a few minutes more, pulling the blanket tight. When she reached out for the three frequencies, they rose readily in her mind. Red, green, blue. She sighed with relief at the connection to the walkers. Not a dream but real, tangible. When Robyn finally looked up, Catherine had gone.

The kitchen table was empty except for Kara tapping away at her laptop.

Kara glanced up at Robyn. "You okay? Next time, don't leave on such a dramatic note."

"I'm good, all things considered." Robyn flashed Kara a weak grin, noticing for the first time how tired her best friend looked.

A delicious aroma emanated from a loaf of banana bread on the counter. A bread knife rested against the cooling rack, already covered in crumbs from the first assault. *Catherine's holding this crazy family together, and what do I do? Run away to sulk.* Robyn sighed and threw some stale sourdough into the toaster. She didn't deserve banana bread. "How long have you known about the list of convergers?"

Kara stopped typing. "I've had my suspicions for a few days, but we were only able to confirm all the names yesterday morning." She leaned back in her chair and rubbed her eyes. "You know, it's been a tad terrifying. You were comatose for three days after the injection, Robyn. I didn't know if you would make it."

"I'm sorry." Robyn braced her arms on the counter, cataloguing the dark circles etched under her friend's eyes and the scattering of coffee-stained mugs on the table.

"And to top it all off, Fletcher somehow caused a green lightshow. You know the scientific consensus is an expansion of the aurora borealis and aurora australis?" Kara shook her head in wonder. "It's freaking crazy. Everything is changing. Kate and I are doing what we know how to do, but it's you the convergers and walkers need. You understand what it's like. You're a converger now."

Robyn stared at the glowing red bars in the toaster. "I'm worried that deep down they hate me." *Fletcher certainly seems to*, she thought.

"Hate you? How could they hate you? They're just scared, Robyn. We're all getting used to it. We've all had to adjust our baseline for *normal*." Kara stood up and rolled her shoulders with a cracking sound as she joined Robyn at the counter.

The toaster popped. "Used to me, you mean. I'm different. I know I'm not the same and it scares me."

Kara rolled her eyes and poured another cup of coffee, tipping in a small mountain of sugar. "Of course you're different. You stood up to the MRI, rescued the walkers and helped free Sara and Jacob. You cracked the genetics. But you're still Robyn, no matter what is happening inside you. You're still my best friend. You did all of that without any crazy enhanced genetics. Imagine what you'll be able to do now?" Kara mimed an explosion with her hands. "It blows my mind just thinking about it."

Yeah, you and me both, Robyn thought as she slathered apricot jam on her toast.

Kara slung an arm over Robyn's shoulders and squeezed. "Give them some time. Everyone's still reeling from … you know."

Robyn closed her eyes. Terence's death. Derek's defection. Thinking of both felt like ripping open freshly scarred wounds. So she did what she'd been doing every day for two whole weeks. She tamped down the pain, sucking it into a tiny space and locking it away inside herself. All this she achieved while eating breakfast. Perhaps if she kept up the regimen long enough she'd make a dent in her guilt.

4

Biochemistry

The Judeo-Christian-Muslim tradition upholds that Nature must submit to human rule. While the Hindu-Buddhist-Jain tradition and Native American beliefs teach us that Nature must be cherished, protected, defended. In such a frame of reference, an isolated mountain in Laos thus becomes the perfect refuge for a cult dedicated to bonds between humans and animals of a significance never before recorded.

Miranda Collins, Working Notes.

Robyn showered and pulled on a clean pair of jeans and shirt, glancing at her bare feet. Despite the cold, she couldn't bear to muffle the zinging energy in her body with shoes. Even socks felt like a barrier. Whenever she forced herself to wear shoes, it made her feel edgy and irritable. Or maybe there was no connection whatsoever and she was slowly going loopy as the activation dose destroyed her brain cells. Robyn wiped the fogged mirror and examined her reflection. She brushed her hair, barely recognising the face staring back at her. She pressed a hand to her right eye, felt the ridge of skin beneath her fingertips. Her birthmark, surgically removed when she was a child, had returned in all its jagged scarecrow-like glory after her visit to the spirit world.

"I think it's kind of badass." Sara leaned against the doorjamb with her arms folded. "Your birthmark."

Robyn jumped and dropped her hand by her side. "Sorry, you scared me."

"You really slept outside, huh?" Sara pushed herself upright. "I visit him. For Ariana, partly. But in a way, he was our brother, too."

"I know." Robyn straightened. "I feel the same way. About you, as well."

Catherine and Ariana had busted Sara out of the MRI's experimental lab in Beijing. She and Jacob were

34

the only survivors of Fang's initial attempts to activate the convergence gene. Ironically, it was only by studying their genetic sequences that Robyn and the others had been able to create the activation dose, the injection which was now in the hands of the MRI. The thought of Fang capturing and experimenting on others like Sara filled Robyn with raw fear.

Sara blushed and picked at the doorframe. "I'm just saying, I don't think Terence would want you to get sick."

Robyn frowned. A flicker of white light flashed in the mirror, gone before she could see what caused it. "Did Catherine send you?"

Sara raised both hands. "Nope. But speaking of, I think she's looking for you. Plus I kind of want a shower."

"Robyn?" Catherine's voice echoed down the hallway.

At the sound of her name, Robyn froze. Sara raised her eyebrows.

There was really only so long she could avoid Catherine in a small space. Robyn was proud of her campaign so far – spending as much time as possible outside with the convergers and walkers, disappearing underneath a stack of textbooks in communal living space and pretending to instantly fall asleep on the camp bed in their shared room. She hadn't had time to slow down, evaluate her feelings. The rational part of her mind clung to explanations she half-believed. That living together had brought them closer, the stress of the last few weeks an allying force.

"Robyn, are you in here?"

Sara sighed and pushed Robyn through the doorway where she collided with Catherine.

"There you are."

"Catherine." The unexpected contact made her skin tingle. How dare her biochemistry betray her like that?

But Catherine didn't seem to notice. "I have new data."

She followed Catherine into the tiny lab space. The ancient chromatograph whirred in the corner, making a rack of vials on the bench rattle. Catherine had clearly been working at full tilt.

"Remember the screening test? I thought maybe we could look at energy production in the convergers in more detail. The walkers are still a bust. I can't get an accurate reading on their energy levels." Catherine pulled a graph from the printer. "It's incredible. Energy production has spiked dramatically and seems to be increasing."

Robyn pulled her gaze from Catherine's loose

ponytail and skimmed the numbers. "This is well beyond the normal range. But they're both fine, right?" Sara had seemed perfectly normal. Robyn frowned as she realised she couldn't *feel* Sara or Jacob's presence like she did the walkers. Fletcher and Eli's frequencies tugged on her mind as she thought of them, that strange combination of light, sound and pressure. She *felt* them as if they were part of her, a pulsing entity rippling through her skin.

"That's the thing. They are," Catherine said.

Kara's twin sister Kate appeared in the doorway, gesticulating with a slice of banana bread and spraying crumbs on the floor. "So these kids are jacked up? Like superheroes or something?" said Kate between mouthfuls. She yanked a power board from the socket and draped it over her shoulder with her free hand. "I'm also requisitioning this."

"Not exactly," Catherine said, eyes flashing with excitement. "It most likely means they'll be able to run faster, jump higher, heal quicker … I mean, we already kind of knew it but this proves it."

"So, superheroes. Got it," Kate called down the hallway as she disappeared into the studio.

Catherine ran her hands through her hair. "I've

never seen anything like it. Because they're on the mitochondrial sequence, the convergence genes are directly linked to energy metabolism. In a way, Kate's right. Jacob and Sara, the convergers, are superhuman. Their biochemical anatomy is distinct. We looked at it from a screening perspective, but their mitochondria can tell us so much more."

My biochemical anatomy is distinct, Robyn thought. *We've only scraped the surface.* She watched Catherine jab at the graph, eyes bright. *And if only you knew what you do to me.* "I … I can feel them. The walkers." Robyn pressed a hand to her ribcage. *I have to tell her. I have to tell everyone that Ariana is all right.* "I'm not sure how, but I can sense where they are, what they're experiencing."

Catherine froze, abandoning her data. She stared at Robyn in utter shock.

"It happened last night. I crossed over into the spirit world again. I can feel them, here."

Robyn pressed firmly against her ribcage. Catherine raised her hand to Robyn's with a frown. "That's not possible."

Robyn took a deep breath, registering Catherine's pulse against her own. "Fletcher. He's still asleep down the hall. He's angry and confused, can't stand hiding here while the MRI are torturing Ariana."

Catherine started to pull her hand away, but Robyn caught it, holding her in place. She concentrated on the pulsing red frequency. "Eli. He's sitting in the sun, watching his osprey, Una, circle above him. Revelling in the majesty of her flight, the sun on his shoulders. Living in the now. He's hurting, too, but concealing it. Knows better than anyone what the MRI is capable of doing."

"And what are the MRI doing?" Catherine whispered.

Robyn closed her eyes, focusing on the wavering blue thread of energy. "Ariana's in a cell, like Eli was." She exhaled, grasping the stuttering, almost pixelated view of white walls, Ariana's dark hair, the mottled bruises on her wrists and ankles. "They're hurting her in some way, but I can't see past the cell, I've tried. She's strong, but it's taking its toll." Tears spilled onto Robyn's cheeks. "She's so alone and so far away."

"But she's alive," Catherine breathed, pulling Robyn into a hug. Catherine's warm breath tickled Robyn's ear, her own tears smudging Robyn's cheeks. "She's alive."

Robyn let herself be drawn in tight, the energy tethers expanding and contracting with her heartbeat. For a long moment, Catherine's arms around her formed her entire world; nothing existed but their twin heartbeats and the persistent ache of the walkers' frequencies swirling in her blood, her bones, her very being.

With a shuddery breath, Catherine stepped backward and wiped away her tears. "I don't know how this is possible, but I believe you. But Jacob and Sara ... they can't cross over to the spirit world. I thought only the walkers could."

"So did I," Robyn admitted. "I don't know if Terence ... well, I'm the only one who's taken the activation dose and survived." She felt shaky after concentrating on Ariana's energy tether for so long, and her fear bubbled readily to the surface. "What if we've inadvertently created a way for Fang to control the spirit world?"

Catherine paled. "No, you don't think ..."

Robyn paced the tiny lab space. The activation dose was specific for the convergence genes; the walkers' gene mutations were impossible to pin down and map. So the odds of the activation dose randomly altering the mitochondrial genes were almost zero. Logic dispelled Robyn's initial fear, replacing it with a strange certainty. It felt *right* somehow, her connection to the walkers.

Like a block had been lifted from her mind. Red, green, blue. Three parts of a whole. She glanced over at Catherine with growing certainty. "No. We'd know. Eli and Fletcher have been travelling to the spirit world every day, trying to contact Ariana. If the activation dose also enabled convergers to cross between the physical and spirit worlds, they'd know."

Catherine rearranged a rack of vials and straightened papers, her eyes unfocused. "How can you be so sure?"

"It's statistically improbable." Robyn took the papers from Catherine's hands, breaking Catherine's semi-trance. "I mean, we're good, but I don't think we're that good," she added with a weak grin.

Catherine finally nodded, a hint of a smile on her face. "We should tell the others," she said, sounding more certain. "They'll want to know about Ariana."

For a long moment, the kitchen was silent. "Well, shit. I guess this is as good a reason as any for a round table meeting," Sara exhaled, leaning back in her chair. By her side, Jacob watched Poppy flit across his knuckles, his face deep in thought. For once, the twins had no joke to lighten the mood.

"What are they doing to her?" Fletcher leaned heavily against Eva's side, his face pale. The brown bear sat at the end of the table, her breath misting in the cool air. Robyn spread her hands across the kitchen table and glanced across at Eli. The air walker sat straight-backed in his chair, the muscles in his neck corded. *He's experienced it before*, she thought. Sara and Jacob nodded faintly in Eli's direction in silent camaraderie. *They all have.*

"I'm guessing she has an implant, like the MRI used on Eli, Sara and Jacob," Robyn said. "It would explain why it's so difficult to get a coherent image of Ariana and her surroundings. I don't think it's purely the distance. When I can feel her, it's like I'm right there in the cell with her."

"I don't understand how this is even possible, how you crossed over to the spirit world again in the first place." Fletcher shook his head as he fisted a hand in Eva's fur. "I thought it was only because you were holding onto me, when …" His voice petered out.

"When you spirit zapped the sky?" Sara joked, though her face was drawn. Fletcher nodded stiffly. The table groaned as Eva rested her head against it.

"They saw what we could do when we escaped from Beijing," Eli said, his voice small. "Now they know about our auras, I'm sure they'll want to control them, find their source."

The kettle whistled in the silence that followed. Robyn thought of Ariana, alone and afraid, completely at Fang's mercy. Fletcher's pain yanked on Robyn's ribcage and coiled into her stomach, where it settled like a dead weight. Her heart went out to the earth walker. *I'm sorry*, she wanted to say. *I don't understand why any of this is happening.* Instead, she watched Catherine push back her chair and gather up a teapot and mugs.

Catherine rummaged through the cupboard, producing a plate of biscuits, then looked up. "Eli and Fletcher, you haven't seen anything unusual in the spirit world?"

Eli looked at Catherine with a wary expression while Fletcher shook his head in exasperation. "Nothing. Lenti has completely disappeared. I was hoping he would know what to do. Anything is better than this." Pain flared sharp against Robyn's ribs as if Fletcher had twisted a knife into her flesh. She gritted her teeth as the moment passed. Eli tipped his head, his expression thoughtful. "You think the activation dose might also include the ability to cross over between the worlds," he said softly.

Fletcher jumped to his feet. "What?" Colour flushed his cheeks. "No way. Screw that."

Robyn took a deep breath, riding the wave of Fletcher's anguish, pushing herself away from the roaring tide with an effort. Catherine squeezed her arm briefly in sympathy, and it was all Robyn could do not to burst into tears at the kindness. She flashed Catherine a weak smile in thanks.

"No, I don't think it does."

Fletcher went silent and Eli turned to Robyn with a frown. "Do you remember what Lenti said when you first crossed over to the spirit world?"

Fletcher's energy tether receded in the wake of Eli's burgeoning hopefulness.

"He mistook me for someone else. Liro." The young boy in orange robes had knelt at Robyn's feet, the name murmured like a prayer.

Eli shook his head slowly. "No. He recognised you for who you truly are." His eyes roamed Robyn's face in wonder. "The guide."

Fletcher balled his fists, but Eli's energy tether gripped Robyn like a vice, drowning out the earth walker's confusion and fury. She stared at Eli. "What do you mean?"

Eli drummed his fingers on the table. "The day you and Terence took the activation dose, I was in the spirit world with Lenti. He told me that he wasn't the true guide. The last guide died a thousand years ago, a monk named Liro." Eli glanced over at the windowsill where Una was perched, preening her feathers. "I think I met him, just for a moment. But when I got back, everything was crazy and I guess I forgot about it."

Liro. The name echoed through Robyn's skull. She felt a strange twinge of recognition, as if she'd turned in response to a stranger's summons. *Liro.*

"It explains why you're connected to us, why you can cross over to the spirit world." Eli's face brightened, his growing enthusiasm infectious. Robyn felt energy ripple along her spine and tingle through her fingertips.

At the end of the table, Fletcher shook, his entire body taut with rage. "She's the reason we're in this mess in the first place," he yelled, his gaze pinning everyone at the table in turn. "The reason my parents are dead, Terence is dead, Ariana captured and tortured." He turned to Robyn, his gaze renewing the twisting pain in her gut, the imaginary knife sliding deeper and deeper. "If you're the guide, then we're royally screwed." He turned and ran out the door, Eva lumbering behind him. Robyn gasped for breath as his energy tether began to fade. Catherine sat frozen beside her, hands still wrapped around the teapot in its knitted cosy. *No, it's not possible. I can't be the guide.* Robyn steadied herself as she raised her eyes to the table. *Fletcher's right. Without me, none of this would have happened.* Eli watched her, his energy tether calm, flickering with strange certainty. Robyn swore she glimpsed a momentary glimmer of red on his skin.

Sara tugged at a loose strand of hair, pushing it back into her ponytail. "Well, I for one would love a biscuit."

Catherine's hands tensed around the teapot, but she gathered herself, pouring steaming mugs of tea on autopilot.

Sara waved a biscuit studded with chocolate chips. "But someone should go after Fletcher."

Jacob reached over and distributed mugs. "Poppy is on it. She's being very discreet."

Robyn imagined his bee tailing Fletcher and Eva, reporting back like a spy. The image dispelled the worst of her shock. "Thank you," she managed, her fingers trembling as she accepted a mug. She'd known Fletcher was in pain, barely tamping down his fear and anger, but the energy tether magnified everything he felt and sent it rocketing straight to her heart like a heat-seeking missile. Catherine forced a biscuit into her hand and she ate it without registering the taste.

"He'll realise he's being an idiot," Sara said. She sat with one knee up, her elbow hooked around it, but Robyn registered the tension in her shoulders. "Even if you're not the guide, if you can see Ariana, we can make a plan to bust her out. Maybe we can even work out what the MRI is planning. And being able to enter the spirit world can only be a good thing."

Jacob nodded as he chewed. "You've guided us this far. Sara and I owe you our lives. I'm happy to call you my guide." Robyn couldn't seem to find her voice as Sara nodded in assent and Eli gave a low bow. "Thank you," she managed to rasp eventually. Light danced across her vision, the familiar flashes of red, green, blue.

5

Communication

The discovery of electromagnetic energy paved the way for the rapid technological expansion we've witnessed over the last two centuries. A unique combination of electric and magnetic fields that does not require a medium for propagation, electromagnetic energy passes just as easily through air as the vacuum of deep space. We are most comfortable with the portion of the electromagnetic spectrum we can see: light. Every form of electromagnetic energy travels at the speed of light ($3x10^8$ m/s), a speed incomprehensible to us. Our atmosphere is an electric conduit of charged particles, carrying more information in a nanosecond than all of our satellites combined. It is impossible to claim we fully understand the workings of the energy that passes through every living organism and on which we depend. We use microwaves to reheat our leftovers, blister under harsh ultraviolet rays and administer X-rays in our hospitals, yet these represent a mere drop in the proverbial quantum bucket.

Brock Williams, Working Notes.

"We need more equipment. You know we do." Catherine stood at the stove, stirring the lentil bolognese with more force than was strictly necessary. Jacob had just left the kitchen with Poppy in tow, confirming that Fletcher was cooling off down by the stream and had repeatedly told the bee to *buzz the f**k off*.

Robyn found the earth walker's energy tether had faded to an almost bearable pang. Knowing she had some weird ability to hone in on the walkers still freaked her out, but she needed to understand it if they stood any chance of saving Ariana. With a sigh, Robyn closed the textbook on quantum mechanics she'd been reading.

Nothing explained the energy tethers linking her to the walkers. "It's too dangerous. The MRI could have the place under surveillance. They're probably expecting us to show up there."

Catherine dunked pasta into a second pot. "One ancient chromatograph won't cut it. Kate and Kara have an arsenal of tech in the studio and we're working half-blind."

Robyn barely saw the twins outside of meals. They basically lived in her mother's art studio, which they'd converted into a high-tech lair. They were working flat out to keep them all safe, to stay one step ahead of the MRI, and what was she achieving? Nothing. Catherine was right, but they needed to stay hidden, keep the walkers and convergers out of danger. "The only reason the MRI haven't found us here is that Derek never knew where *here* was. My society-phobic parents never listed it anywhere. We're completely off the grid and I want to keep it that way."

Catherine stopped stirring and turned around. "I know, Robyn, believe me, I do. But I need to be doing something. If I don't keep busy …" Catherine shook her head. "Forget it."

Robyn tapped her fingers along the spine of the textbook. She knew how Catherine felt. Plus, they really didn't have any other option. "Fine. But I get to drive."

Catherine smiled at her and cracked open the window to yell, "Eli! Lunch is on the stove. Don't let it burn."

Robyn frowned. "We're going now?"

Catherine wiped her hands on a tea towel. "Right now."

The track was more overgrown than Robyn remembered. She skirted around a rotting log, and the ancient Delica spluttered as she shifted into third gear. Kara had found the van on Gumtree after Derek stole their only car. The twins had trekked from the compound into town to collect it while Robyn and Catherine grabbed their notes and destroyed samples. Thinking of that day made Robyn's stomach twist. Terence barely in the ground when Derek snapped. If only she'd been more aware, seen it coming, she could have stopped Derek. None of this would have happened. Ariana would still be safe.

Robyn flicked a glance over to Catherine as they hit the bitumen. "Thank you. For staying, for working, for everything."

Catherine looked affronted. "I would never just up and leave. Not now ..."

"Not now we've helped the MRI control the world's convergers?" Robyn regretted her brusqueness the moment the words left her mouth. *Great, alienate the one person still trying to follow the crazy science with you,* she thought.

Catherine stared straight ahead. "I was going to say, not now we know the world's in danger and we have a responsibility to help all the convergers we can." She glanced sideways at Robyn. "But your reason is why I can't sleep properly."

"Me, too." Robyn focused on the road, tightening her grip on the steering wheel.

Catherine picked at a thread in her jeans. "We haven't talked about it."

Robyn flushed. "Talked about what?" Her heart thudded in her chest as her mind whirred into overdrive. Did Catherine know how she felt about her? How exactly *did* she feel about her? Oh God, what if Catherine was about to let her down gently? Robyn stared straight ahead, blood pounding in her ears, regretting she'd agreed to come. A situation like this was exactly what she'd been hoping to avoid.

"You. You're stronger, faster."

Robyn sighed in relief. "Yes."

Catherine tipped her head. "You're the reason none of the doors have working handles anymore."

Robyn laughed. "Yeah. I tried to fix them."

"I think you succeeded in making them worse." Catherine's grin lit up her entire face, washing away the remnants of Robyn's unease.

"Probably." Robyn rolled her shoulders, remembering how much she enjoyed spending time with Catherine. *Stop making everything more complicated*, she admonished herself. *Catherine is your friend, and you have few enough of those as it is. Don't screw this up.*

Catherine turned her head. "What's it like?"

Robyn glanced quickly over at Catherine before returning her attention to the road. The colours of the forest seared her retinas, the static pressure of the air in the Delica prickling her skin. The dull ache of the walkers' frequency tethers pulled at her ribcage. "You really want to know?"

"I do," Catherine said quietly.

Robyn tapped her fingers on the steering wheel as she tried to figure out where to begin. "It's like I'm tapped in to a force greater than myself. The ground seems to feed me energy, loops it through my body's circuit then earths the remainder. It's overwhelming. I'm not sure I'll ever get used to it."

Catherine nodded, eyes trained on the road. "No wonder you've been quiet the last few weeks. I thought maybe …"

"What?" Robyn tipped her head.

"I thought maybe it was because of Derek." Catherine's voice was soft.

Robyn's birthmark throbbed. *Shit.* She'd been so terrified Catherine was going to talk about their not-quite-a-relationship that she'd pushed all thought of Derek out of her mind; now it all came rushing back. "I'm worried about him. I can't believe he gave up on us like that." She glanced across at Catherine, butterflies thumping against her ribcage. *I have to tell her the truth.* She drew a deep breath. "He … he kissed me. Right after the activation dose, before I fell into the coma."

Catherine's hands curled into fists on her knees.

"But it doesn't mean anything," Robyn rushed out,

remembering the suddenness of it, the shock of his lips on hers, the dizziness from the activation vector making her feel as if she were swimming through molasses.

"Sure." Catherine looked away.

Robyn grimaced. She didn't need an energy tether to know Catherine hadn't liked her answer. Robyn didn't know how to explain the way her body had reacted to Derek's touch despite his invasion of her personal space. She cared about Catherine and it confused the hell out of her. *Why do I always manage to screw things up?* Robyn cranked up the radio and let Triple J fill the gaping silence, but it didn't make the trip any shorter. Catherine didn't press her on the subject of Derek, just sat ramrod straight with her eyes on the road. She didn't move or speak until they reached the outskirts of the compound and she uncapped a pair of binoculars.

Robyn slowed down. "See anything?"

"Nothing. It looks empty," came Catherine's terse reply.

Robyn pulled into the lot. "I guess we hope for the best, then."

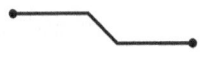

55

Robyn stood in the middle of the empty lab, trailing a hand along the counter. Weeks of emptiness had filled the room with a sort of heaviness, a muggy sweetness. The kitchen was no better. The stainless steel felt almost alien when not so long ago it was the bustling centre of their unusual family. Robyn was surprised to realise how much she missed it.

"Hey." Catherine stuck her head around the door. Her mouth was a thin line. "I think we're ready to go."

Robyn nodded as she sat on a stool. Clearing the lab hadn't taken long. She and Catherine had carved out a few key machines, stuffing the Delica with several months of reagents and lab consumables. It was as if they'd come in with a scalpel, excising only what they needed.

"There's nothing here for us anymore." Catherine rounded the lab bench, her gaze suddenly fierce. "But at least now if Derek comes back, there's nothing for him either." Her lips curled into a sneer as she uttered his name.

Robyn's chest tightened. A wave of energy rolled through her ribcage. "It feels weird to abandon ship," she said, shaking away the unsettling energy.

"We're not abandoning it. We're retreating with full intent to return later." Catherine glanced around the empty lab and Robyn caught a momentary flicker of sadness on her face.

"It's still abandonment," Robyn said.

"*Strategic* abandonment," Catherine insisted. "There's a fundamental difference."

"I know we can't stay here. Even the farm isn't completely safe." Robyn propped her elbows on the laminate lab bench and cupped her chin. "But it scares me, that the MRI hasn't shown up on our doorstep."

Catherine frowned. "Why?"

"Because it means maybe Derek didn't tell Fang about the lab. That we're wrong about him." Robyn sighed as Catherine's expression hardened again. "Or worse, the MRI no longer judges us a threat. They've surpassed our research and no longer need us."

"Derek betrayed us. All of us."

The ice in her voice startled Robyn.

Catherine swept an arm to indicate the room. "This is all his fault. He was the one determined to push through the trials. He left *us.*"

Robyn regretted speaking Derek's name again. The

anger etched onto Catherine's face sent guilt crashing through her system. She didn't want to relive the betrayal in Derek's eyes as he saw her and Catherine together. The hurt in Catherine's voice made her feel sick to her stomach. *I can't be what anyone needs right now*, she thought. *I don't even know who* I *am.*

But out loud she said, "We need to focus on what we can do now. We can't afford to dwell on what Derek did or didn't do."

"Fine." Catherine turned away, the hurt on her face palpable.

"Good," Robyn replied with more menace than she'd intended.

They drove home in silence, the van jolting over every pothole.

6

Earthed

Every frequency of the electromagnetic spectrum is visible as unique colours, but not to our eyes. Imagine if we could see in ultraviolet or use X-rays to peer into the workings of plants and animals. Imagine if we could transmit and receive radio waves, allowing instantaneous communication across vast distances. If the entirety of the electromagnetic spectrum were open to us, we would interact with our world in an entirely different, more intimate, way. Did we ever have the capacity to receive signals from different portions of the electromagnetic spectrum? If so, why did we lose them as we evolved? A world understood in terms of visible light only is a sensorily poor one.

Brock Williams, Working Notes.

Robyn fell into the new routine at the earthship like an uneasy visiting grandparent, unsure of the rules, afraid to linger in any one room for too long. The twins locked themselves away in the studio, emerging only for food and to enforce the convergers' correspondence work. The lab space came alive with the addition of the new machines. The space was too small for them to work together easily, so Robyn and Catherine took shifts. The long hours split between the sequencer and the chromatograph still gave Robyn too much time to think. She listened to Catherine clatter in the kitchen or answer questions about the convergers' schoolwork while she stared at pages of data. Day after day, Robyn willed it to connect into something tangible, for the secrets of the walkers' gene mutation to reveal themselves. The muted reverence on everyone's faces except Fletcher's stripped her raw. *I can't tell them I have no idea what I'm doing.*

Robyn left the sequencer humming and pushed into the studio. Kate turned around with raised eyebrows. "What can I do for you?"

Robyn frowned at the empty chair. "Where's Kara?"

"Had to go to Canberra for a few things. She'll be back in a few days."

"Oh. She didn't tell me."

Kate shrugged, already turning back to her computer. "She left early. We're pretty busy."

"Right. Sorry to interrupt." Robyn returned to the lab. *Everyone's busy, making progress, except me.*

Who could she talk to? None of this was fair. Her whole life had been turned upside down. Her parents were hundreds of kilometres away on the cruise they'd been looking forward to for years. If you could call a group of die-hard environmentalists on an old CSIRO research ship a 'cruise'. According to her parents' last postcard, they'd been busy harrying whalers, collecting ocean data and doing stints of mainland volunteer work. They thought she was happily ensconced in her lab in Canberra. Her best friend had a secret life as a computer genius. The first time in her life Robyn had a proper circle of friends and everything had imploded. She didn't know how to pick up the pieces, tessellate them together into something whole. Terence dead. Derek gone. Catherine prickly and quiet. Robyn never seemed to say the right thing at dinner, always felt underfoot in the kitchen. It was as if they were working in parallel versions of the same earthship.

Back in the lab, she stared at the data for another forty minutes before admitting defeat.

Sara and Eli grinned at her as she entered the kitchen. "We on?" Sara said, pushing her schoolwork away. Fletcher and Jacob looked up from their textbooks. Robyn nodded, forcing herself to tamp down her excitement. They were eager for the freedom of the run, not her company.

The days were becoming shorter. They had to start their runs earlier and earlier, racing the sunset back to the smoking chimney of the earthship. Robyn had never been a runner. Now the only time she felt remotely at peace was on her afternoon run, when the energy flickered to life in her body, washing everything away except the sound of her heartbeat. Her birthmark tingled as they formed a jagged line of moving bodies, disappearing down switchbacks and realigning on the spine of the ridge. She allowed her mind to drift, snagging on the taut energy tethers connecting her to Eli and Fletcher that seemed to pierce the very core of her being.

They made it back as darkness descended, as rapid

as if a celestial switch had been turned off. Fletcher's sullenness counterbalanced Eli's calm, measured movements at dinner. Their tethers pushed and pulled at Robyn's ribcage like a physical force, prickling her skin in the wake of the easy flow of the run.

Robyn feigned sleep on the camp bed as Catherine sank onto the proper mattress. She waited until she heard Catherine's slow, even breathing before she pushed back the blankets and padded into the kitchen.

The fridge door bounced off its hinges onto the floor with a solid *clunk* as she pulled it open. "Damn it," Robyn whispered, wary of the sleeping forms down the hallway. The coiled energy in her chest tightened as she brushed the newspaper clipping taped to the front. She'd read it nearly a dozen times. Kara insisted on its prominent position as a reminder. Robyn could recite the headline from memory. *Unprecedented extension of the aurora borealis and aurora australis leaves scientists puzzled.* Or, in reality, the time Fletcher somehow triggered a huge magnetic disturbance in the sky. *Which I'm still no closer to understanding*, Robyn thought as she wrestled the door. There. Robyn swung the door more carefully. It held. She poured herself a glass of milk and leaned against the kitchen counter.

Sleep no longer came easily. When she did manage to fall into an uneasy sleep, she felt the threads of blue, green and red in her bones, her blood, in the neurons firing through her synapses at impossible speeds. Robyn sipped her milk, thinking of her mother prescribing it when she was little and plagued by bad dreams. This certainly qualified.

The fridge door wasn't the first casualty. It was as if she didn't know her own body anymore. A weird second puberty that left her more uncoordinated than ever, except when she ran. The energy coursing through her limbs gave her new strength. *It's too much. I don't know what's happening to me*, Robyn thought. Light darted across her eyelids and her birthmark burned. She gasped as energy zipped through her spine and the glass imploded in her hand. Sharp fragments skittered across the kitchen floor as blood welled from her palm. Head pounding, Robyn shoved her hand in the sink, letting the frigid water blast the remaining glass away. The earth walls around her seemed to breathe, contracting and releasing in time with her own breath.

Damn it. Tears prickled behind her eyelids. She didn't know how to be what the convergers and walkers needed. She'd never had a brother or sister before, much less a responsibility for anyone other than herself. She couldn't think of Terence or Derek. Too many people she'd failed.

The cold water numbed her hand and wrist, slowing her hammering heartbeat. Through the kitchen window, the Milky Way lit up a cosmic path of burning gas that would outlive all of them. Desperate for fresh air, Robyn stepped onto the cold dewy grass, leaving the claustrophobic embrace of the earthship behind. In the darkness, it was as if the stars were everywhere at once. Like she was floating. A pleasant buzz wound up her calves, circling her hips, loosening the tension in her neck. Robyn raised her hands as pins and needles erupted across her skin, leaving the flesh pink and whole. The cuts on her palm were gone. Catherine's voice echoed in her mind: *run faster, jump higher, heal quicker.*

Robyn climbed the side of the earthship and lay on the grass, the contact lulling her to sleep as the stars watched overhead.

7

Temple

Posted to International GeoPhysics Forum by Hypatia

Topic: Implications of the auroral extension

The bright green magnetic disturbance in the sky is more than just a momentary lightshow. It's a warning. This has happened before. If we do not heed history's lessons, we are doomed to repeat the same mistakes. The solar storm of 1859 caused a geomagnetic storm that ravaged our atmosphere, crippling the communication system of the day: the telegraph. We've come a long way, but if we are hit by a geomagnetic storm of the same (or, heaven forbid, greater) magnitude, all our technology will be stripped from our hands. I'm sure the Québécois remember the surge in 1989, and that was just a glancing blow. A superstorm narrowly missed us again in 2012 and it took NASA over two years to reveal the data. Is no-one taking this seriously? Why do we even have dedicated satellites trained on the sun?

Kara stood at the rusted gate, the duffel strap biting into her shoulder. The mildewy one-level shack was wedged in between two towering apartment buildings, both with tiers of glassed balconies conspicuously free of grubby fingerprints. Oases to child-free public servants. One was sided with copper, already corroding in trendy blue veins. The smell of frying oil wafted from the burger van in the car park down the road where she'd managed to find a park after no less than three passes.

Braddon. Just as eclectic as always.

She wasn't entirely sure Aster would welcome a visit, but she needed equipment. Kara pushed open the gate and navigated the weedy overgrown garden spilling over the driveway. Up close, she spied the state-of-the-art satellite dish cleverly camouflaged among three broken ones.

The door opened, the security screen rattling. He'd probably been watching her from a security camera while she dithered.

"Hi, Aster."

"Kara. Long time no see."

The interior hadn't changed, the hallway littered with cardboard boxes and the lingering smell of congealed grease. Aster was unlike anyone she'd ever met. Gaunt and tall, he probably weighed less than her despite the crap he ate. She'd met him in her first year, pulling credit card numbers in Civic. Wearing stained jeans and a ripped flannel shirt, he'd been weaving his way through the intoxicated crowds when she spotted him. A good disguise, but Kara saw through it when she registered the calm collected look in his eyes. The scanner was high quality, way more sophisticated than anything she'd come across before. He could tell she'd made him, turning on his heel and disappearing. But she'd managed to get a pretty good look at him and tracked him down to this crack shack. They weren't friends, exactly. Rather acquaintances with similar proclivities. Over time, he became her dealer, of sorts.

"Haven't heard from you in a while." Aster led her through to what should have been the dining room. A long narrow table abutted the kitchen counter, crammed with computers and partly operated-on circuit boards. He whirled around. "Can you pay?"

Kara shrugged the duffel off her shoulder and dumped it on the chair. Aster unzipped it and let out a low whistle. "That's a nice lot of pineapples." He leaned against the counter with a grin. "What are you after?"

Kara handed him her list.

Robyn sat in a triangle with the two walkers, a wonky isosceles. Their frequency tethers pulled her toward them, yanking just above her ribcage. Fletcher had taken some convincing, but he'd finally agreed to travel with them for Ariana's sake. Robyn shifted to get comfortable, trying to ignore the flare of energy swirling through her body at the walkers' proximity. She felt the walkers at a cellular level, could read their moods, their energy levels. It was like an invisible umbilical cord.

"Are we going to do this or what?" Fletcher sat with

his eyes already closed.

"It's kind of hard to describe. Like meditating, maybe? You have to sort of consciously let go of what's happening around you." Eli rested his fists on his thighs.

Great, thought Robyn, *meditation for dummies*. She closed her eyes and concentrated on her breath. Light danced beneath her eyelids. Unbidden, images flashed across her mind. Derek, looking at her with disgust, holding the rack of activation vials. A roaring sound filled her ears and the image shifted, blurring into Catherine. Even as Robyn smiled, Catherine's face soured, pointing to a body dangling from chains. The unspoken accusation lingered. *You did this.* The body was Ariana, pale and bloody, unnaturally still. Jericho, her salamander, lay eviscerated on a table next to her like a high-school frog dissection, pins separating entrails from brain and scales.

No. Sweat beaded on Robyn's forehead. She shoved the images aside. Breathe. *Breathe*. Red, blue and green light blazed across her eyelids and white light engulfed her, jerking her into a weightless limbo. Robyn kept her eyes firmly shut until she felt solid ground beneath her feet. Gasping, she rested her hands on her knees and fought against the rising nausea in her gut.

Eli and Fletcher appeared with a red and green flash of light. Una hopped from Eli's shoulder onto the ground, expanding in size like a bag of microwave popcorn. Eva humphed at the display, already the size of a tank herself.

Robyn stared. She hadn't had time to appreciate either animal's spirit form before. It was enough to clear the lingering nausea in her system.

Eli grinned at Robyn. "I knew you could do it. Easy, right?"

Robyn wiped the sweat from her forehead and didn't answer. *Not exactly*, she thought.

"Hey. Where are we?"

Robyn turned around at the concern in Fletcher's voice, taking in their surroundings for the first time. They hadn't crossed over to the glade; instead, they stood exposed on a rocky outcrop devoid of vegetation. Steps chiselled into the stone led up into a clouded peak. Wind whipped around the three of them as they huddled together.

"I don't like this," said Fletcher.

Robyn gazed up the steep stairs. She was certain she'd never been here before, but the place felt familiar.

She peered into the cloud. "I think there's something up there."

Fletcher stared at her as if she'd just suggested they amputate one of his legs to use as a walking stick.

"Let's go see." Eli leapt astride Una's back and the osprey soared above them.

"I'm staying here." Fletcher crossed his arms and leaned against Eva.

"Fine." Robyn turned to face the ascent. She was only ten steps up when Una swooped low and Eli reached out a hand, pulling her up behind him. Equal parts terror and exhilaration coursed through her as they lifted high into the air, transforming Fletcher and Eva into tiny stubborn dots.

Robyn concentrated on breathing as they ascended into the milky clouds. Condensation formed on her skin as the wind chilled her to the bone. Her thighs ached as she clung to Una's back, shifting perilously every few seconds with the osprey's powerful wingbeats.

Abruptly, the cloud disappeared. Una slowed as they reached the top of the stairs. Robyn stared over Eli's shoulder as an ornate building appeared on the crest of the mountain above the reach of the ring of cloud. It looked as if it had been carved from the stone, more a part of the landscape than an addition to it. Thick, contorted vines grasped it like a giant's fingers.

Una coasted in for a landing and Robyn jumped down, her bare feet curling against the cool, damp stone.

Eli pressed a hand to one of the vines, forehead creased in thought.

"It's a temple." Robyn joined Eli at the entrance, pushing aside the hanging vines. "I think," she added at the walker's curious glance.

"Maybe we should wait for Lenti," Eli said. "Wherever he is."

Ignoring the concern in Eli's voice, Robyn pushed open the wooden door.

The interior took her breath away. A circular hole in the roof allowed a cylinder of light inside, catching the golden ceiling and flooding the room with brightness. A mosaic frieze swirled around the walls like a serpent. It was the most intricate artwork she'd ever seen. Red, green, blue. It felt like stepping into a dream, as if she'd been here before.

Maybe she had, in another life. *Could I really be the guide?*

"Walkers," Robyn said, tracing the coloured tiles.

Eli joined her, frowning. "Lenti's shown me this before. That day I told you about, when I met Liro?" He took Robyn's hand, seemingly insensible of the glittering ceiling, and led her to the rear wall. "Lenti was worried about this."

Robyn followed Eli, puzzled. He pointed to a circle of the mosaic encapsulating three figures.

"Oh." Robyn exhaled. Two boys and a girl stood with a bear, a bird of prey and a dragon. "It's you. All of you."

Eli motioned to the rest of the temple. "The lineages. They all end here."

Robyn traced the outline of the circle. There was knowledge there, in the back of her mind, but she couldn't quite catch it. She followed Eli's hand. Each of the three swirling lines did meet here, in the circle.

She hovered a hand just above the tiles. "You're right."

"Don't sound so surprised," Eli commented dryly.

"It's your history." Robyn turned around, taking in the sparkling lineages. "All your reincarnations." A turtle surrounded by blue tiles, a red raven, a horse circled in green. Robyn pressed a hand to the horse's mane and felt a shock of energy ricochet up her arm, sending her flying backward. A wave of choking darkness washed over her, crushing her chest and sending a shiver down her spine.

She grimaced and pulled herself upright as the temple ceiling let out a deep grating sound.

Eli stepped back toward the temple entrance. "This ruin isn't stable. Let's get out of here."

"But we've barely looked around," Robyn protested. The walls shook and plumes of dust rose from the stone floor. "Or maybe that is a good idea," she added.

Una screeched, clawing at the ground outside the doorway. The walls trembled again and Robyn coughed up dust as the familiar pressure began to build behind her right eye.

"Robyn, come on," Eli called. He grabbed her arm and half-dragged her through the temple, pulling her over the threshold as the door slid shut behind them with an ominous *boom*.

Robyn didn't have time to process what was happening. Her feet left the ground as white light engulfed her.

Robyn blinked, feeling the warm grass beneath her toes. The smell of vegetable soup hovered over her alongside the pull of Fletcher and Eli's frequency tethers. *I'm back.*

"What the hell was that?" Eli jumped to his feet, dislodging Una from his shoulder. She squawked and hopped onto the grassed mound of the earthship.

"Fletcher?" Robyn crawled over to the unmoving walker. His head lolled onto his shoulder when she poked him. "He's still there."

Eli sighed. "Waiting at the base of the stairs like a stubborn git." He closed his eyes. "I'll be right back."

"Wait!"

Faint red light retracted from Eli's skin. "What?"

"You said Lenti showed you the temple before. What did he say about the mosaics?"

Eli bit his lip. "He was part of a special order of monks dedicated to helping the walkers." Eli flicked his gaze over to Fletcher. "There's more. I didn't want to say anything the other day."

Robyn waited, her skin still tingling with energy from the spirit world.

Eli raised his eyes to his osprey as she shook her feathers. "Nyx escaped before. That's why Lenti was in the spirit world in the first place. The last guide, Liro, stopped Nyx somehow, but he died in the process. All the monks of the order died except Lenti. Liro transported him into the spirit world; a lone monk to help future walkers should the guide not return."

"There was a whole order of monks dedicated to the walkers?" Robyn said in disbelief. People who lived and breathed the rich history of the walkers, who kept fastidious mosaic records. People who knew about Nyx, about what the guide was tasked to do. She didn't have any training, any real understanding of what the walkers could do. She had no idea how to stop Nyx, and if the last guide had barely managed it, how on earth was she supposed to, even if she miraculously learned how? Robyn's shoulders slumped. Eli was still looking at her, his face solemn.

"Lenti also said that we might be the last walkers. Ever."

Eli's energy tether felt like a lance through her gut. Robyn thought of the mosaic version of Eli, Fletcher and Ariana, the tiny bright tiles, the circle encasing them all. Could Lenti be right? Her head spun, and for a moment Robyn thought she would vomit.

Eli ducked his head. "I'm going to get Fletcher."

Robyn nodded as red light flickered on Eli's skin, her mind far away. *The last walkers. No. I can't believe it.* She sat frozen between Eli and Fletcher, their calm, slack expressions so at odds with the turmoil inside her. Their energy tethers felt muted and dull. She took a few deep ragged breaths to overcome her dizziness, pressing her hands to the ground to steady herself. Energy trickled through her fingertips and swirled through her spine, slowing her racing pulse. *Even if I'm not the guide, I owe it to the walkers to try. Try to find a way to save Ariana, destroy Nyx, save the convergers that Fang is creating.* Clenching her fists, Robyn stood there revelling in the energy coursing through her body.

8

Connections

"It's beginning. Crop failure across Central America, famine in Africa, mysterious mass deaths of animals throughout Europe."

"I thought we had more time."

"Time is exactly what we don't have, Brock. The Greeks dubbed her Nyx, goddess of night. An apt name for a primordial entity with power beyond their wildest dreams."

"I've read Hesiod, Orpheus and Homer's assessments, Miranda. If you believe the poets, even Zeus feared her."

"An incorporeal, intergalactic, living organism. An entity beyond even our grasp today. Who knows her origins? A remnant of the dawn of time? The temple doesn't enlighten us."

"Past truth slowly becomes myth, legendary to those reading about it thousands of years later. Every era has recognised the power of beings beyond humans."

"Ah, but so few have come face to face with such power."

"And you think we'll fare any better than those before us?"

"My dear, I'm counting on it."

Kara hiked her duffel higher until it sat flush against her shoulder, sweating as she reached for the next branch. She pulled herself up into the crown and leaned against the main trunk to catch her breath. She'd chosen well. From here, the main road was visible as well as a nice straight section of the track to Robyn's farm. Kara dug out two cameras and strapped them to opposite sides of the trunk where they whirred to life. She pulled out her laptop and checked the feed, adjusting the camera trained on the road before packing up and clambering down.

It had taken three full days, but she'd managed to encircle the entire property with the electronic tripwire she'd sourced from Aster. Kara stepped out past the tree, holding her laptop. Onscreen, one of the connected dots blinked, tripping the camera she'd just installed. Kara saw herself standing alone on the track. Satisfied, she closed the laptop and yanked the duffel bag over her shoulder. The farm was as safe as she could physically make it. Pulling her coat closer, she started the long hike back to the earthship.

Eli, Fletcher, Jacob and Sara were sitting outside in a sliver of sun, notebooks on their laps. Kara watched them as she approached, trying to decide whether they were concentrating or chatting. Ming leapt up to lean against her chest as she reached them. Kara scratched behind the cat's ears. Chatting, she decided.

Sara shielded her eyes. "Can we finish now? You know how much I hate maths."

Kara leaned over Sara's shoulder and checked her scribblings. "Okay."

Sara jumped to her feet with a dazzling smile. Eli, Fletcher and Jacob clapped shut their books.

Kara walked inside. She found Robyn seated at the kitchen table, pouring through a textbook. Robyn raised her head, briefly making eye contact with her friend.

"Still looking for the temple?"

Robyn closed the book. "You don't understand. It was majestic. It felt like I was *supposed* to find it. Yet I can't get back there. We've all tried." Robyn jerked her head toward the shrieking outside. "How about you? Perimeter safe?"

Kara dug out her laptop and showed Robyn the circle of dots.

"Thanks. For shouldering so much of this," Robyn said, rubbing her eyes.

"It's not a problem." Kara tucked her laptop under her armpit. "Is Catherine here?"

"Yeah." Robyn raised her head. "Analysing the convergers' energy levels."

"And you're –"

"I'm fine," Robyn snapped, grabbing the textbook again.

"Right." Kara headed to the studio. She dumped her duffel with a sigh and rolled her shoulders.

Kate was already plugged in. She grunted in the direction of the coffee pot and Kara refilled the two stained mugs, pushing one over to her sister.

The gentle hum of the computers was soothing, a sound she'd come to associate with a feeling of calmness, of control. On the internet, it didn't matter if you were a 23-year-old law student. You could be anyone.

"Door shut?" Kate said without looking away from the screen.

"Yeah." Kara sipped her coffee. "Shoot."

"The death toll has exceeded all estimates. Edging on four million now."

"Shit."

"Should we tell Robyn?"

Kara shook her head. "She's just finding her feet again. We'll get a handle on this before we let her know." One less thing for Robyn to be responsible for. "Anything else?"

"Bunch of new column requests. Do you think Hypatia should take any of them?"

Kara glanced over her sister's shoulder at the list of five or six moderate online newspapers. "Nope. We wait until the big guns come to us."

"Roger that."

Kara worked her way through the forums she'd tagged, replying to the mundane comments without much effort and toying with her responses to the more astute ones. It had taken time, but their ideas were gaining traction. First, a frontal assault on the major discussion boards, the online marketplaces where the global village traded in ideas and anonymity was as commonplace as crude usernames. Still, they routinely had to shut down impersonator accounts. They'd both attracted followings.

Hypatia argued the moral necessity of preserving the planet and rallied for uniform international environmental legislation. Her eloquent posts documented gruelling environmental atrocities covered up by governments around the world. At first, Kara painstakingly dug up proof herself, but as Hypatia slowly became a household name, whistleblowers began coming forward. Too terrified to risk their own jobs and wellbeing, they delivered the information like an offering to an oracle. And Hypatia obliged them, freeing them of their guilt and trumpeting the information to the masses. Of course, only after taking a deep hard look down the mouth of each gift horse. The people clamoured for more. Deep distrust of their governments plus the quality of the information she leaked proved an irresistible combination, just as Kara had envisioned. Now parliaments in Moscow, Beijing and Washington debated her posts. Serious talks were underway as to whether the United Nations should be granted actual legislative power.

BeyonceKnows worked at the opposite end of the spectrum, steering entirely clear of political and environmental issues. Her syrupy, gossip-laden posts spread quickly, picked up and distributed through other networks by legions of users. An army of plugged-in youth unwittingly seeded their IP addresses with the bots Kate encoded in each post, giving her millions of pairs of eyes.

Kate had been the one to suggest the pen names. No-one would guess that Hypatia and BeyonceKnows worked side by side in remote rural Australia.

Kara swirled her mug and settled in.

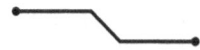

"This is useless. I don't feel anything." Fletcher opened his eyes with a sigh. Eli sat cross-legged next to him, the picture of serenity. A stack of pallets sat teetering across the clearing from the earthship, still very much intact.

"We've both done it before. We must be able to control our auras somehow. We just need to figure it out," Eli said. Una soared overhead, sending her shadow racing across the grass. Eva sat beside Fletcher, the warmth radiating from her skin better than any heater.

Still your mind, young one. The air walker is right. You can control the energy within, the energy without.

Fletcher's mind refused to calm down. The inaction was crippling. He'd failed so many people: his parents were dead because of him, and he could have saved Ariana if he'd told her about Terence's death, urged her to come home. *Home.* He didn't really have one anymore. The earthship wasn't home. Everyone's forced smiles were beginning to chafe him raw.

You must let them go. Empty your mind. Enter the void.

Eli cracked open one eye. "In Beijing, the energy just danced at my fingertips."

"We're wasting our time here. I know it, you know it," Fletcher groaned.

You're frustrated.

A brilliant observation. What a keen mind you have, Fletcher projected.

Eva humphed.

"We need to connect with who we are. Our lineages. The temple …" Eli began.

"Enough about the damn temple. You said it yourself, it was a ruin."

Eli shook his head. "You should have seen the mosaics. Ariana talked about an in-between place, a void she reached when she trained with Atlantis, and Lenti talked about opening the channels to our past lives."

"We should be *rescuing* Ariana, not sitting around," Fletcher snapped. Then he faltered. "Eva mentioned a void, too."

You actually listened to me? I should make a note. Eva scratched her side and rolled over. Fletcher ducked his head in silent apology.

"Somewhere between the physical world and the spirit world," Eli continued. "Una says it should be possible for us to reach it, to control the energy."

A faint rumbling of thunder echoed through the valley as fat droplets began to fall. Wind snuck past the edges of Fletcher's coat, chilling the sweat beneath. He leaned back against Eva.

"We have to learn how to control our auras if we're

going to save Ariana," Eli said, raising his voice over the brewing storm. Una curled downward to land on his shoulder.

He's right, young one.

Fletcher clenched and released his fists, willing his body to relax, his mind to slow down.

Empty your mind. Enter the void.

Eli controlled his breathing as he calmed his mind. He couldn't think of Fletcher by his side, or Ariana in the MRI's clutches. He had to embrace the present moment as if nothing existed beyond his heartbeat. Una dug her talons into the padded leather on his shoulder as the storm intensified. The familiar pressure of crossing over to the spirit world descended, but Eli held on to his grip on the physical world, teetering wildly between the two until he pushed through into blackness.

Eli stared, struck speechless as he hung suspended in nothingness, neither standing nor falling. It was like hanging in deep space, the entire cosmos swirling around him. His limbs tingled, and a red glow blossomed on his skin. Una merged into her spirit form and released him. He blinked, and suddenly he was standing in a dusty alleyway lined with ramshackle huts. People passed him but seemed not to notice his presence. The smell of rancid frying oil made him gag.

Where are we? he projected to Una.

"You're in India. Duh."

Eli whirled around at the voice. A small girl stood in the middle of the dusty street in a brightly coloured sari, arms crossed. She smiled at Eli as if he were an old friend. On her shoulder sat a dark raven. The bird tipped its head and studied Eli with wise eyes.

Eli took a step forward. "You can see me? Hear me?"

"Oh boy." She stroked the bird on her shoulder.

Eli looked between them, registered the mirrored positions of their birds. As he watched, Una and the raven spiralled upward into their spirit forms. Red light blazed simultaneously on Eli and the girl's skin. "You're the last air walker," Eli breathed.

The girl's smile widened. "The name's Clara. Glad you finally made it."

As he took a step toward her, the blackness gathered them up. Clara now hung beside him in the void, wreathed in red light. She studied his jacket with interest, staring at the zipper. "It's been a long time since

I was air walker," she said, her voice laced with sadness. "That means Notos has been adrift for centuries."

A deep voice rose in the depths of Eli's mind. *Our separation has only made it easier for the dark one to regain power. The rippling has begun.*

Notos? Eli thought. The red light on his skin flared. "You're ... a part of me?"

Clara's arm jangled with dozens of bracelets as she touched his arm. Eli reeled as a vision flashed across his consciousness, a line of people moving as one, raising their arms and shifting their weight. Not quite dancing, not quite fighting. Notos' voice rose once more in his mind: *It is dangerous for you to attempt the bridge to me. There is not much time. You must learn to direct the energy inside of you. What you feel now is only the faintest stirrings. Seek out the old ways. Some among your kind still practise the art.*

The pinpoints of light around him began to disappear. Una let out a nervous cry as Clara began to fade, her arm raised in farewell.

Perhaps this time will be different, the air spirit intoned.

Eli's vision blurred as Una encased him in her wings, the blazing red of his aura surrounding both of them. He felt his body jerk sideways as the blackness engulfed him.

Fletcher listened to the storm, felt the air crackling around him. He felt the beginnings of the slip into the spirit realm and deliberately stopped himself. It was like balancing on the edge of a precipice. His whole body rebelled against it, jerking as if he'd grabbed hold of a live wire.

Eva?

I can't hold us here. Eva's voice was laced with fear.

Fletcher felt a wave of darkness wash over him. He couldn't move, couldn't think, couldn't see anything but blackness. Dread filled him, thick as ink. Time swirled around him – had he been here only minutes, or hours?

"Fletcher?" Strong hands shook him, sent the darkness rippling around him. Fletcher recognised Eli's voice, but it sounded distant, echoey. He tried to push back from the blackness toward Eli's voice, but it wouldn't let him go. Fighting panic, Fletcher concentrated on the pull of Eva's mind, felt the dark begin to lift.

He came back to himself like a drowning man, clawing for breath. Eli was shaking him. Fletcher felt a throbbing pain in his skull as his sight returned. Eva panted beside him. It felt like he'd been running hard for hours.

Eli released him and took a step backward. Rain pounded against his skin, though the air walker barely seemed to notice.

What was that? Fletcher projected, but Eva remained silent. Her fear curdled in his stomach. His legs shook as he stood. Eli caught him as he stumbled, sending prickling energy racing across his skin. Fletcher wrapped his sodden coat tight around him. Only the faintest edge of sunset pierced the trees. *How long was I out there, in the void?* Fletcher wondered.

Sara and Robyn appeared in the doorway as Eli turned to the stack of pallets. Red light flared around his body as he lifted his arms, moving them in a figure of eight in front of his torso before pushing both hands outward.

Boom.

The pallets exploded in a flash of red, jagged planks rising high into the air. Fletcher shielded his eyes against the dazzling brightness. The light on Eli's skin retracted to a faint glow.

Fletcher lifted his arms, but there wasn't a hint of green on his skin. *It didn't work*, he realised, fighting the throbbing pain in his skull.

"How?" Robyn demanded, seemingly oblivious to the rain as she ran over.

"I found the in-between place, the void between our world and the spirit world. It was like floating out in deep space, and then ... I met the last air walker." Eli's eyes welled with tears. "A girl named Clara – she had a raven." The last remnants of red light faded from his skin.

Fletcher shook his head under the combined weight of Robyn and Eli's gaze. "I tried but I ... got stuck."

"Lenti talked about opening the channels, but I never dreamed ..." Eli continued, eyes wide. "I never dreamed it would feel like this. I felt the air spirit – it's part of me. It told me that I had to learn to direct the energy, that I had to seek the old ways."

"It looked like you had the directing part under control," Sara said, motioning to the steaming remnants of the pallets.

Eli shook his head. "I don't think I could do it again. I have to learn to funnel the energy." He took a few steps away and repeated the movements, but the red energy didn't come.

Robyn chewed her lip. "Ariana talked about specific movements she used to channel energy, to actively break down bonds between carbon, hydrogen and oxygen."

Fletcher barely took in the conversation happening around him. He shuffled over to Eva and wrapped his arms around her neck. *What happened to us?*

I felt the darkness, couldn't fight it. Eva shuddered under his arms. *It is not as it should be.*

We can try again, I'm sure –

No.

But we have to try. What happened to 'empty your mind, enter the void'?

I was wrong. Never again.

Fletcher looked up as Robyn called his name from the door, realising he and Eva were alone in the clearing. He felt hollowed out, like he might topple over at any moment.

Inside, Robyn spread a sheet of butcher's paper across the dining table. She drew a straight line across the page, writing *radio* at one end and *gamma* at the other. In the very centre, she wrote *visible*. Catherine emerged from the lab and peered over her shoulder as Eli and Sara shucked their wet jackets onto the floor. "I heard a bang. Is everything okay?"

Robyn nodded, not looking up from the table. She tapped the centre of the spectrum. "Visible light. We can see your auras, but you can wield all sorts of energy, not just visible." Robyn dragged her pencil across the line toward *gamma*. "Gamma rays. Higher frequency but shorter wavelength. We can measure the gamma radiation you're emitting with a Geiger counter, like Kara did back at the lab. But it's more than that. I think each of you is tapped into a particular set of *frequencie*s. You're able to speak with animals from specific biomes because you're clicked into a specific set of frequencies. Radio frequencies would be my best guess."

Water dripped steadily from Eli in the ensuing awed silence. "A human radio?"

Robyn nodded and tapped the paper. "Somehow you can receive and transmit energy in that range, like the gamma power of your auras." She straightened. "I think that's what the energy tethers are, too. Specific frequencies connecting us."

Catherine's mouth drew into a little 'o' of understanding as she stared at Robyn's drawing.

Fletcher wondered if Robyn could feel the fear still shuddering through him, the turmoil roiling in Eva's mind. Eli had reached the void and returned whole, but Fletcher had come face to face with something terrifying. Eva flinched as he rubbed her flank. He saw a flash of darkness in her eyes, gone as quickly as he registered it. Fletcher slumped back against Eva, hooking a hand in her shaggy fur. He felt drained, beyond exhausted. *If I can't use my aura, what chance do I have of saving Ariana? Of helping anyone?*

Eva wailed softly into his side, but for once she had no words of wisdom.

9

Spirits

"With the chip, the girl poses no threat, Miranda."

"Yet they're torturing her. Vulcan is an imbecile."

"I'm doing my best."

"And the new convergers?"

"You should be here to see them yourself. Anything less pales in comparison."

"It's not the right time."

"What will the mid-year solstice tell you that you don't already know?"

"You can't honestly believe that hogwash about the aurora expansion. We're not due for a geomagnetic reversal for decades. I need to know if the timeline has changed. There's much we still need to do."

"I'm no geologist, Miranda, but I think Vulcan is

a more pressing concern. Or have you forgotten the madman in charge of the lives of every converger pair popping up across the planet?"

"I'm surprised their existence hasn't yet been revealed. Soon it will be beyond containment."

"You're right. It's only a matter of time before the world is aware of these children and their capabilities. Before the world is aware of our existence. Come back."

"After the mid-year solstice, my dear. Don't worry."

The bare room reeked like a hospital ward. The freshly painted white walls left no cracks for her to count. One tiny window near the ceiling she had no hope of reaching. A single bed, toilet, sink. And, of course, a camera in the corner. Foolishly, Ariana had thought her confinement would be temporary. She should have known better. Stupid, so stupid, not to start keeping track of time. She lost weeks in the early blur of meals on plastic trays and slanted fingers of sunlight tracing their way around her cell. She made her own calendar by pressing her fingernail into the hem of her shirt until it tore. The rows grew.

Each morning, a woman in a lab coat arrived with breakfast and to take her blood before wheeling her down the hall to the shock chamber. The treatment left her weak and shaky, only lucid enough to think by the late afternoon. The electrode burns scarred her flesh, yet by the next day, her skin had always healed. *Increased mitochondrial energy production*, Ariana thought, remembering her brother's words.

The blood samples and treatment made Ariana increasingly paranoid. She knew it was unlikely Fang would be able to do anything with her gene sequence. Terence had told her of the flux-like complexity of the walker convergence sequence, of the impossibility of mapping or replicating it. Yet her certainty began to waver as more and more vials of crimson left her body, as each day she spent in the shock chamber sapped her strength. Was Fang better than her brother? What did it matter? Terence couldn't help her now. Her brother was gone. Jericho was gone. Not dead – they wouldn't kill him while they still needed her. The very fact that she was alive meant they still needed her. She was an asset.

But she was only human. Isolation was designed to

break people, reduce them to snivelling messes eager to please their captors. She was determined not to be one of them. Yet in the confines of her cell, her mind taunted her. Memories rose in the unused hours like ghosts. Sitting in her father's study with Terence, enthralled by a story. Her mother, Val, in the garden, dirt-smeared and smiling. The warmth of the memories made Ariana shiver, knowing the farm stood empty. The gardens had probably gone wild, her father's study covered in dust now that he'd left on his odyssey. They'd never be together again, not now Val and Terence were dead.

But she still had a family, in a way. Fletcher and Eli wouldn't abandon her. She clung to the hope of rescue with religious fervour. *They're coming.* She spent hours repeating it like a mantra in her mind as she practised the movements Atlantis had shown her. To whoever watched the camera footage, she was simply exercising. A fully defensible action for someone locked in a cell. No-one came to stop her. So she trained, filling the long hours with the only action she could take. The flow of movements calmed her, even though the chip at the base of her skull stopped the familiar push and pull of energy.

When she reached five rows of tears in her shirt,

Ariana felt the first hints of full-blown panic. *I can't go on like this. I have to get out of this cell.* She rolled over and stared at the ceiling. The door mechanism clicked open and the familiar female scientist pushed her wheelchair through the doorway. Ariana didn't know her name. *I don't know anything: what's beyond the corridor, how many people there are in the building, where they're keeping Jericho.*

Ariana held out her arm for the needle and ate her porridge. The woman scrawled in her notebook as she packed away the crimson vials. "It's time."

Ariana sat in the wheelchair, her face strained. Fear descended on her like a stranglehold. She closed her eyes and focused on breathing, imagined the spirit energy coursing through her body. By the time she reached the shock chamber, her heartbeat had levelled. She felt the chip release its hold of her the moment the doors sealed shut. Fang held the receiver aloft behind the glassed wall. Jericho was already in the room, immobilised as usual.

Jericho. Ariana felt oddly calm. *I don't care anymore. There's nothing else they can do to me.*

Pain can be overridden. It is temporary. Jericho raised his head as far as his restraints allowed.

Everything is temporary. Ariana stood and raised her arms, staring blankly toward the glassed wall as the scientist closed the wrist cuffs and secured her ankles. The electrodes felt cool against her skin, like water.

As the door closed, Ariana focused on her breathing. She heard the crackle of electricity, knew it must be coursing through her body. But she was floating away, beyond its reach.

"Something's wrong." Fang frowned as the monitor flatlined. "Stop the current, then give her a short burst."

The scientist at the controls nodded and complied. The heart monitor didn't change.

"Again."

Ariana's body convulsed under the current, hanging heavy from the restraints.

Sweat beaded on Fang's forehead. Derek pressed his hands to the glass. "Do something," he urged, his gaze never leaving Ariana's face.

Fang turned back to the monitor, heart racing. "Again," she said evenly.

Ariana floated in blackness. Around her tiny lights

flickered like stars. Jericho hovered in his spirit form. She felt Atlantis' presence even though she couldn't see the whale.

Do you feel that?

In every fibre of my being, Jericho said.

Atlantis' voice echoed in the darkness. *Come.*

Ariana felt the familiar building pressure of the transition to the spirit world and closed her eyes. Sound washed over her. Seagulls, crashing waves. Her feet sank into a soft shifting substance. She opened her eyes and a beach strung with palms materialised. *Where the hell am I?* A ship swayed offshore. Ariana spun around and nearly fell over as she registered the strange man sitting cross-legged in front of her. A half-naked, bearded man.

Am I in the spirit world? Am I dead? This is it. It's all over. Calmness descended on her. She turned back to face the man. "Is this … heaven?"

The man laughed, the sound booming and jovial. "Unfortunately, no." An enormous turtle crawled from the water and the man reached out to stroke its shell. Blue light arced between them.

The man wore fitted trousers and a thin vest. He had bands around his wrists and intricately inked tattoos spiralling up his arms.

"You're a walker." Ariana's dreams from her time with Atlantis came rushing back. Coral, the gleaming underside of a turtle, a dark-skinned boy. "You're the boy from my dreams?" She wasn't convinced. "But you're so …"

The man smiled. "As you can see, I'm not a boy anymore. But yes, that was me."

"But how are you here, now?"

"You're ready to meet me," said the man. "The name is Yves."

"But this – the chip stops me from entering the spirit world," Ariana protested.

"Ah, but we are not in the spirit world. We are somewhere infinitely more complex, a place in-between the physical and spirit worlds. You have touched the edges of this place before, but never truly entered it."

"Atlantis." Ariana thought of the galaxy-like darkness she'd entered. The feeling lingered in her chest, sending blue light skimming across her limbs. *Every time I've trained with Atlantis, I've felt a strange presence. I always assumed it was the brink of the spirit world.* "Beijing," she spluttered. "I reached a place where I could call Jericho into his spirit form while still in the physical world."

Yves nodded. "It is the fusion between spirit and human that allows your consciousness to drift here. You are young to have made the journey – I did not achieve this until I had near thirty summers." He stared at her with sorrowful eyes. "But you have been through much for one so young."

Ariana turned away, staring out over the calm water. "I wanted it to end."

"But what is an end but another beginning? There is much good for you still to do. We are all fleeting specks of humanity, called to do what we can in the time we have." Yves pushed himself to his feet. "But controlling it is another matter. You automatically trigger into this state when your life or that of your partner is at risk. Entering it at will takes total command of the energy flowing through your body and mind."

Ariana lifted her hands. "I managed to do it."

"Yes. And you will be able to do it again. But you are vulnerable here." Yves clapped his hands and the beach disappeared, replaced by the eerie, floating blackness. Blue light surrounded them both.

Yves uncurled his hand to reveal a seashell. He

thumbed the smooth ridges. "Look."

Ariana frowned. "It's a shell." Not even much of one, just the interior scaffolding of some grand swirling mass. She weighed it in her palm as Yves passed it to her.

"But once it was an enormous palace with many passages, completely enclosed. So it was with the dark one. Long ago, the spirits trapped Nyx. But time has a way of eroding boundaries."

Ariana stared at Yves in horror. "Nyx escaped."

"Briefly, yes. The walker before me found a new shell to trap her in."

"Another prison."

"But perhaps it is not as sturdy." Yves crushed the shell in his palm. Sparkling white dust disappeared into the abyss when he opened his hand. "Soon Nyx will be free on the wind, everywhere. The sun song is coming."

Despair washed over Ariana. What good could she do trapped here? "How do we stop it?"

Lights flickered in the dark like so many stars. "Our bond to Atlantis sustains us here. Atlantis is of the spirit world and you the physical. Together you can drift between both, by the strength of thousands of years of walker connections. But Nyx too comes from the in-between, this space as old as the beginning of time. If you should die while your consciousness is tethered here, the walker lineage will be broken, the reincarnation cycle destroyed."

Ariana watched as the lights behind Yves expanded into a ghostly formation of men and women, all wreathed in blue light. Tears pricked at her eyes. *Past sea walkers. All of them.* She felt a surge of belonging, of peace.

"Do you understand?" Yves stood at the head of the group, taking a step backward into their midst. He began to fade.

"Yes." Ariana bowed to her past selves as the lights dimmed, leaving her alone in the darkness.

Atlantis' voice rose in her mind. *Now you have earned your scales.*

Fang hunched over the monitor. Five minutes, forty seconds unresponsive. In the shock chamber, Ariana lay on the ground, the electrodes in place but the restraints hastily removed. Derek pumped her chest, paused to check her pulse, then continued his attempt at resuscitation.

Fang pressed the intercom. "Derek. She's gone."

Somehow, she managed to keep her voice level despite the fear paralysing her limbs. Fang thought of the failed subjects in Beijing, but that was different. Miranda had upped the experimental dosage at Vulcan's insistence; it hadn't been her fault. She stared through the glass at Ariana's slender, unresponsive body. Not this time. *I killed her. I pushed too hard, and I killed her.* Horror flooded through her veins.

Derek shook his head. "No. Try it again."

Fang took a ragged breath and nodded at the scientist. Current surged through Ariana, sending her legs and arms into a jerky spasm. Then she lay still. Derek kept going. "Again," he urged. He worked like a man possessed. Fang could only watch, frozen into inaction. Bracing herself against the desk, Fang was just about to nod her approval when Ariana sat up with a huge shuddering gasp, her eyes wild.

Derek let out a choked sob.

Fang clutched her own chest as she watched the heartbeat re-establish itself on the monitor. *Impossible.* Relief surged through her like a drug.

Derek stormed back into the room as two scientists lifted Ariana into the waiting wheelchair. "No more. I won't allow it."

Fang straightened with a nod. "You want to integrate her."

"It's time, Fang. Vulcan agrees with me."

10

Integration

Every single atom of our body is on loan to us from the universe. The iron in our blood, the calcium in our bones, the carbon in our DNA — all were sent tumbling toward Earth by distant stellar explosions. Each atom is recycled anew here on Earth, millions upon millions of times. Many educated people sneer at the concept of reincarnation, but it's already happening all around us at the atomic level.

Brock Williams, Working Notes.

Ariana's eyelids fluttered as she lay half-awake on her bed, clutching the threads of her conversation with

Yves. For two days she'd lain undisturbed, thinking. No-one came to take her blood or take her to the shock chamber. The memory of Derek's terrified face flashed through her mind, his hands shaking as he lifted her into the wheelchair, smoothing the hair from her face. "Thank God, Ariana," Derek had whispered. "No more. I promise you."

He seemed to have kept his promise. So far. She rolled over onto her side and traced the healed skin where the bruises and electrode burns had disappeared. The chip in her neck still stilted the flow of energy in her body. *I won't be able to get back to the in-between with this thing controlling me.* She replayed the image of the legion of walkers, all crackling with blue energy, all standing with her. *I'm not alone. I'll never be alone.* Ariana lay in a half-doze until she heard the door security mechanism.

Derek.

She sat up as the heavy door closed behind him with a *thunk*. Ariana steeled her expression. "What more can you possibly want from me?" Her voice was hoarse and weak. Ariana dropped her head, heart pounding. *I have to look damaged, broken. I can't let them know I've discovered truth beyond their comprehension.*

Derek remained near the door, hunched over his hands. "I've spoken with the Chief Director. I never intended for you to be ..."

Ariana straightened and Derek paused, looking momentarily uncertain.

"We're going to integrate you with the other students."

Ariana stared blankly at Derek. So there were others, other convergers co-operating with Fang. She swallowed the barrage of questions that surfaced, remembering the camera. She had to play her part. She had to co-operate. For now.

"Others?"

Derek turned and wrenched the door open. "Come and see."

Men in dark fatigues lined the corridor, holding guns across their chests. Ariana walked behind Derek, focusing on the feel of the floor against her feet, the echoing sounds of Derek's footfalls. She didn't understand why the soldiers were necessary. *Why now?* Ariana thought. *I'm not dangerous with the chip.* Only real threats required such a show of power. *They're still scared of me*, she realised. *Of what I can do. I can use that. Even though they expect a broken creature emerging from the mental ravages of near-solitary confinement, that creature still merits guards.* Ariana processed the information in an instant, only raising her head when Derek passed her a slim metal case.

"Your tablet. You'll need it for classes and recreation. Your uniform will be waiting for you in the dorms."

Ariana swiped a palm across the screen and it lit up. *Welcome, Ariana Jones.* Handprint-activated. She slid it under her arm as Derek stopped in front of a door. The flanking guards hadn't moved. They stood at attention against the walls. Watching. Ariana ducked her head again. *Classes, uniform. A school?*

"You're a new student. You don't mention anything about convergence, walkers, anything. We'll be watching." Derek had one hand on the door. Right. Because *student* sounded better than *prisoner*. Ariana nodded, eyes trained on the floor. *Look submissive, intimidated by the guards. Let them think you're a scared little girl.* Voices carried from beyond the door, increasing in volume as Derek pushed it open. A group of teenagers stood in the middle of a huge warehouse lined with laboratory benches. Ariana imperceptibly scanned the machines whirring in the centre. At the back of the lab, an enormous aquarium rose almost to the ceiling, splaying eerie dappled light across the walls. An orca hung suspended high above the scientists, as if floating in a dark sky. A wetsuit-clad girl sat on the edge, feet dangling. Ariana stopped dead in the doorway, taking it all in. Derek pushed her gently forward and she almost tripped before regaining her footing. The door slammed behind them and the knot of teenagers turned.

Convergers, Ariana realised as she saw the animals. She assessed each new pair as the girl in the wetsuit slid down a ladder set into the wall. Apart from the animals, they looked totally normal. She felt their eyes on her as she walked across the laboratory with Derek. Some of them whispered excitedly to each other. *A new laboratory and new research subjects.* If Derek called them students, then they were willing participants. Ariana felt her anger rise and deliberately tamped it down. *I have to stay calm, to learn everything I can.* The crowd of people, the enormous room: it was overwhelming after so long on her own. By the time she had her emotions under control, they had reached the small group. Derek nodded once at her and then strode to the front. He looked steadier, more capable than she remembered. *He's all steel. The Derek I knew is gone.*

"Welcome to the MRI." Derek flashed a smile at the group. "You represent a genetic leap, a step forward for humanity and the planet. I think you'll find you've come to the right place to explore your abilities." The other convergers nodded with rapt attention. Derek pointed to the blonde girl in the wetsuit as she wrapped a towel around herself. "This is Spencer, one of our most promising students."

Spencer wrung out her long ponytail and wrinkled her nose. "Call me Spence. Only my mother calls me Spencer."

A smatter of laughter echoed through the cavernous space. Ariana watched the others fidget, noted their wide-eyed glances at the machines. As far as she could see, none of them had implants. She wondered what story the MRI had concocted to convince them to walk into their trap. She scanned the nearest laboratory benches for anything she could use as a weapon – a scalpel, syringe – but they were bare. When she looked up, Derek was staring at her, almost as if he'd read her mind.

"Spencer, I mean Spence," Derek rubbed the bridge of his nose, "is going to show you around. You've been briefed already and you each have your tablets. I'll be monitoring your progress, so work hard. Again: welcome and good luck." Derek turned and walked away.

Ariana stiffened. *Jericho.* She'd missed her chance to ask Derek about Jericho. Spence set off toward a corridor on the opposite side of the lab. Ariana turned her head and pinned Derek's retreating form with her gaze, trying to look as pathetic as possible. *Please turn around. Please.*

He did.

"Later," he mouthed, as he was engulfed by a group of scientists emerging from the same door she'd come through only moments before.

Raising her head, Ariana scrutinised the upper glassed level wrapping around the lab. No doubt Fang was up there somewhere. Watching. Waiting.

"Ready for the tour?" Spence called. The new convergers stood on the opposite side of the laboratory, waiting. They all turned to face Ariana, eager and smiling. Her stomach knotted. *They have no idea what they've walked into.*

Ariana cast a final look around, committing the

layout to memory. She lingered at the back of the group as Spence led them into the corridor, nattering about schedules and practice times.

I'm out of my cell, and I'm going to make them regret it.

11

Emergence

Sun worship permeates nearly every culture, and for good reason. Without its prodigious energy output, we would not exist. Earth would be just another barren, frozen rock hurtling through space. It keeps us Goldilocks warm – not too hot, not too cold. Plants harvest its energy via photosynthesis, gifting us both oxygen and food. And, of course, this blazing star illuminates our daily lives, keeping us safe from everything that goes bump in the night.

Brock Williams, Working Notes.

Ariana stepped through the door into a parallel corridor

that fractured into a series of rooms. Spence stopped at the first, swinging open a door to reveal a huge room with two lines of partitioned single beds. Each had an overhead shelf, all made of the same metal as the bed frames. It reeked military.

"Here are the dorms. This is ours, the boys are next door. Handprint-activated entry. No boys in the girls' dorm and vice versa. You'll get your assigned beds later today, and your uniforms." Spence waved the group further down the corridor. Human voices and animal calls bounced off the walls as Spence stopped again.

"Ready?" Spence grinned as she braced her arms on the door in front of her.

The group shuffled closer. *Ready for what?* Ariana thought.

Spence opened the door wide. The subsequent wave of sound hit Ariana like a physical force after the enforced quiet of her cell.

"Hey, Spence, bringing in the fresh meat, huh?"

Someone else wolf-whistled.

"This is the cafeteria." Spence ignored the running commentary and strode through the room to a long counter. Wary, the new convergers followed her. Ariana stood still and surveyed the room. She felt lightheaded. How many? Sixty, maybe eighty? There were tables and tables filled with convergers: joking, eating, bickering. The whole time she'd been locked up, there had been this many convergers in the building and she had had absolutely no idea. *If only Fletcher and Eli could see this.* Fear replaced the momentary giddiness. *What were the MRI doing with so many convergers?*

Spence jerked her head toward the counter. Following the new group, Ariana grabbed a tray. The server dolloped porridge into a bowl. Ariana nodded her thanks and eyed the tables more closely as she stepped into the middle of the cafeteria. Five were marked with a stripe of colour. Spence sat down at the table divided by a blue line.

So there's a hierarchy.

Ariana headed toward the empty row of tables at the back of the room, ignoring the curious glances thrown her way. She needed to watch, get a feel for how things worked. A lion yawned behind a boy further down the hall. A gorilla scratched its head next to a dark-haired girl. Ariana stared at the enormous blonde bear sitting next to a tall boy. She couldn't help thinking of Eva, of

Fletcher.

One of the new girls walked over to the boy with the bear. "Hi," she said, her face bright. "Can I join you?"

A girl at the table sniggered. "I don't know. Can she, Daniel?"

The table quietened. The boy – Daniel – looked up, his face unreadable. "I'm sorry," he said, his voice like flint. "But we don't entertain rooks here."

The girl shrieked as the bear lurched to its feet, snarling. She stumbled backward, the tray skidding from her grip to the floor as she landed awkwardly on her forearm. Ariana heard the crack of bone before the girl's wails began echoing around the room. The table erupted with laughter.

Ariana ate her porridge. A medic led the injured girl away, the room already thrumming with resumed conversation.

Standing at the window in Vulcan's office, Fang stared at the bustling laboratory, Ariana's determined gaze seared in her mind. There was no rational way the walker could have survived. It was an accident, but even with her rapid healing, Derek shouldn't have been able to revive her. Fang had frozen, completely useless. If Derek hadn't been there … she didn't want to think about it. Fang caught a glimpse of her own reflection in the glass. Her face was a cool mask, expertly hiding the disturbance within. She'd spent years cultivating that expression, as much a mask as a shield, but for a moment it threw her off balance as she thought of the woman who'd taught it to her. She missed Miranda, the security of knowing her place in the food chain. Where Miranda was fire, passionate about finding the walkers and furthering the science, Vulcan was all ice. Miranda would never have put an asset like Ariana at risk, but Vulcan had demanded it. Maybe Miranda was right. There was more to these walkers than she realised. Even so, Vulcan's methods were brutish. She hated constantly having to prove her worth, hated fighting the underlying unease that followed her everywhere like a shadow. If she didn't come up with results soon, who knew how Vulcan would react?

The door swung open and interrupted her thoughts. Derek nodded at her before turning to the desk. "It's done. I stand by my original recommendation of Athena."

Vulcan leaned back in his chair. "Whichever team you think is best. Are we ready to start choosing sequencing targets to create the commercial vectors?"

Fang watched the vein in Vulcan's neck pulse. "Soon," she said. "We don't have enough data to proceed."

Vulcan narrowed his eyes, but Derek stepped in. "What Fang means is that the initial skirmish rounds have proved promising but we can't discount any of the students yet. Commencement of the games will give us plenty of statistics to work with."

Vulcan nodded, satisfied. "Good." He laced his fingers together. "Dismissed."

Fang ducked her head in acknowledgement and left with Derek. He strode down the hallway with a determined look in his eye. "It's coming together."

Fang nodded, still unsure how to treat Derek. He'd been quiet since Ariana's accident in the shock chamber. She wondered if he realised he was as much a pawn as she was, being moved around the board at Vulcan's whim. God, if only Miranda were here. Everything would be different. She'd have control of her research again, someone sane to discuss it with. But Miranda was dead and Fang had to make do with the pieces she'd been given, so she decided to make an attempt at diplomacy. "Your activation dose has proved extremely successful."

Derek frowned. "We still have so few of the convergers. There should be hundreds."

"Three hundred to be precise. And we'll find them. I'll find them," Fang amended. The extraction unit was all Vulcan entrusted her with now. Hours in front of the computer instead of the lab. Punishment for her failure to extract the secrets of Ariana's energy aura.

Derek seemed to sense the tone of her thoughts, because he tensed at her side. "I can speak to him, if you'd like."

Fang shook her head as she stopped in front of her office. She still wasn't sure how everything had inverted so quickly, but she was not about to place any reliance on Derek, no matter how damn polite he was.

Derek nodded and disappeared back downstairs to the lab, making a beeline for the command centre.

Fang paused with her hand on the doorknob. The goddamn prodigal son returned. Vulcan's fawning was getting on her nerves.

"Fang?"

She turned at the familiar voice. Brock stood clutching a folder in the hallway. "Director."

He waved away the title. "Call me Brock, I insist."

Fang smiled despite herself, her shoulders relaxing a fraction.

"I see you've integrated the walker with the main students. Do you think that's wise?"

Fang pulled the slim receiver from her pocket. "She'll be well controlled."

Brock's hand itched forward. "May I?"

Fang nodded. Brock held up the receiver, examining the buttons. "It's incredible how she wields electromagnetic energy, isn't it? I've watched the video feed from the shock chamber. Imagine the good we could do if we could harness it. We could save the planet, you know." The folder fell from his grasp. "Goodness."

"Let me." Fang dropped to her knees and picked up Brock's files. Her fingers froze over a familiar photograph – the three walkers on the wall of the temple. It wasn't that long ago that she'd discounted Miranda's theory about the walkers. Now she didn't know what to think. If only she had listened when she had the chance … "These are Miranda's." Fang smoothed out the photograph.

Brock straightened, passing back the receiver. She pocketed it without looking. "I've been going over the archaeological work Miranda completed. I can't get anything out of her notes." He paused. "Here. Why don't you see if you have more luck?"

Fang opened her mouth to protest, but Brock pushed the folder into her hands. Fang clutched it tight against her chest. It could be the second chance she was looking for. She thought of Ariana's strange blue energy field, the way Eli had brought down the research operation in Beijing. *Miranda knew more than she told me*, Fang thought. *Maybe the answers will be in here.* Her hands trembled at the possibility. "Thank you."

Brock nodded. "If you ever need anything, I'm just down the hall." He turned away, stopping after a few paces. "She'd be proud, you know."

Fang stood frozen, gripping Miranda's legacy. She'd figure this out, show Vulcan she wasn't to be trifled with. "Thank you," she whispered as Brock's office door closed.

12

Games

It felt too normal. The cafeteria, the dorms, the classroom and study halls. Ariana studied the bare walls of the classroom as the teacher balanced equations on the flashy projector screen. Her assigned seat placed her next to Spence, who split her attention between the teacher and doodling on her tablet. The snug band on her wrist looked too modern to be a simple watch. The boy on her other side had one, too. Ariana tilted her head. All down her row, the wristbands stood out.

She decided to risk the question. "Hey, what's this?" Ariana tapped her own wrist in demonstration.

Spence glanced at her, frowning as if annoyed by the interruption. "Monitoring during the games. Heart rate, vitals, stuff like that."

Games? Ariana nodded her thanks and returned

her attention to her tablet. The delineated tables in the cafeteria made sense then. *Teams.* Which made the wristbands shackles.

Ariana abandoned her equation and investigated the tablet. A library, extra coursework, videos, a holo-link to what looked like an oversized terrarium filled with rustling trees and ferns. She skimmed the extensive library. Physics, mathematics, biology, chemistry, military history. No internet access, only the internal network. *Great.*

The bell rang and conversation immediately rose around the room. Spence swiped her tablet and the screen dulled. "Game time. You'll love this, rook."

Ariana sincerely doubted it. She palmed off her own tablet.

Animal calls echoed along the corridor as Ariana was caught up in the crush of people headed toward the dorms. Hoots and yells rose around her. Girls pushed past her to their beds. Ariana stepped inside, curious but careful not to get in anyone's way, the cafeteria incident fresh in her mind.

Spence beckoned her over. "Guess this is yours." Spence pointed to the neatly made bed beside hers.

"Thanks." A stack of clothing lay beside a pair of boots. Ariana lifted up what looked like some kind of bodysuit and a wristband rolled off onto the blanket.

"Here, let me help you with that." Spence picked up the band and snapped it closed around Ariana's wrist. It fastened with a magnetic-sounding *clunk* before flashing to life. Ariana examined the sleek bit of gadgetry with its narrow clock-like face set into a thick padded material. A tiny heart symbol in the upper corner read 80 bpm.

"You can put down the bodysuit, rook," Spence said, pulling a dark pair of pants and a matching shirt from Ariana's pile and handing them to her. "You're not going to be on the field today. Takes at least a week to get placed. Even then, only if you're really good."

The girls around Ariana were already half-dressed. Apparently, there was no place for self-consciousness here.

"Hurry up and get dressed." Spence pulled off her tracksuit and stepped into a bodysuit.

It looked like a lightweight neoprene wetsuit with a vertical blue stripe along the side, and Ariana realised it's what Spence had been wearing in the aquarium earlier. Different-coloured stripes assaulted her when she turned around. Blue. Green. Yellow. Red. White.

"Check out the rook."

"Doesn't know how to get dressed."

"Baby's waiting for Momma."

Ariana blushed at the taunts, stripping off her pants and shirt and pulling on the tracksuit. She was lacing her boots when her wristband beeped in symphony with the rest of the dorm. Ariana found herself propelled along by the eager group, noting with relief that not everyone wore a bodysuit. It meant there was always a moderately sized pool of 'rooks'. The slang was foreign but simple enough to understand. *Rookies.*

The space that opened up before them was enormous, easily the size of a football field, and surrounded by several tiers of elevated seating. Ariana stopped to gawk and convergers pushed past her, climbing up onto the stands. Unlike a football field, it was divided by a long, jagged body of water running parallel to the sidelines through undulating terrain. Ariana followed the stragglers up the steps. From up high, it was like looking into a valley or basin. Thick plastic plates projected outward toward the arena. *So whatever this is, it's a spectator sport.* The plates formed a semi-roof over the arena below. Because that's exactly what it was, Ariana realised, *an arena.*

She took a seat on the top tier behind Spence and a group of convergers wearing the blue stripe. Spence was the only one who'd shown even a shred of kindness toward her, so even though she was not about to foist herself onto the blue team, neither was she stupid enough to stray too far.

The group hushed as someone in a suit raised a hand. Derek? Ariana stared to convince herself it was really him. She'd never seen him in anything other than jeans or track pants. Some of the girls in front of her whispered among themselves. Giggled. Honest-to-God giggled. Ariana wondered if they were the same girls who'd mocked her in the dormitory.

"This is the first official tournament round. I hope you're all ready to show us what you've got." Derek's voice echoed across the arena. Ariana registered the tiny microphone on his lapel and bud in his ear. Cheers rose from the convergers in the stands. Ariana's heart sank as she caught a flash of movement from a glassed private box. Fang and a serious-looking man sat inside, watching Derek.

She stared at the arena in despair. The school had to be a front. A way of inducing a feeling of normality, to make whatever else the convergers were required to do less threatening. You didn't build an arena unless you were serious about what was taking place inside it.

"Ares and Enyo, if you please." Derek's voice interrupted her thoughts.

Two groups whooped and rose to their feet. Red and yellow stripes disappeared down the stairs back into the hallway. Ariana examined the field below more closely. At first glance, the rock looked real enough, but she realised it was fake. Tufts of grass dotted the artificial landscape, but the water through the midline was real enough. She closed her eyes, felt its presence. *There's water below the arena.* She glanced up at Derek and remembered the enormous aquarium. *There must be a connection between the aquarium and the arena.* She looked at the artificial rivulet with longing as the doors burst open again. The two teams congregated on opposite sides of the field, now with their animal partners. Ariana recognised the boy with the lion from the cafeteria. He stood in front of the red team, gesticulating positions. The other convergers jogged to match his placement as he pointed.

On the other side, the girl with the gorilla positioned her team members. She planted a red flag behind them.

Capture the flag, Ariana decided, *but undoubtedly with its own peculiarities*. Derek jogged down the arena steps and onto the field. She tracked his progress as he disappeared into a door set into the northern end of the field.

Derek raised his phone to his ear. "I'm on my way." He stood in the doorway of the command centre until his eyes adjusted to the semi-darkness. Technicians worked at the bank of monitors in the centre. Light skittered across the screens from the glass-walled tunnel that took up the entire rear wall.

"Arm devices. We are go." He turned to the screens as one of the teams immediately dispersed into smaller groups.

"Classic Ares," grumbled Spence. "Guerrilla-style attacks."

Ariana watched a boy slip into the water with a crocodile and submerge. A girl with a black bear ran hard up an incline. A falcon from the yellow team, Enyo, took to the air, banking sharply as its human partner stood still in concentration. The bird dived for the Ares flag, wings pinned against its sides.

Too easy. There had to be more to it than that.

A hawk appeared in the air from the Ares side, knocking the other bird from its trajectory. The falcon flapped fiercely as it regained its balance before simply freezing and dropping out of the air.

"Here comes Mikey," Spence muttered.

Ariana watched, mouth agape, as the boy with the lion – Mikey – stood with his hand extended, the gun-like object still pointed at where the falcon had been only seconds before.

Ariana replayed the blue jolt of electricity in her mind. Tasers. Capture the flag with *tasers*.

The falcon's partner gripped her head in pain before sinking to the ground and collapsing. Ariana shivered, running her fingers over the implant embedded at the base of her skull. So the MRI has graduated from electroshock implants to actual weapons.

The girl with the black bear reached the top of the incline only to meet a small contingent of Enyo. Her body jerked under the force of the electric current, and she rolled back down the slope to land heavily on the uneven ground. The bear dropped where he stood, grunting in pain. The sound echoed around the tiers of empty stands.

No-one was giggling now. All eyes were trained on the carnage.

The water rippled and the crocodile lunged forward, rushing the two Enyo combatants. Its thick, armoured tail swatted them backward with a sickening crack. Ariana winced in sympathy as bone smashed.

The crocodile's partner plunged his taser into their fallen bodies, which jerked with the voltage, as the crocodile sank below the waterline. A second later, it shot up into the air, contorting wildly, on the nose of a seal. Ariana's mouth fell open. A boy gripping a saddle on the seal's back tasered the crocodile's partner in one slick movement before descending back into the water. The dark water surged in its wake as bodies convulsed on the ground.

This is insane, Ariana thought. Half the fighters on the field were incapacitated, their prone forms scattered across the landscape. It had all happened so fast she hadn't even seen the other skirmishes.

The remaining members of both teams reached the centre of the field. The Enyo leader, the girl with the gorilla, stood flanked by two convergers. They all heaved for breath.

Mikey had three.

The lion growled as the gorilla stood up and gave an ear-splitting roar. Goosebumps rose along Ariana's arms. Two of the most powerful animals in the world, facing off. It should have been a special on *National Geographic*. Instead, it was happening right here, in real time.

Spence leaned forward. The stands went deadly silent.

Mikey leapt astride the lion and pounded into the Enyo group. Keeping his head low, Mikey plunged his taser into the gorilla's exposed chest. The girl's knees gave way and she fell to the ground as the gorilla flailed, landing with a human-sounding scream and a ground-shaking *thump*. Mikey's teammates dispatched the remainder of Enyo with unnecessary force, landing kicks and jabs before shooting their tasers. Only then did Mikey snatch up the enemy flag. Still astride his lion, he waved the flag above his head. Ariana felt sick to her stomach as medics jogged into the arena to carry off the injured students.

Derek's voice came over the speakers. "Athena, Eris. You're up."

Spence rose out of her seat, freezing halfway. "Shit." She glanced backward at Ariana with a frown. "You Ariana?"

Ariana nodded. Her wristband buzzed and flashed blue, the words *Athena* illuminated in blocky text.

"Looks like you're going to see action after all."

13

Rook

All living organisms must adapt to stress, or die trying.

Brock Williams, Working Notes.

"Come on, rook. Don't get underfoot." Spence's words washed over her as Ariana stared at the bodysuit-clad convergers clambering over the seats. *No. Spence had said it herself, it was too soon.* She felt curious eyes on her as she sat frozen in her seat.

"Rook." Spence nudged Ariana's shoulder in frustration. "Get up. I'm not happy about this little arrangement either."

Ariana stared at her feet as she followed Spence

down the row of seats, regretting positioning herself at the back. But how was she to know she'd have to walk past a gauntlet of stares?

The rest of Athena bounded after Spence. Ariana ran to catch up, recalling the terrible arcs of electricity and the convulsing bodies. Her mind jerked unbidden back to the shock chamber, and a shiver ran down her spine. She'd had no preparation, didn't know any of the convergers jogging in formation behind Spence. *The captain*, Ariana realised. *She had to be.* A sandy-haired boy dropped back to her side as muffled moans emanated from the door at the end of the corridor. "Don't worry about the tasers. The pain from the shocks doesn't last long. It's more important to make sure you don't hurt yourself when you land."

"Awesome," Ariana managed. Spence pushed past an enormous door and the rest of Athena disappeared inside. The animal noises heightened. The boy stopped and ducked his head by way of greeting. "I'm Chris, by the way. I don't think a rook has ever been promoted to a team so fast, much less on their first day."

Great. Unfairly advanced before my time. Now I'll be a target.

Chris held one hand on the door. "Ready to enter the Dome?"

None of this made sense. *What the hell was the Dome, and why advance me before the other rookies?*

Ariana raised a hand to shield her eyes against the light as she stepped inside after Chris. Thick panels rose in a cage-like fused ring, enormous trees barely grazing the top of the enclosure. All around the Dome, convergers rushed to greet their partner animals. An enormous vampire bat dived from the ceiling to land on a girl's arm while a jaguar stalked out of the trees to a dark-skinned boy. Ariana stared. The terrarium-feed on her tablet was really the interior of the Dome. "Wow," she breathed.

"This is where our animals hang out during the day. Except for battles and training, of course." Chris strode into the centre of the Dome. "Pretty cool, huh? The rooks always geek out in here."

A huge shaggy white bear ran toward them. Ariana took a step backward. *A polar bear.*

"Iki," Chris exclaimed, wrapping his arms around her neck. He grinned at Ariana.

She managed a weak smile. If it wasn't for the damn

chip, she'd be able to communicate with her.

"Everyone ready?" Spence called. "Athena, let's get going."

Other convergers called taunts as they filed out of the door. "Babysitting today, Athena?"

"I can babysit and wipe your ass on the field, Eris," Spence yelled back. "It's called multi-tasking."

The reminder of what waited for her on the field made her insides clench. Ariana wrenched her gaze from the menagerie to follow the rest of Athena, focusing on slowing her breathing as the Dome rapidly emptied. As Chris opened the door, Derek appeared, his hands clasped behind his back. Ariana stopped in the middle of the Dome.

Spence yelled from further down the corridor, throwing a final curious glance her way, and Chris closed the door reluctantly. Derek's face remained calm as he pulled a small cage from behind his back.

Jericho. Ariana ran forward and pressed her fingers through the bars. The salamander flicked his tongue against them.

"Your implant will be partially inactive for the duration of each match, similar to the prior … testing procedure. Jericho can stay with you full time, but we'll be watching."

Derek's words washing over her in a rush, Ariana nodded. Anything to have Jericho back. He opened the cage and pressed a button on a slim metal receiver in his other hand.

Ariana felt like crying as she dipped into the shared thread of consciousness again. Blue light fizzed on her skin as Jericho stepped onto her palm.

Jericho. You're all right.

"One condition."

Ariana opened her eyes. The blue light faded from her skin.

"Any sign of your aura, and your implant is back online and you're back in your cell." Derek turned down the corridor. "Now hurry up, or you'll miss your first match."

Ariana stood in the Dome, clasping Jericho to her chest for a long moment. Smart. Dangle freedom in her face, reunite her with Jericho, then threaten to snatch it away again. She hated it, hated Derek. Because it would work. She'd do whatever it took to keep Jericho by her side.

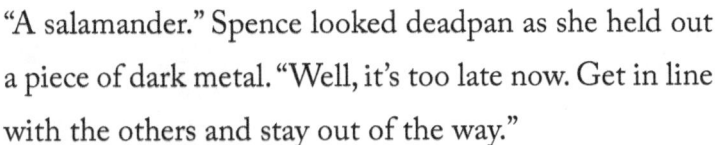

"A salamander." Spence looked deadpan as she held out a piece of dark metal. "Well, it's too late now. Get in line with the others and stay out of the way."

Ariana accepted the taser without thinking. It felt heavy and foreign in her palm. She shuffled past the other convergers, still not believing this was really happening. She stopped behind the girl with the bat, glancing at the others. Their bodysuits had a sewn-in holster. Ariana glanced down at her tracksuit. She was in no way prepared for this, so why throw her into the games on her first day? Some sort of test, or just pure spite?

Perhaps both. Jericho's tongue tickled her ear. *But we are free, and stronger than they know.*

Ariana turned her attention to the animals around her. Jericho catalogued them: *jaguar, vampire bat, Arctic wolf, Komodo dragon, polar bear.*

The girl with the bat checked her weapon and threw a glance toward Ariana. "Don't worry. Spence is tough, but she's a good captain." Blue sparks erupted from the gun. The girl looked up from it and grinned. "Nice and toasty."

I was right. Spence is the captain.

The orca's name is Flint.

Orca? Ariana remembered the aquarium. *Spence's partner is the orca?* She closed her eyes and extended her mind, brushing against the killer whale's mind, flitting to the polar bear's. Tears threatened to spill onto her cheeks at the long-suppressed connections. Ariana turned back to Spence, who stood alone at the head of the line talking rapidly with Chris, who nodded every few seconds.

Ariana's mind raced as she looked out onto the field, the bright lights flooding her vision. *I'm not ready.*

We have to be.

The siren blared. Ariana froze as the others sprinted onto the field. She'd been given no direction, nothing. Her indecision cost her precious seconds until Jericho skimmed her thoughts again.

We must play along, little one.

Right. Ariana swept her gaze across the blue-striped figures and followed the girl with the bat. "What's your name?" she called.

The girl turned to look over her shoulder. "Lucy."

Ahead, Chris dived into the water with his polar bear as Spence disappeared below the surface.

"Come on, rook," Lucy called. "We're on diversion duty."

Ariana turned back to the water, but Spence and Chris had disappeared. She ran up the first slope in Lucy's wake. Scree tumbled from her grip and she slipped. Adrenaline coursed through her as she scrabbled for purchase, clammy with sweat. The memory of the terrible pain of the electrodes coursed through her, had her gasping for breath.

Pain is temporary. We have overcome it before, we can do it again. Together.

"Hey, numbskulls, over here!" Lucy waved both arms overhead as she pelted downward. Heads turned in their direction.

"Shit," Ariana mumbled, picking her way among the loose rocks. Whoops and cheers rose in the air as Eris convergers loped easily toward them. In seconds they'd be surrounded.

"Lucy, you have a plan, right?" Ariana whispered. Without using her energy aura and revealing Jericho, she couldn't do anything. Damn Derek.

"Sure, rook. Just gotta hold out a little longer." Lucy flicked her gaze to the other end of the field. Ariana followed her line of sight to where Chris breasted the water on the polar bear's back, holding a finger to his lips. The flag hung only ten metres away.

"You turds going to take us on, or what?" Lucy hollered.

The ring of Eris convergers tightened. Ariana and Lucy stood back to back.

"Lucy, you're asking for it. And this rook needs to learn how things work around here." A boy with a wolfhound raised his taser. "No-one's good enough to get placed first day, no way."

Lucy buzzed her taser in reply. "Lots of talk, no action. I bet this rook could take all of you."

Sniggers rose around them, and Ariana's stomach plummeted. Lucy couldn't have drawn a bigger target on her forehead even if she'd wanted to.

Wait. That's exactly what was happening.

"What are you doing?" Ariana hissed.

"Sorry, rook." Lucy's bat spread its wings, hooking its feet around the collar of Lucy's bodysuit and launching them both into the air. Lucy drew up her legs into a ball, clearing the knot of enemy convergers. The boy with the wolfhound grinned. "Let's roast us a rook."

Ariana grimaced as multiple tasers hit her simultaneously. She closed her eyes and focused on her breathing, on calming the energy rebelling against the current. Limbs jerking, she hit the ground, her implant burning against her neck. Blackness washed over her. A mercy.

14

Athena

"What happened to your mixed thoughts about our cosmic deadline?"

"What do you mean?"

"Your summaries, Brock. The team names."

"I thought you'd get a kick out of that."

"Indeed."

"I admit, the longer I spend observing these children, the more I find my beliefs eroded. They are very much real."

"As such, Vulcan's use of tasers seems barbaric. Why not the laser weapons we developed?"

"Much too tame for Vulcan."

"So his alternative is military-grade electroshock weapons. Of course, it makes complete sense."

"The convergers can take the shocks. Their

enhanced energy production means rapid tissue regeneration, less fatigue. That's the official rationale, anyway."

"But they still get hurt."

"Yes."

"And the walker?"

"She's been integrated. Nearly two months in solitary will leave anyone in poor physical form, but I'm confident she'll improve."

"Vulcan is wasting her potential."

"You've seen the data. The flux in the gene sequence is extraordinary, too rapidly changing to harness."

"Still, she's a resource we can't afford to squander."

"Your cosmic deadline, I know. Don't worry. I'm looking out for her."

"Like a proud grandparent. I'm not worried about that."

"Then what are you worried about?"

"Everything else, my dear."

"Morning, rook."

Ariana sat bolt upright, feeling disoriented. *What time is it? Where am I? Jericho?*

I'm here. You were injured. They brought you back to the dormitory. Ariana felt Jericho's reassuring weight on her shoulder.

Spence leaned against the end of her bed, grinning. Ariana grasped a vague memory of a white hospital room, of the cloying smell of antiseptic. She winced as she remembered the taser shots. *Lucy just left me there. She must have known what would happen. Spence, too.* She glared up at Spence. "What do you want?"

"No bad feelings, yeah? You proved you can take a hit. Welcome to Athena. Breakfast is at seven thirty. Don't be late." Spence turned on her heel and left the dorm.

Ariana blinked, realising she was the only one still in bed. The dorm was empty. To make matters worse, her wristband read 07:26. "Shit," she muttered, wrenching off her blankets and wincing at the pain that erupted along her side. Jericho skittered to the relative safety of the headboard as she stripped and pulled on a clean uniform. She desperately wanted a shower, but there was no time. A cheap power play by Spence, setting her up to be the last to breakfast. The dumb rook, sleeping in after being barbecued in the arena.

She left her dirty tracksuit in a pile and ran for the door, unlaced boots clacking against the concrete.

07:29. The cafeteria was quiet, the tables full. A knot of convergers clustered against the side wall, gesticulating at a screen.

"Rankings board." Chris grinned as he grabbed two trays. He passed one to her and Ariana nodded her thanks. She twisted her shoulders and felt yesterday's bruises on her arms and torso already fading.

"Ranking what, exactly?" Ariana tried to gauge Chris' age. He looked older than her, eighteen maybe. Muscles strained against the dark material of his shirt. Ariana averted her gaze, focusing on her tray.

"Team and individual rankings. Hits are scored. Pure statistics. No points for strategy." Chris slapped down his tray and it was filled with toast and eggs. Ariana received a smaller plate. She frowned at it.

Chris smiled at her confusion, waggling his wrist. "Everything is controlled by the wristbands. Portion size according to dietary needs."

"Of course." Ariana looked at her wristband. Out of

her cell but not free. Of course not.

Patience. Jericho slipped out of her shirt and perched on her shoulder. Ariana froze, her eyes widening as she realised she'd been talking to Jericho all morning. It felt so normal she hadn't even thought about it. *I thought the chip …*

Someone is helping us.

Derek? Ariana wondered, her hand grazing the implant on the back of her neck. *Would he have given us this chance? Can we –*

No. The spirit world is still closed to us, little one.

Ariana stroked Jericho's nose, grateful for the connection after months of solitude.

Chris jerked his head toward the table with the blue stripe. Ariana felt eyes on her from the rook tables. Envious, or glad not to be her? Athena lapsed into silence as she approached. Ariana sat next to Chris, a blush blooming on her cheeks. Spence glanced up at her once before returning her attention to her plate.

Lucy slid down the salt and pepper. "Nothing personal, rook. You did good." She reached out and clapped Ariana on the shoulder. "Went down like a sack of potatoes, just like you were supposed to."

Spence snorted as she cut her toast.

Ariana looked around the table. What she said next mattered. They'd expect her to crave their approval and acceptance, be embarrassed about her performance. Not too pushy, not too submissive. For all she knew, one or all of them reported to Derek or Fang. She had to play along.

"I think I can do better than being a human lightning rod," Ariana said, adding a shrug for effect, as if yesterday's battle meant nothing to her. Water under the bridge.

Chris spluttered over a mouthful of eggs.

A dark-skinned boy shook with laughter. "I like her." He flashed a grin down the table.

Spence rolled her neck, seemingly satisfied. "Rook, meet the team. This charmer is Jason." The boy's grin widened. "You're already chummy with Lucy, you know Chris, so that leaves Sia and Basil."

Ariana nodded at everyone in turn. Sia's caramel skin contrasted with Basil's snowy complexion. She wondered how far everyone had travelled to be here. If they'd come knowing what lay in store for them. She doubted it.

"We're a solid third." Spence jerked her head in the

direction of the rankings board. Mikey stood beneath it, stroking his lion's mane.

"After Ares and Perses." Chris gesticulated to two tables with his toast for Ariana's benefit. "Our good friends."

Lucy reached over the table and shoved him. "She'll believe you, idiot." Lucy turned conspiratorially to Ariana. "They're kinda the pits."

"I thought all animals had to stay in the Dome?" Ariana scanned the room as Jericho slid back under her shirt, out of sight. She recognised the Enyo captain, but only because the girl sat with her gorilla.

"Captains only," said Spence. "And Mikey's just an asshole. Strutting around like that."

Ariana looked at the convergers with new interest, wondering how the team captains had been selected. Sheer strength of their partner animals? Brains?

Malleability to their will? Jericho added.

Daniel dumped his tray in the disposal unit. His bear scratched its ear a few paces behind him. Different to Eva now that she looked more closely. Shorter, with shaggy blonde fur.

"That's Daniel and his grizzly," Chris confirmed.

"Perses captain."

The bear rocked back on its haunches as it waited for Daniel, surveying the cafeteria.

"He's bad news. Trust me." Chris frowned as he watched Daniel and the bear exit.

Ariana remembered the machines in Beijing, the cannula bruises on Sara and Jacob's arms. It made sense. Derek must have given the MRI the activation vector that killed her brother. Ariana pushed aside the familiar ache that rose when she pictured Terence's smiling face. She had to think, couldn't afford to break down now. While she'd been in her cell, Fang had been using the vector to activate the convergers on the list. This whole place was testament to that. So why were they running a school, co-ordinating these battle games? Ariana glanced around the table. Everyone was wearing the standard dark, long-sleeved shirt, so she couldn't see any telltale bruises. "They don't ... inject you with anything here, do they?" Ariana had to know if Fang was still experimenting, still toying with people's lives.

Chris laughed. "No way. They take blood samples, but no drugs." He flexed his arms. "This is all natural."

"Yeah, naturally narcissistic," Lucy added.

Jason whooped, slapping the table top as he laughed. Ariana's plate jumped, dislodging her scrambled eggs from their island of toast.

Ariana smiled weakly along with the others. If it wasn't an experiment, then what the hell was it? Chris nudged her shoulder, bumping her out of her reverie. "Earth to Ariana. Time for class."

08:00. Ariana glanced at her wristband and nodded, forking a huge mouthful of eggs as she left the table.

She barely took in anything during the morning's lessons, distracted by the whispers floating across the breadth of the room, all centred on speculation derived from the rankings board. The teacher outlined the main components of the mitochondrion on the projector screen. Bored, Ariana picked at her wristband until it beeped at her to desist. She knew all of this. Terence had drawn her mitochondria and chloroplasts when she was still in primary school. He had made everything interesting. Ariana squeezed her eyes shut. She couldn't think of her brother now, or she'd fall apart. It was more important to figure out what Fang was up to and get word to the others. But first, she had to survive the battle games. Real fear gripped her. What chance did she have with Jericho only as a salamander?

Only? Jericho nipped her shoulder.

Ow. Ariana flinched. Spence tapped her shoulder and pointed to the board. Mouthing *sorry*, Ariana annotated the diagram on her tablet from memory.

It's not you ... it's this place, the chip. It's all wrong, Ariana projected by way of apology to Jericho.

We will find a way. The fact that we can communicate at all is testament to that. They can take everything away but you will still be a walker. Always.

Ariana sighed. If she couldn't use her energy aura, she'd have to rely on her brain. Take apart everyone's motivations, figure out what's driving the battle games, the forced normality of classwork.

It's the only way.

15

Training

"Have you come across a demagogue named Hypatia online?"

"Her column in the New York Times is quite diverting, I'll admit. I like her stance on clean energy. You don't?"

"It goes beyond that. The UN Secretary-General has drafted orders for international legislation regarding use of environmental resources. It goes to a vote in less than two weeks, largely due to Hypatia's voice."

"It's not exactly one more step to a hegemony, Miranda."

"Perhaps, but it is the beginning of the climb."

"The UN is in no position to claim power."

"Not yet. But if Hypatia's star continues to rise ..."

"I'd have thought you'd be pleased to find such a rational voice among the rabble. Your motives are not so different."

"Her power makes me uneasy. She's herded parliaments in the West into pens of her own making, and the powers of the East are not far behind. I did some digging, but the Times won't reveal who's behind the moniker."

"Vulcan scoffs at her environmental rhetoric."

"Exactly. Which is why I want her on-side. She will be useful when the time comes."

Ariana's wristband flashed again at 12:00 hours. Lentil soup and flat bread. She ate like a robot, barely listening to the conversation at the table. The gossip floated over her as a blanket of disjointed sound. At 13:00, Spence stood up.

"What's next?" Ariana asked as all around the room convergers jostled toward the door. She felt uneasy and unprepared. The sooner she learned the routine, the better.

Lucy elbowed her, grinning. "We've got gym until dinner. Come on, before the others get all the good stuff first. It's not all about being big. Small and fast is good, too." She ran past her with the rest of Athena, heading toward the Dome. Ariana stood alone in the corridor. She didn't need to pick up Jericho. He was – quite illegally – already with her. Derek hadn't mentioned the captains-only rule yesterday. She frowned as the doors to the Dome closed. The sound of running feet and whooping voices coiled from the arena toward her.

Ariana walked through onto the field – except it wasn't a field anymore. The waterway was gone, the ground uniformly flat. It looked like a school gymnasium, albeit one ringed by spectator stands. A fully customisable arena for every set of battles. Convergers filled the space, lifting weights or running between sprint markers. Ariana stood still, entranced by the fluidity of movement of humans and animals. *They're so unbelievably in sync.*

Like us, projected Jericho.

More and more convergers filed in. Ariana swept her gaze across the gym floor. Mikey ran between a set of markers, paced by his lion. She watched the graceful movements of the enormous animal, one of nature's ultimate killing machines. Mikey skidded to a stop, flicking his hair out of his eyes. Ariana could've sworn he leered at her. A ripple of apprehension ran through her.

Or maybe not like us, Jericho amended.

She gazed toward the northern end of the arena and saw Derek high up in the stands, arms braced on the railing. Watching.

"Ariana, catch!" Spence called.

She jerked sideways and managed to catch the heavy medicine ball that appeared in the air. It knocked the air from her lungs. Ariana gasped for breath as her teammates zigzagged, tossing medicine balls between them. Chris took the ball from her and her lungs expanded in a rush. She fell into line with him, concentrating on co-ordinating her legs and arms as she ran.

"Don't worry. Spence is tough but she respects us." Chris spun the ball around his torso before tossing it back. Ariana caught and returned it without any flair. They passed a group of convergers doing push-ups. The grizzly bear's paw reverberated off the floor in sync with Daniel and the rest of Perses. *Keeping count*, Ariana realised.

Her wristband flashed, and Ariana realised each team had twelve minutes at a station. They finished the medicine ball torture dance and headed toward the sprint markers. *Without my energy aura, I'm just a regular girl.*

Not exactly regular, Jericho projected.

You know what I mean.

Lucy bounced on the balls of her feet as she waited for Basil to return the length of the arena. He tapped her hand and she pelted away. Ariana steeled herself for her turn as Basil jogged past her, panting.

Lucy returned and Chris sprinted off, leaving Ariana alone at the front. She shook out her arms, wishing for the water underneath the floor. During one of her spirit world check-ins while training with Atlantis, Fletcher had told her about Derek's training sessions, but she hadn't run since last year's sports carnival. Ariana shuddered at the memory, all tripping limbs and burning lungs.

Too soon, Chris slapped her outstretched palm. Ariana took off, coaxing her knees higher as her lungs burned. It felt like an eternity before she reached the opposite marker. Halfway.

It is strength they want, little one. Push through.

Ariana felt eyes on her as she pounded back toward Athena. Her breath came in short, choppy bursts. She crossed the final marker at a jog.

"Room for improvement," called Mikey as Ariana braced herself on her knees, heaving for breath. If she could summon her energy aura, she would throw him across the room, consequences be damned. Scattered laughter rose around the echoey space.

Ariana raised her head to meet Derek's placid gaze.

Patience, little one. You will become stronger. If you are not a threat, they will underestimate you.

Ariana straightened as Chris clapped her on the back. "Don't worry, it gets easier."

She wasn't so sure. Her legs felt wobbly and her next few circuits were even worse. It was a relief when her wristband flashed again, though short-lived. Push-ups next. Sia and Lucy set a punishing rate while Jason and Basil were somehow completing that aberration known as the clapping push-up.

I can't do this. Ariana watched in horror.

Yes, you can. We can. We must.

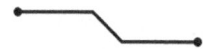

Exhausted, Ariana leaned against the wall of the shower as warm water pounded her back. She ached in places she didn't know she could. Jericho hung from the ceiling tiles, enjoying the steam.

I'm glad you're having a great time. Groaning, she turned off the tap. If only they'd trained in the damn pool.

We need to hide our true strengths here. At least for now.

Without my energy aura, I don't have any strengths to hide. I'm going to be a punching bag.

The reality stung. The afternoon's training had shown her just how far behind the others she truly was. Chris' encouragement did little to mask Spence's obvious dismay at being burdened with such a useless rook. Patting herself dry, Ariana reached for a clean set of clothes. The lactic acid in her legs made them seize every time she took a step, and her arms felt heavy and leaden.

Why does it hurt so much?

You'll catch up. You'll heal overnight, you know you will.

And then I'll have to do it all over again. Ariana threw her sopping wet towel into the laundry chute along with her sweaty uniform, sending an unspoken apology to whoever had to deal with them. She shuffled out of the bathroom thinking longingly of sinking into bed.

"Hey, rook," someone said, pushing Ariana into

the corridor wall. She gasped as her cheek hit smooth concrete. Hard.

"You're a pretty one. Shame you're pretty useless."

Hot breath ghosted across her cheek. Ariana squirmed against the firm grip on her shoulders. "Get. Off. Me."

"Just wanted to officially welcome you." Sniggers rose behind her. More of them? Ariana sagged against her assailant, preparing for the inevitable beating. If she could twist and protect her kidneys, get a knee up into her assailant's groin, she could maybe slip away …

"Michael." Derek's voice echoed along the corridor, and the hands on her shoulders disappeared. "Is there a problem here?"

"No, sir. No problem at all."

Mikey. She should have recognised the venom in his voice. She'd heard it often enough already in the cafeteria.

Ariana didn't move until the sniggers faded and she heard the boy's dormitory door close.

"Thanks," she said, turning to face Derek. He nodded. "And for this," she added, cupping Jericho in her palm.

Derek glanced over his shoulder before returning his attention to her.

Of course he's being watched, Ariana thought. For the first time, he looked uneasy. Restless.

"Returning Jericho to you was a courtesy, nothing more." Derek glanced at his watch. "21:25. You should be in bed. Lights out in five minutes."

Ariana nodded and turned on her heel, feeling confused. Maybe he didn't realise she could communicate with Jericho outside of the battles. Maybe he wasn't the one helping her. Either way, she probably would have preferred taking the beating. Now Mikey had yet another reason to hurt her. *Teacher's pet.*

Lying in bed, she tried to examine the inflection in Derek's voice, but her exhaustion won out.

16

Sensei

"They don't know about the boy, do they?"

"Even if Robyn is the one, it will take time for her to figure it out. If she ever does. It took me nearly twenty years."

"I would urge you not to underestimate her twice, Miranda."

"I know you care for her and I agree, she is brilliant, but we still have the upper hand. To think, we've had two within our grasp, yet the most important of all three still eludes us."

"Vulcan has samples from all three."

"Samples don't compare to the real thing. The boy is a walking bomb, but if we defuse it –"

"You mean kill him."

"– he'll simply be reborn into another body."

"And there's 350,000 babies born each day, four every second. The earth walker may not even be reborn in our lifetime."

"It's possibly already too late."

Sensei Mick had been called Sensei for so long, some of the younger kids in his classes thought it was his first name. He'd never thought of retiring, not seriously. Too many youngsters in the musty church hall Tuesdays and Thursdays, the teenage classes Wednesdays and Fridays. When he ran into the primary school kids on the street, they ducked their heads and chanted almost reverently: *Sensei.* The older ones did, too, just more softly, until they managed to emerge from their puberty chrysalis free of hang-ups of status and ego. Not all of them did.

He was an oddity, the elderly Japanese man responsible for the town's solar energy systems and, for four nights a week, their children. He heard the whispers that painted him as a widower, leaving his home country for a fresh start in the south. He felt their pity mingled with admiration as they picked up their children in the weak light of the hall. He stacked the sweat-tinged mats, saying little, the mystique entirely misplaced but already firmly rooted. He'd grown up in Jannali, not Japan; didn't remember his birth country beyond his mother's soba. He'd never married. He grew vegetables, tinkered with circuits, accepted the bottles of cheap sake after grading each year. It was enough.

Kara frowned as the perimeter line was broached, tripping the cameras directed at the main road. She watched the faded ute pick its way down the rutted track, its sole occupant a white-bearded man surely edging toward his eighties.

"Robyn?" Kara yelled.

"What?" Robyn called from the kitchen table.

"We expecting company? We've got a visitor, incoming."

"I called a friend."

Kara peered at the image she'd captured from the camera feed. *Robyn had other friends?*

Sensei Mick sat in his ute outside the earthship, admiring his handiwork. The solar panels on the roof gleamed. It was good to see a system still going strong after a decade or so. He remembered Robyn, the shy gangly teenager who'd taken his judo class until she was sixteen. Thursdays. He was entirely unprepared for the young woman who stepped out of the front door. She strode across the grass with a confident step.

"Sensei," Robyn called, bowing lightly.

Sensei Mick carefully got out of the car. Robyn reached him just as he closed the door. His fingers unfastened slower than he'd have liked, arthritis creeping up on him like the reaper himself.

Once inside, Robyn brewed a pot of green tea. She had remembered the scones he liked, the pumpkin ones. Another young woman had made them, but she didn't stay to talk. Sensei Mick sipped his tea and focused on Robyn's words. They came to an agreement. Of course he would teach her cousins. His days were gaping with holes now that he was handing the business over to younger men. Men able to clamber on rooftops and scurry down ladders. He didn't want payment. He could start straight away.

Fletcher woke feeling groggy to find Eli tapping him on the shoulder. "Come on. It's getting late."

Fletcher threw off his blankets and pulled on a clean

shirt, running his fingers through his hair as he padded down to the kitchen, Eva his constant shadow.

Coffee and toast filled the yawning pit of his stomach.

"Eva has to stay here," Eli warned. Fletcher turned to the bear, but she was already shuffling back down the corridor. He followed Eli out into the sunshine, gaping at the scene in front of him. Sara and Jacob moved in almost a dance. In front of them stood a wizened old man in a faded tracksuit. Fletcher joined the others, widening his stance and bringing his arms up in imitation of their poses.

"Robyn found us a teacher," Eli whispered, eyes bright. "We'll be able to master our auras, Fletcher."

"And we're just here for shits and giggles," murmured Sara.

Fletcher forced a grin even as Eva's words flashed through his mind. *Never again.* He swallowed thickly and turned his attention to the movements, his breathing, trying to get lost in the flow.

Tai chi was an essential part of Sensei Mick's daily practice. The movements Robyn described had been practised for centuries by warriors and farmers alike.

He had spent more than three decades teaching all kinds of teenagers karate, aikido and judo, yet there was something different about these four. Older than their years, faster to learn, eyes hungry for more. He came every morning at seven and joined Robyn and her 'cousins' for breakfast before leading them through two hours of practice. He noticed the animals right away, sun dancing on fur in his peripheral vision, the shriek of a bird of prey. He pretended not to. Just as he pretended not to see the shimmering red light on Eli's skin, or the fear and uncertainty radiating from Fletcher.

He simply led them through the flow.

"It's like the old people in the mornings near Lake Burley Griffin." Kate sipped her coffee in the weak sunlight penetrating the studio window. It felt like an age since they'd been normal – well, almost – uni students in Canberra.

Kara looked up from her computer as Sensei Mick led Robyn, Sara, Jacob, Eli and Fletcher through a series of exercises. Slow-moving arms, gentle lunges. The sun danced on their shoulders as they moved.

"Robyn thinks it's important. Something to do with

the sun's energy, the whole spirit energy loop."

"I know."

"Maybe we should join in one morning. You know, get the blood flowing."

Kara sighed. "Absolutely not."

After only two weeks, Robyn's cousins had matched his level of skill, moving as fluidly as water. Robyn, too. Sensei Mick didn't want the arrangement to end. He tried to pinpoint his motivation. It wasn't just the breakfast company, the normality of a shared meal he'd eschewed in his bachelordom. Nor was it the pleasure of easy communication between teacher and student. He *felt* it, the energy the movements produced, in a way he never had before. His arthritis ebbed away, a gentle tide receding until he no longer remembered the constant pain he'd endured for so many years. He walked with a new spring in his step. His students in town noticed, and people whispered as they always do. His mystique grew.

17

Communion

Jacob followed the steep track, picking his way carefully over gnarled tree roots and loose rocks. No-one seemed to notice his disappearances except Kara, who'd told him how necessary they were. Now they were training with Sensei, the twins had backed off on the correspondence work. After training, he simply slipped away, only returning in time for the gruelling evening run. Everyone was locked in their own little worlds. Those few hours in the afternoons were his alone.

He stopped to appreciate the view. It was hard to imagine a future in which the internet was useless, but the twins clearly could.

Jacob sat in his usual spot, a tiny round clearing in the forest. Only the gentle creaking of the giant trees above broke the silence. *I wonder if this is what it feels like, crossing over to the spirit world*. He always felt peaceful waiting for Poppy to return, as if he only existed in this present moment, connected to everything.

He heard the thrum of wing beats as the hive swirled back into the clearing. The buzzing noise intensified as the bees flew closer together, a vortex of russet fur, before merging with a flash back into a single bee. Poppy. She coasted down onto his shoulder and nuzzled his skin.

Every day he learned more. Poppy worshipped the earth, spoke reverently of the flowers that unfurled for her kind season by season. She offered up their troubles free of self-pity: fields of death, the clinging sticky pesticides infecting hives like a plague; bitumen where wildflowers once held sway; hundred-year-old colonies desecrated as trees were brought down. The atrocities committed by humankind made Jacob sick to his stomach. He closed his eyes as images flashed across his consciousness. Wilted flowers at fresh tombstones, discarded bouquets in hospital dumpsters.

More people are dying every day.

The activation vector. Jacob focused on his breathing, trying to quell the rage. *Derek.* Kara had made him promise not to tell the others, but the knowledge hung heavy on his shoulders. Derek had killed so many people, whether inadvertently or intentionally.

Whispers of another, but she was gone by the time we reached her. Taken to the faraway place with the sea walker.

Jacob grimaced. Every time Poppy picked up the trail of a new converger pair, the MRI always seemed to get there first.

Her hold is slipping. The trees, the flowers, they feel her pain. She cannot sustain them like she used to. Poppy flashed an image of dried-up fields filled with decaying wheat stalks across his mind. *She has held on for so long, waiting, but the sun dances ever onward, calling to the dark one.*

Jacob felt the pain in Poppy's words. He tried to understand. *Who is she? A spirit?*

She is our everything. Gaia. The one who has kept the darkness in check for thousands of years.

The earth spirit? Jacob pressed.

The sun is shifting into twin positions, slowly, slowly. She is vulnerable. She cannot help him.

Him? Are you talking about Fletcher?

She cries rivers of tears for him, her heart warm as a hundred geysers, but she must preserve herself. The sun song is building. Now she wraps herself in stone, and she waits.

Poppy buzzed onto Jacob's outstretched palm. He watched as she cleaned her wings, flickering ever so slightly, like a glitch in a video game.

Fletcher wiped the sweat from his forehead and rearranged his legs into a more comfortable position. He was determined to reach the void, no matter what it took. What good was he as a walker if he couldn't? Eva sat by his side, her eyes tracking Eli as he paced the clearing in front of the earthship. Her unease curdled in Fletcher's stomach, but he gritted his teeth and ignored it.

"I don't think you should do this," Eli said.

"You just don't think I *can*." Fletcher closed his eyes, thinking of the day he met Eva, when the solid green sphere of energy had surged from his body, as simple as breathing. And later, in the mad rush in the van, the energy had jumped from his fingertips to protect them all. He remembered Robyn's awestruck expression, her face illuminated by the wreck they'd left behind. Fletcher clenched his fists. *I need to be that person again. I need to figure out how to control my aura.*

"I'm saying it's *dangerous*." Eli turned to face Fletcher, hands on his hips.

Listen to the air walker, pleaded Eva. *He speaks truly.*

"Ariana knew how," Fletcher continued stubbornly. "She'd been training with Atlantis when she was taken."

"But she's not *here*, Fletcher. Maybe she understands this more than we do, but she's trapped on the other side of the world. We're doing the best we can."

"We've been training for weeks. I'm ready."

Eli rubbed his face in exasperation. "You don't understand, Fletcher. This place – it's not like the spirit world. It feels old, primordial even."

Fletcher uncurled his fists and stared at Eli. "That doesn't make any sense."

"I'm explaining it as best I can. It's like … a state of consciousness."

"The walker state?" Fletcher sassed.

Eli nodded, eyes unfocused as he thought. "Yes … that's it. That's exactly what it is. Total control of the spirit energy." Eli exhaled sharply.

Fletcher closed his eyes, felt Eva's uneasy presence beside him. *It is too dangerous, young one.*

But apparently not dangerous enough for you to tell me

why? Eli can do it. So can Ariana. Why not me?

Eva was silent, her face stricken.

"Well, I'm not going to sit here and do nothing. I'm going to try," Fletcher announced.

"Fletcher, don't –" Eli began.

Fletcher clapped his hands to his ears, heard the blood pound against them. *Breathe.* His breath expanded in his ribcage and contracted down into his stomach. He imagined the energy shifting inside him with each inhalation, each heartbeat. It began stirring within him, strengthening with each new breath. Then he was wrenched out of his body.

Fletcher opened his eyes. In front of him stood Eli, Una hovering above in her spirit form. He looked around in confusion and saw Eva watching him with mournful eyes.

It didn't work.

"We're in the spirit world," Eli confirmed.

No. Fletcher stood up and stormed to the edge of the glade, clenching his fists. *I need to get to the in-between, the walker state.*

"Don't," Eli cautioned. "Remember what happened last time."

"So what?" Fletcher roared.

Listen to him, young one. Anger only hinders you.

You're hindering me. You're the one stopping me from reaching the walker state, aren't you? Fletcher stormed into the trees, feeling sick with the realisation. Eva followed, padding over the forest floor as the canopy shifted under a gentle breeze. Fletcher powered ahead, his mind whirling.

It is never easy. Especially now the sun song is building. Eva's mind was filled with tenderness. *Each walker must learn anew, but the ability lies within you. I only fear that once you reach the walker state … you will not be able to return.*

I'm not giving up. I'm trying as hard as I can. You're the one stopping me from controlling my aura.

It is not that simple, earth walker. I'm trying to protect you.

By making me powerless? Ariana needs our help.

Which you cannot provide with a mind clouded by fear and anger.

Fletcher stopped walking. He was back in the glade, Eli sitting in its centre. "What the hell?" He turned to Eva and the bear nudged him forward.

You cannot run from yourself.

You did this. You brought us right back here. Fletcher didn't understand why Eva wouldn't talk to him, wouldn't explain why she kept stopping him from reaching the walker state.

You seek harmony the wrong way. Listen to the air walker.

Fletcher closed his eyes, summoning the familiar jerking sensation of returning to the physical world. When he opened his eyes, Eli sat unmoving on the grass. He waited, but Eli hadn't yet returned from the spirit world. Fletcher turned to Eva. *Leave me alone. I have work to do.* He ran up the track leading away from the earthship, head pounding, not stopping until he reached the lookout point at the top. He could see Eva below, standing motionless in the clearing. Fletcher leaned over, sobs wracking his throat. He just felt so useless, so raw. Nothing worked for him. He'd spent countless hours practising Sensei's forms, and for nothing. Not even a flicker of green light. Cool wind snatched up his hair and chilled the sweat on his skin. *I've only ever done this twice before, and both times I didn't control it.* Fletcher closed his eyes, remembering the armed men running toward his home and the helicopter attacking the van. It had been reflexive, beyond his control. *But both times I was in danger. Mortal danger.* Fletcher stepped closer to the cliff edge, loose rocks tumbling into empty space. What would happen if he jumped? Would his aura flicker to life, cocooning him from injury, or would he just plummet to his death?

Maybe it was worth it, just to find out ...

"Fletcher?"

Fletcher turned abruptly, almost overbalancing as he did so.

"Whoa," Jacob squeaked. "Careful."

"What are you doing here?" Fletcher demanded.

Jacob shrugged. "Went for a walk." Poppy burrowed through his hair. "You?"

"Wanted some time to think," Fletcher muttered, carefully stepping back toward safety. His heart thudded in his chest, matching the tempo of the splitting pain in his skull. *Stupid, so stupid. It would never have worked, anyway.*

Jacob perched on a tree stump. "Awfully close to the edge there."

Fletcher sighed and joined Jacob. Poppy buzzed up

in an angry orbit around Jacob's head as Fletcher moved closer.

"What?" Fletcher paused at the look of alarm on Jacob's face. "Is something wrong?"

"Nothing." Jacob shook his head and jumped to his feet. "I should be getting back, that's all. We're running soon, right?"

"Right." Fletcher caught a glimpse of Jacob's pale face as he retreated down the track.

18

Frustration

"I've been distracting myself from the grim realities of the present by reading the ancient poets. Your spirit world has a long literary tradition, Miranda."

"Orpheus? Homer?"

"Parmenides."

"Ah. You've been reading 'On Nature'. You know, I believe the Laotian temple is the 'gates of the ways of Night and Day' he describes."

"Parmenides pre-empts Plato's allegory of the cave. Escape the darkness and cross over to gain truth and wisdom. Yet the darkness guards the attainment of such wisdom. Parmenides doesn't name her explicitly, but it must be –"

"Nyx. Yes, I am well aware. He writes that only the divine persuasion of the sun can overcome the

boundary between the worlds."

"Philosophically, he could mean there's a difference between our perception of reality and what is truly real."

"Why can't both be true? In 475 BC, neither Parmenides nor Plato knew of the mysteries of energy and matter. As a species, we've always strained for meaning. The electromagnetic power of our blazing star can tear down the boundary, bring us into the true light of wisdom."

"But only if we overcome the darkness. We will all face judgement if the spirit is liberated."

"And you doubt we will be marked worthy? I thought you didn't believe in spirits or gods."

"Forgive me if I rank my intelligence beneath that of the possible existence of a primordial cosmic entity."

"Ah. This is why I hate arguing philosophy with you. Always straight to the self-pity."

"It's hardly pity. I'm being frank."

"Much has happened in the thousands of years since."

"Exactly. We've looked extinction in the eye and

barely won the staring contest. The ice doesn't lie."

"I thought you'd find that heartening – we've overcome this once before. Why not again? It's our nature to cling to survival."

"Last time there was no solar storm, yet the prolonged glaciation nearly wiped us out."

"Oh, now you're being over-dramatic. This is my life's work, Brock. I don't intend to die just yet."

Kate swirled her tepid instant coffee as she sat at her computer. 3 am. She had two emails from persistent clients needing evidence of a cheating spouse and a swindling business partner. She ignored both, instead pulling up the encrypted comms link. Two surveillance video feeds popped up. One showed a busy marine biology lab in the Netherlands. Kate focused on the frizzy-haired woman hunched over a microscope. Sara's aunt checked out. She'd found the newspaper article detailing the car crash easily enough – it was on public record – but Kara found herself treating Sara differently. More gingerly, now she knew the grief she'd already endured.

The second video feed was a sun-drenched Greek marina. A parade of luggage-laden donkeys darted across the frame as Kara pressed fast-forward. Jacob's family's cafe didn't have security footage, but they were conveniently located across from the marina, which did.

Eli's family had been considerably harder. Kara ripped open the letter on the bench and skimmed the doctor's report. The funds she'd transferred had been used as she'd intended. A new prosthetic for Eli's father and money for Eli's parents to disappear into the wilderness for a while. She fingered the paper, feeling uneasy. She hated relying on people, preferring the infallibility of machines, but she had no choice.

No-one is going to get close to the convergers' families without me knowing about it first.

Robyn pushed onward, climbing higher and higher, the steps slippery and damp underfoot. The cloud-covered mountain beckoned to her, calling her name. Her skin thrummed with white light. There must be something in the temple she was meant to find, that only she would understand.

"Robyn ... Robyn ... Robyn." Her name echoed

around the valley, swirling with the wind. The voice was familiar.

Robyn felt herself floating upward, away from the stairs, the temple fading from sight. "No," she cried.

"Robyn, wake up. You were having a nightmare."

Jerking upright, Robyn registered Catherine's voice. Cool air nipped at her arms.

"You kicked off all your blankets. You must be freezing."

Robyn rested her feet on the floor, the contact anchoring her. She was on the camp bed in her room.

A dream. It had felt so real.

"I'm pretty sure you didn't cross over. None of the walkers have ever screamed and kicked like that. They're a tad more serene," Catherine teased, though her voice sounded strained.

Robyn ran a hand through her hair, feeling disoriented. She blinked at Catherine. "Sorry, what did you say?"

"Okay, we're switching, no arguments." Catherine pulled Robyn to her feet and led her to the bed. "It's rare enough you sleep inside at all, you deserve the real bed."

Robyn sat on the edge, still clutching the edges of the dream. The cool stone steps, the wind. "Thank you, but just tonight." She pulled the blanket around her shoulders, uncertain how to broach the silence that followed. Her skim thrummed with energy, making her twitchy. She closed her eyes until the swirling prickling stream settled. *I have to get to that temple. I know there are answers inside.*

Catherine lay down on the camp bed. "I'm worried. What if we can't do this?"

Robyn opened her eyes and shuffled backward until she leaned against the headboard. "I'm worried, too."

"I – I see Terence when I close my eyes." Catherine's voice was small. "I'm sorry I left you by his grave that morning. I couldn't … couldn't face him."

"I see him every day," Robyn admitted. "I think I see him at the stove or by the chromatograph … but then I look properly and it's you. It's always you."

Catherine choked back a sob, the sound vibrating in the still night. "He liked me and I never did anything about it. Does that make me a monster?"

"You could never be a monster, Catherine. Terence and I, we chose to have the injections." Robyn closed her eyes. "The only way I can move forward is by holding on to that. He wouldn't want us to give up. He'd want us to keep going."

"There's so much we still don't know. We've lost Terence and Ariana … I don't want to lose anyone else."

"You've got me. I'll always be here." A blush stole over Robyn's cheeks.

"Everything is … I feel responsible for these kids. If anything happens to you, where does that leave me? I … I can't lose you, too."

"You won't. I'm too stubborn for that." Robyn curled onto her side and faced Catherine. "Tell me something about your life. Before a crazy girl came to your apartment and screwed it all up."

Catherine snorted and rolled over on the camp bed. "Like what?"

"You lived in a van?"

"Yeah. Until I was sixteen." Catherine waved a hand in dismissal. "But it wasn't that exciting. A new city every few nights, home school, laundromats. No time to make real friends because we were never in one place long enough."

"But some of it must have been fun," Robyn persisted.

"I learned a lot about people. How to gauge whether someone means you harm or good." Catherine glanced upward. "I think that's why I let that crazy girl into my apartment."

Robyn smiled at the memory of the tiny apartment cluttered with books and tapestries. She worried the edge of the blanket as she worked up the confidence to ask her next question. "Did you – did you always know you were gay?" Robyn stared at the ceiling, blood pounding in her ears.

Catherine propped herself up on one elbow. "I think I always knew deep down that I was different. My parents basically encouraged me to try everything once."

Robyn baulked, banging her head against the wall. "Everything?"

A sly smile spread across Catherine's face, her eyes fixed on Robyn's. "Everything. Motorbikes, soft drugs, hard liquor, and yes, boys *and* girls."

Robyn felt her face redden as the heat in Catherine's gaze sent warmth pooling low in her stomach. She tried to imagine her conservative Christian parents sitting her down at the kitchen table and urging her to explore her sexuality. The ludicrous image made her giggle. "They did what?"

Catherine laughed and rubbed her eyes. "I mean, I

made out with boys when I was younger, just to try it out, but it never made me *feel* anything. When I met my first girlfriend, it all clicked."

Robyn remembered the feeling of Catherine lying next to her, how it just felt so *right*, so peaceful. As if nothing existed beyond the island of the bed and Catherine's touch. Was that what Catherine meant when she said *it all clicked*? Robyn didn't have that swelling certainty, only two parts of herself at war: her brain, telling her she was overthinking everything between her and Catherine; and her heart, tugging at her limbs to step off the bed and pull Catherine into a kiss. Afraid Catherine might see the battle reflected in her eyes, Robyn looked down at the bed and forced a grin. "No, the other things. The drugs and liquor."

"Only the motorbikes stuck. Don't worry." Catherine grinned. "What about you?"

"Me?" Robyn jerked half-upright.

"Twenty questions goes both ways. Now it's my turn. Where do you sit on the Kinsey scale?"

"I'm … I …" Robyn felt energy collect in her stomach and rocket along her limbs. "I don't know."

"Somewhere in the middle, maybe?" Catherine gazed

up at her, that damn sly smile on her lips again.

"Maybe," Robyn echoed, terrified to look at Catherine again. *Will she see the truth in my eyes? Will she be able to tell me what I can't figure out?*

"Okay."

"Okay?" Robyn spluttered.

"It's a start. Goodnight, Robyn."

"Goodnight."

Robyn lay down and waited for what felt like an eternity before Catherine fell asleep. She should have articulated her thoughts better, told Catherine that when she'd woken up after the coma wrapped in Catherine's arms, she'd never felt more at peace. Catherine must have felt it. Robyn wondered if they'd ever have it again, if Catherine even thought of her that way, truly. She pushed herself upright with a sigh, energy still zinging through her limbs. It felt like she'd downed a double shot of coffee. Grabbing a jacket, Robyn padded into the hallway and out into the night air, climbing the earthship to lie on the turfed roof. She watched the stars until they lulled her to sleep, the energy in her system finally calm.

19

Energy

The frenetic tempo of Fletcher's frequency woke Robyn. She crawled to the edge of the roof and peered over. The night was still and open under the sliver of moon. She saw Fletcher standing in the middle of the grass, arms raised, moving through the series they'd practised with Sensei Mick. Robyn glanced at the stack of pallets across the clearing, saw Fletcher kick the ground, sending a tense spike through his frequency tether.

Eva humphed and moved out of the darkness of the forest to nudge the pallets. Her fur was alive with a kaleidoscope of greens.

Robyn slid off the roof edge and dropped onto the grass.

Fletcher wheeled around. "What are you doing up?"

"Stargazing. You?"

Fletcher threw his arm toward the pallets. "What does it look like? I'm trying to get the energy to come."

Eva wandered over and rubbed against Fletcher's side. He sighed and hunched in defeat. "I'm supposed to be some great protector and I can't even move a block of wood. Eli sent that thing thirty metres into the air without breaking a sweat."

Robyn reached out and touched Fletcher's forearm, gasping as energy spiked up through her calves in a rush. The trees at the edge of the clearing flickered with light, tendrils of energy dissipating into the air. Energy gathered behind her ribcage, making her heartbeat jittery. Fletcher's frequency blurred and distorted. Robyn watched in horror as darkness spread across his body from where they touched. Eva snarled, spittle flying from her jaw, and the sound echoed around the clearing.

Robyn yanked her hand away and screwed her eyes shut. Energy pooled in her spine. She vaguely registered Fletcher calling her name as she sank onto her hands and knees. The thrumming feeling gradually dissipated, energy rocketing into the ground.

"Are you okay?" Fletcher said, kneeling beside her.

"I think so." Robyn shuddered as Eva wailed in concern

and sniffed her hair. She pushed aside the sudden fear and willed herself to calm down. *It's Eva, not some wild, crazed beast. But I saw something, felt something.* Robyn stood up and dusted off her pants.

Fletcher ran his hands through his hair and picked up the thread of conversation as if nothing had happened. *How could he not feel that?* Robyn wondered, eyeing Eva warily.

"It's just ... I don't know what I'm doing. The MRI are hurting Ariana, really hurting her. I can't stop thinking that if we'd told her about Terence's death she would have come back. She'd be safe here, with us." He kicked at the ground again. "And where the hell has Lenti disappeared to?"

I've been wondering that myself, Robyn thought. At least Lenti had seemed to know something about the walkers, the threat of the sun song. Now they were running blind. She straightened as she felt the familiar tug of Eli's frequency. The front door swung open to reveal Sara and the air walker in their pyjamas.

"Thought I heard voices." Sara yawned. Ming wove through her legs as she joined them. "You can't think like that, Fletcher. Trust me, we've all been kicking ourselves over what we did and didn't do, but the past is dead, gone."

"Dead," Fletcher repeated, his face pale. "That's exactly what I'm worried about."

"No. Ariana is alive," Robyn said. She tried to focus on the faint thread of Ariana's energy tether, but Fletcher's rage made everything fuzzy.

"I know, I know, you get your little glitchy energy updates about her. But what good does that do us? We're not doing anything about it, are we?" Fletcher yelled. Robyn blinked to clear her vision. She could've sworn she'd seen the dark light around Fletcher again, for a split second.

"We're not going to leave her there. No-one's saying that," said Eli, joining them. "I know what it's like to be the MRI's prisoner. So do Sara and Jacob. We're on your side, Fletcher."

"Terence was a brother to all of us, and Ariana is our friend, too. We can only make this right if you get your shit together." Sara crossed her arms and scowled at Fletcher.

"I trusted Derek and he betrayed all of us. Handed Ariana over to them." Fletcher raised his arms in frustration.

"We all trusted Derek," Sara said, her voice glum. "He tricked us into thinking he cared."

He had cared. Right up until he didn't. Was it all a punishment? Some form of twisted payback because Robyn had not returned his affection? The alternatives were worse. Maybe Derek had lied from the beginning, biding his time until they came up with an activation dose that worked. A plant. The thought made bile rise in Robyn's throat.

Sara reached out to touch Fletcher's shoulder in sympathy. He flinched at the contact but didn't shrug her away. Robyn's heart ached at the pain and anger twisted through his energy tether. *He's not angry with us, he's angry with himself,* Robyn realised. Fletcher swayed with exhaustion, barely holding himself together. How could she not have seen it? She kicked herself for not being there for him. *He needed me, and I left him in his own darkness.*

Sara squeezed Fletcher's arm, and it was as if a wall broke down. Fletcher's chest heaved with silent, agonising sobs. He choked down air, wheezing as he battled tears. "But we're not doing anything. We need to storm in there and destroy everything in our way to get Ariana back. And I'm useless. I can't even use my own damn aura. How am I going to be able to save her?" Fletcher swiped tears angrily from his eyes, reminding Robyn how young he was, how much he'd already been through.

I should have been there for you, she thought. *Instead, I've been too damn wrapped up in my own life.* Robyn took a step forward and pulled him into a crushing hug. He gripped her tightly, as if she were a life buoy thrown into a stormy sea. His energy tether made it hard to breathe. "You're not useless, and you're not alone," she whispered. Fletcher's shoulders shook against her arms and Robyn felt tears threaten at the corners of her eyes.

"Ariana has Atlantis, Eli has Notos. I have no spirit to help me," Fletcher spluttered. Eva nudged Fletcher's ribs and the boy twisted a hand in her thick fur. They stood together for a long time as the storm within Fletcher subsided. Robyn held him tight, his words filling her with anxiety. *He's right – there's something missing. If only I could get into that damn temple again.* The pressure of Fletcher's energy tether began to fade as Robyn slowly released him.

Sara picked at her pyjama top, an old one of Robyn's featuring different kinds of cats. "I'm not really dressed for it, but let's do this." She moved several metres away and set her stance wide, flicking her hair out of her eyes. "Let's go. We practise until we get it."

"Now?" Fletcher stared at her with dead eyes.

"Yes, now. There's still some time before dawn. We'll practise until Sensei arrives. Together."

A flicker of hope dawned on Fletcher's face. They formed a line in the clearing and moved in unison, flowing through the movements until they felt as natural as walking. Robyn felt herself buoyed by the energy rising to replace her fatigue. She barely noticed the sun rise.

Kara listened to the hubbub outside as she sat at her monitor. Light crept into the valley, illuminating the figures moving outside. Robyn moved with the grace Kara had come to associate with her, so different from her awkward old self. She sighed, rubbing her eyes with the heels of her hands. It wasn't exactly lying, keeping everything she and her sister were doing from Robyn, but it wasn't much better. Kate leaned forward in the chair beside her. "It's up."

Kara glanced over her sister's shoulder at the first scholarly paper Hypatia had ever published. Kate had pushed it into the approved pile of a senior editor of *Nature* last week.

The satellites orbiting Earth controlled a dizzying amount of data, slinging it from receiver to receiver as their algorithms dictated. It was a challenge tapping into the flow of information but one worth the effort. Kara chose key satellites, slipping inside like a genie to observe the machinations of governments across the world. Dozens of space weather satellites dredged the cosmos for data. Put together, the numbers were startling but overwhelming in their raw form. Little wonder no graduate student had persisted with unravelling news of the impending disaster. Someone was bound to notice it eventually, but Kara wasn't willing to take the chance. Every month of inaction was crippling. So she and her sister did it for them. They filled spreadsheet after spreadsheet, comparing current solar flare activity against the eleven-year solar magnetic cycle. They fed the data into models, simplifying the trend and removing background noise until it became painfully obvious. The commentary on the complex dataset was easily distilled into the concluding paragraph:

"The inescapable conclusion is that we are due for a solar storm of previously unimagined force. A direct hit to our magnetosphere will render satellite communications and power networks useless. This devastating blow will have consequences spanning the next several decades. Urgent action is required to protect the Earth against such an onslaught. If we fail to act now, we will enter a dark age from which we may never recover as a species."

Within the hour, copies of the concluding paragraph had been forwarded to key members within the UN. Twenty minutes later, the Secretary-General herself sanctioned an emergency meeting of the General Assembly.

There, that should do it. Kara stood and stretched before slipping into the kitchen. She needed more caffeine. As the kettle boiled, she watched Robyn and the others through the window. A second mug clanged down beside hers.

"I can't believe they didn't wake me up," said Jacob,

looking peeved. "How long have they been out there?"

"A while." Kara filled their mugs. "Fletcher had a bit of a meltdown."

Jacob sipped his tea as Kara heaped sugar into her coffee. "Are you *trying* to become a diabetic?"

"I run on caffeine and sugar."

"I think you mean sugar and caffeine, in that order." Jacob rummaged for yesterday's loaf of bread and set about making toast. "Jam or tahini?"

Kara made a face. "What do you think?"

"Jam for you, tahini for me. Got it."

Kara paused to watch the seamless progressions outside as the sun rose, dappling Robyn's shoulders with light, before disappearing back into the studio.

"You know, I think there might be something up with Fletcher." Jacob turned around with two laden plates. "Kara?"

20

Walker State

Eli closed his eyes and moved through the movements from memory. Sara, Fletcher and Jacob flanked him, moving in synchrony. The energy welled in his abdomen, spreading through his limbs. He felt peaceful, separate, as if he were nothing and yet everything at the same time. *Two months of training. Real training. I feel stronger, more connected.*

"Good." Sensei Mick's voice penetrated the quiet of his mind, bringing Eli back to the clearing, to the most immediate state of consciousness. Sensei Mick stood tall in front of him, moving with a limberness incongruent with his age. "Now go deeper."

Eli sank lower into his stance, bringing his arms in front of him as if he held an enormous ball. Una perched on his shoulder, but he didn't register her presence as an external weight; rather, she felt like an extension of his own being.

"Let the energy flow. Let all thought leave your mind except for the feeling of the energy moving through your body."

Eli tamped down the fear rising in his mind. *I have to do this.*

Una's mind strengthened his own. *We can do this.*

Every external stimulus receded. Eli didn't register the feel of his feet on the ground, the eyes trained on him, the potential for failure. He felt only free-flowing emptiness. He broadened his mind, encapsulating all the recesses of his consciousness. He felt the slip into the in-between and paused, hovering on the brink, as his limbs flared with red light. Peacefulness washed over him as he entered the walker state, simultaneously existing in the in-between while rooted firmly in the physical world. His body seemed to recognise it, an instinctual merging completed by hundreds before him.

Eli opened his eyes to see Una shift into her spirit form, flying high above the earthship and issuing a piercing cry. Red light surrounded his body in a pulsing sphere.

We did it. Eli concentrated on maintaining control of the walker state, felt his mind become accustomed to straddling two states of consciousness.

"Steady now." Sensei Mick raised his hands, his eyes bright with wonder. "Bring it back, slowly."

Eli closed his eyes and pushed back from the brink. The division between the two states increased until he felt the walker state recede completely.

He opened his eyes to see Sensei Mick smiling at him. "Congratulations."

Sara and Jacob were clapping, eyes bright, but Eli saw past Fletcher's forced smile to the despair within.

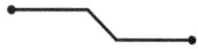

Jacob sat in the narrow clearing watching the movements of the bees. His mind thrummed with images; his head hurt from attempting to link them with meaning.

I still don't understand. Jacob frowned at the swirling mass of bees.

Poppy gently tugged and pried at his mind. *She says the sun dance comes, the younger twin. A chance. The older has not yet come to pass.*

Please, Poppy, I don't get it. Twins? Young and old?

The bees condensed to form a shifting floating sphere. Four smaller groups of bees detached, hovering in a quadrant around the enormous mass. *The sun dance.*

This represents the sun? Jacob indicated the large mass.

Yes.

The two small spheres above and below the sunsphere pulsed with movement. *A whisper of a crack.* The spheres stilled and the ones on either side expanded. *The younger and the elder. A gaping chasm.*

Jacob stared at the orbs, his mind working overtime. Then it clicked into place. He clapped his hands together. "Two equinoxes. Incoming solar radiation is equal in both hemispheres, meaning day and night is exactly the same length."

A whisper of a crack, Poppy repeated.

"Two solstices. Incoming solar radiation is greatest in either the northern or southern hemisphere. We experience the shortest and longest days."

A gaping chasm. The bees forming the sun began rippling.

"That's the deadline." Jacob jumped to his feet. "The solstice at the end of the year, that's when the solar storm will hit. And Nyx will be able to use the energy from it to break free, won't she?"

The mass of bees condensed further, turning back into Poppy with a flash of light. The bee hummed in confirmation. *She says you must be ready.*

21

Battery

"*You're frazzled, Miranda.*"

"*I can't find the group responsible for Hypatia's column.*"

"*What makes you think it's a group?*"

"*She's everywhere at once. Deforestation in the Amazon, crude-oil spills off Peru, the carcinogenic leak in Armenia. No bias, every nation under the microscope. Governments are in damage control the world over. It's a group. Well-connected and with a motive I can't fathom.*"

"*Some would call it a balancing of power. Indeed most of her supporters have, if I'm not mistaken.*"

"*You don't understand. This is power.*"

"*Yet she's given it to the UN. Very humble of her.*"

"*A smart move. Win over the people, use it to*

reinvigorate belief in an institution with lofty goals that has long lapsed into a relic. Brush it off, tantalise the people with peace. Then throw a name of your choosing into the ring for Polemarch."

"Revive the ancient Greek tradition of supreme commander? Obviously. Jump from protecting the planet to dictatorship over it."

"I can't stand your sarcasm. As I've said before, it's a step toward it. Toward hegemony. The UN is not perfect."

"Hypatia has levelled most of the petty feuds between European members. Every nation has accepted the increased discretionary powers. Every last one. She's done the unfathomable."

"Yet my sources report movement of troops in China, Russia and the United States."

"The old powers are always restless."

"Not like this. I'm not the only one who has made the intellectual leap. You've seen the responses circulating on the net. The conservatives are having a field day. It won't take much for the UN to increase the scope of their powers. An international government."

"This isn't the Cold War."

"Yet I'm willing to bet there are some jumpy fingers hovering over launch codes."

Robyn screeched in frustration as she dislodged the power board, tripping over the tangle of extension cords trailing the tiny lab space like snakes. *There's too much junk in here*, she thought. *And that's even with the blood samples in the kitchen fridge.* She sat up with a frown.

The machines didn't miss a beat, their droning hum filling the room with sound. Energy skittered up her spine and white light flickered across her skin. Robyn stared at the plug in her hand, the empty power socket.

"I heard a crash. Is everything all right?" Catherine appeared in the doorway with a tower of folders in her arms.

Robyn frowned. "Not exactly." She held up the cord and Catherine's eyes followed it backward.

"Oh," she exhaled, carefully placing the folders on top of the DNA sequencer. "Oh my goodness."

Robyn dropped the cord and stumbled forward, energy prickling her skin, pins and needles amplified by a factor of ten. Catherine caught her.

"Robyn, it's okay. I've got you."

From her vantage point on the lounge, Robyn watched Catherine pace the length of the living/dining room.

"Everything is connected. Everything. Imagine what it must have been like when the two worlds *weren't* separated, the energy that would have been available." Catherine looped between the dining and coffee tables. "You're a walking battery, for heaven's sake." She joined Robyn on the lounge. "And you're tired."

Robyn nodded and leaned back into the lounge. "Apparently batteries can still get tired."

"Good."

"Good?" Robyn glanced sideways at Catherine, who shrugged, a slight blush on her cheeks.

"It means you're still human. Still you."

Robyn considered. "I guess you're right."

Sensei Mick poked his head in the door, tool belt slung over his shoulder. "Solar energy system is offline. Might be that a storm dislodged the capacitor. By the looks of it, it's been loose for two months or so, but it's back up now." He shook his head. "I didn't even think to look. Everything seemed to be working fine."

Robyn shared a glance with Catherine. "The backup generator –" she began.

"There's no generator, Robyn. I may be old but I'm not blind." Sensei Mick grinned. "I saw the bird today, the true bird. No pet, that one. Nor the bear or leopard, for that matter."

Robyn stared at him. "Una?"

Sensei Mick's grin widened. "Never seen a creature so beautiful in all my life."

Robyn sat bolt upright. "Eli reached the walker state. You saw Una in her *spirit* form."

Sensei Mick turned on his heel. "See you all tomorrow." He paused outside the earthship. "Don't worry, my lips are sealed."

Robyn stared at the empty doorway, feeling shaken.

Catherine misinterpreted her silence. "I'm sure we can trust him – he's worked with the convergers for months now. He's almost a part of this – this family."

"It's not that. Eli did it. He finally did it," Robyn murmured. Without thinking, she added, "Derek would have loved to have seen that."

Catherine stiffened.

Shit, Robyn thought.

"I should check on the lab, make sure –" Catherine gestured vaguely toward the hallway.

It's now or never. "He left because of me," Robyn choked out, locking eyes with a confused Catherine. "Derek left because he saw us together that morning, in your bed."

Catherine froze. "He thought we were together." She closed her eyes. "But we weren't. Because you like *him*. I get it Robyn, really, I do."

"No. Derek was right. Not that we were together, then, but now –" The words tumbled from Robyn's lips. "I like *you*, Catherine, more than I've liked anyone before, and it scares me."

Robyn looked up at the ceiling, her cheeks reddening. The words had poured out of their own volition, bypassing every filter in her head. What if Catherine didn't return the sentiment? A lot had changed since the morning she woke up in Catherine's arms, sunlight in her hair. Maybe too much.

"Robyn."

She slowly turned to Catherine whose eyes were bright, a smile tugging at the corners of her lips.

"Me, scare you?" Catherine's grin widened.

Robyn's skin crawled with goosebumps. She brushed her arms and Catherine reached out and grabbed her hand.

"Not possible. Because I really like you too."

Robyn locked eyes with Catherine. The warmth she found there anchored her.

Catherine slid a hand around Robyn's waist and framed her cheek with the other. Robyn's heartbeat accelerated as Catherine bent her head down. *This is happening, really happening.* Robyn rushed upward, crashing their lips together. Catherine let out a muffled gasp of surprise and their lips parted for a moment. Robyn smiled up at her before Catherine captured Robyn's lips again. Her entire world contracted to the feeling of Catherine's hand on her spine and the softness of her mouth. She'd never been kissed like this before. Slow, careful. Catherine slid her hand down Robyn's cheek and ran her thumb over Robyn's lower lip. Robyn shuddered as Catherine's lips found hers again, but with more pressure this time. She tangled a hand in Catherine's hair, pulling them closer together. Warmth filled Robyn's stomach and her legs quivered. It felt right, blissfully right. Her entire body felt electric, energy zipping along her limbs.

Her birthmark blazed and white light filled her vision. *Oh no. Not now.* Robyn's feet left the ground and she jerked sideways, landing on the plush grass of the glade.

Kara dropped her stack of dirty mugs, mind blank, as she took in the scene before her.

Catherine's head snapped up at the sound.

Kate bumped into Kara's back and her payload tipped onto the floor as well. "What the hell?"

Kara and Catherine stared at each other as plates rattled to a stop.

"I think she crossed over." Catherine gently retracted her arms and propped Robyn against the lounge.

Kara punched the air. "Yes, I win!"

Kate picked up the fallen dishes and dumped them in the sink before pulling a wad of bills from her pocket.

Catherine watched the transaction in confusion. Slowly, the realisation dawned. "You had a bet going on us."

Kara sank into the lounge opposite. "Yeah. Sorry about that. Limited means of entertainment."

Jacob stuck his head around the corner. "Did you tell them?"

Catherine placed a cushion under Robyn's head and stroked the hair from her eyes.

"We found something," Kara said, glancing back at Jacob's thinly veiled excitement.

Robyn came to with a gasp, eyes wide, displacing Catherine's hand from her hair.

"I – we were kissing, and I crossed over, and now – you?" Robyn said in a rush, looking at the twins in shock. "You're here?" She looked over the edge of the lounge. "And Jacob ... hi."

Kate grinned. "Didn't mean to interrupt, but this is *technically* communal space, so ..."

Kara slapped her sister. Robyn sank lower into the lounge. "An invisibility cloak would be perfect right about now."

"Sorry, Harry. Laundry day."

Catherine reached out and clasped Robyn's hand. "What were you saying before? Have you found something Kara?"

Robyn straightened. "What?"

"Jacob figured it out. You know when you told me

about what Eli said, about meeting Liro? We've been backtracking, looking at dates."

Catherine tensed beside Robyn. "And?"

"It was the equinox. Day and night exactly the same length. Only happens twice a year. The tilt of the Earth's axis is perpendicular to the sun's rays."

"The day I got the injection. The day Eli met Liro. The equinox," Robyn echoed, mind whirring as the implications became clear. "When's the next solstice?"

"Not until June," said Jacob.

"That's it. You're geniuses." Robyn's birthmark flared with light.

"Whoa, Harry, calm it," Kara said.

"That's when I'll be able to speak with Liro." Robyn squeezed Catherine's hand. "The mid-year solstice."

Kate cleared her throat. Kara leapt to her feet. "Anyway, we have work we should be doing, so I guess we'll be, er, going."

Kate nodded. "Yep, exactly."

The twins disappeared back down the corridor. Jacob stood uncertainly in the hallway until Kara called, "You, too, Jacob."

Robyn waited until Jacob was out of earshot before

speaking. "That was embarrassing." She rested her head on Catherine's shoulder, swallowing the soft moan rising in her throat as Catherine stroked her hair.

"Which part? You passing out, or the twins' running commentary?" Catherine teased.

"Both." Robyn traced her birthmark with her free hand. Energy whispered through her synapses as the walkers' frequencies tugged on her mind. Then Catherine leaned forward again and Robyn's mind emptied of all rational thought.

22

Courage

UN ORDER 177665

In light of the current crisis, the Security
Council has decreed that all ongoing military
conflicts are to cease immediately. Provision of
funds is required by all member countries to
the major space foundations in Russia, China
and the United States. Failure to comply will
be considered a breach of the peace, and
appropriate action will be taken as per Articles
41 and 42. The General Assembly shall appoint
no less than thirty and no more than ninety
persons to form the Planetary Emergency
Committee. First and foremost, this committee

is to oversee the safe disabling of all nuclear weapons, removing them from any proximal power sources. Secondly, the committee is to oversee stockpiling of sufficient resources including fuel, non-perishable foodstuffs, medical and water sanitation supplies. It shall also plan for staggered evacuation of major cities with more than 70% connection to the electricity grid. These plans shall be submitted for approval in ninety days.

UN ORDER 177666

The contents of Order 177665 are to be kept strictly secret until the Planetary Emergency Committee has submitted their plans. Enforcement of the terms of Order 177665 will not begin until after this date, excepting the immediate provision of funds to designated space foundations.

The murmurs in the dormitory were muted. Ariana pulled on her jumpsuit, trying to push the lingering dreams from her mind. In them, Mikey crushes her chest into the dirt, laughing. Or Daniel's bear swipes a bloody paw across her throat. As she splutters, the bear transforms into Eva, her green eyes sorrowful even as Ariana's blood drips from her claws.

Ariana shivered as she zipped up her suit.

They are just dreams, illusions. Do not dwell on them. Jericho skidded down her sleeve to perch on her elbow.

I'm trying, Ariana projected. Without the spirit energy at her fingertips, she wasn't safe. She'd been put down hard and fast in every game. Always on diversion duty. The needless waste of her potential stung, made her work extra hard during training. *I'm as fast and as strong as any of them.* She took the blows because she didn't have a choice, but inwardly she seethed. *I'm not a rook anymore.*

Beside her, Spence's wristband beeped. "Enyo," Spence announced, glancing up. Lucy and Sia joined them as Ariana laced her boots.

"That gorilla is big, Spence." Lucy crossed her arms.

"So's my brain," came the captain's terse reply. "Come on."

Lucy snorted and they left the dorm for the cafeteria. Ariana's stomach knotted at the smell of eggs and mushrooms. She waved away the protein and sat down with two pieces of plain toast. An elbow connected with her spine and the plate clattered to the floor. Ariana whirled in her seat to grab the offender's wrist. Mikey. She twisted, thrilled when Mikey let out a low squeal of pain.

Grunting, he stumbled backward. "Jeez, it was an accident," he sneered. "No need to overreact."

"Reflex," Ariana offered, turning back to the table. She took a few shaky breaths as the rest of Athena sat down.

Chris passed her a piece of his toast, his eyes hooded in warning. "Be careful messing with Mikey. Don't rise to him. He'll get bored with you soon enough."

Ariana nibbled the toast, her appetite now completely gone. By stepping in that night, Derek had marked her. Since then, Mikey had been on her case. It had escalated from nudges in the cafeteria to pushes in training, unnecessary force in the games. Derek protected her and now she was paying the price. Throwing Jericho into the equation doubled her attraction as a target. There wasn't another converger here with such a small animal partner. She was an anomaly. To Mikey, she was weak.

As Ariana swallowed her dry toast, her wristband blipped. Getting beaten up on the field was not the answer. *I have to get more information about the MRI's plans. I have to figure out what they are capable of, and I can't do that in isolation. I need allies.* She pondered the idea as they headed toward the arena and the Dome. Unless that's what they wanted her to do. Let down her guard. The battle games were clearly a means to an end. The rankings board a thinly disguised means of ensuring co-operation. Do badly and you'd be publicly shamed. The stats didn't lie. Ariana hated it. It turned everyone on each other, reinforcing team loyalties above all else.

So I can't reach out to anyone on the other teams without raising suspicion. It has to be Athena. She stopped inside the Dome, the sunlight prickling her shoulder blades through the suit. Who had placed her on Athena? Derek? Ariana didn't know if he could be trusted. Yes, he'd freed her from her cell, restored Jericho, and stopped Mikey and his gang from roughing her up in the corridor. But that might have been a show on his part, a way to gain her trust. *The Derek I knew is gone. I can't trust him.*

In the Dome, Chris' polar bear climbed out of a frigid pool, slipping in her haste to reach Chris. Ariana swallowed past the lump in her throat. Athena weren't her friends. Her real friends were a hemisphere away.

Yet she couldn't afford to remain solo for much longer. Mikey could very well kill her. In training, in the corridor or on the battlefield. Pretend it was an accident. Then she'd be no use to anyone. Perhaps the MRI didn't care. Maybe they would turn a blind eye.

And Fletcher. Closing her eyes, she conjured his smiling face. She missed him.

"Ariana. Come on."

She opened her eyes and saw Spence waving from the doorway.

Now she'd spent so many gruelling afternoons training here with Athena, the arena was less threatening, but Ariana was still glad she had not eaten a big breakfast. Dirt and gravel crunched beneath her boots. Clusters of boulders stood either side of the arena, separated by a wide pool of water extending the width of the field. Ariana brightened. *We might get to swim today*, she projected to Jericho.

She jogged to join the huddle, trying to ignore the faces in the stands, the bright lights overhead. She squatted next to Lucy, whose vampire bat scuttled around her feet.

"Ariana, you're with me. We'll hit straight through the centre," Spence said.

Ariana almost toppled over – Lucy reached out to grab her shoulder, grinning. "Not a rook anymore."

"Chris, you make a pass on the right. Distract them," Spence continued.

"Nice and loud. You got it." Chris grinned. "My specialty."

"Everyone else. Wedge formation. Stop those assholes getting through."

"Yes, captain." Lucy saluted.

Ariana reeled as Spence took up position beside her. "You're sure you want me?"

Spence nodded, looking out at the field. "Being small means you can slip through. No-one will be expecting you."

For the first time, Ariana wondered if she'd underestimated Spence. Repeatedly, she had sent the rook into unwinnable skirmishes, so the enemy learned not to bother defending against her. Until it was too late.

The siren blared and Ariana sprang into action. She sprinted to the first cluster of boulders with Spence on her heels, then tore toward the water. Heads appeared on the other side, followed by angry shouts. Ariana heard the familiar hum of a taser gun.

All sound disappeared as she dived into the water, the cool embrace making her limbs tingle. Her gills flared and blue light skimmed across her skin. It felt like going home.

Lights flickered around the edges of the enormous pool, illuminating the gloom. A recess set into the opposite wall disappeared as a bulky shadow filled it. Spence swam toward it.

On their edge of the pool, the polar bear hit the water. Ariana grinned, bubbles spewing from her mouth, as Chris' legs followed.

The dark shadow rose upward from the depths of the pool. Hanging off the orca's saddle, Spence whirled upward to join Chris.

Ariana hung suspended in the water, skin thrumming with faint blue light. A stuttered flow of energy swirled through her system. She concentrated on the abrasive stop and start sensation, coaxing a rhythm from the disjointed bursts, straining for a coherent flow. The implant seared her skin, bubbles erupting around her head, but she kept going. The blue light on her skin grew brighter and her limbs convulsed as the implant's hold disappeared. Ariana stilled as her mind filled with voices, consciousness upon consciousness brushing against hers in wonder.

You have to keep my secret, Ariana projected. *None of us are safe here.*

Energy flowed through her limbs like a gentle caress as she rose to the surface, careful not to let any bubbles betray her presence. Thirty metres or so to the enemy flag. Completely unguarded.

Ariana launched herself out of the water, running the moment her legs hit the ground. The sounds of the skirmish behind her receded.

Ten metres. She bristled as the polar bear's pain flared across her mind, a roar cutting through the air as it collapsed on the bank. The smell of singed flesh soured the air; Ariana tasted it in her throat.

Duck. Ariana dropped to her stomach at Jericho's command, skidding along the ground, as electricity arced above her. The sounds of the battle rushed back toward her as she scrambled to her feet. The taser gun in its holster on her hip felt like an abomination. She threw it onto the ground in disgust as her pursuers reached her. The ground shook under the force of the running gorilla. The beast was massive, taller than her and more than twice as broad. Ariana held her ground as the Enyo captain slowed down beside it.

Ariana gritted her teeth. "I don't want to hurt you."

The girl snickered. "That's a shame, because I want to hurt you." She raised her taser, blue sparks igniting. Enyo doubled back to their captain with a cacophony of yells.

I can't use my aura. Derek will know the implant is damaged.

But you can use the energy itself, Jericho projected.

She stepped backward. The girl followed her.

Ariana leapt forward, kicking the girl's gun arm and sending her weapon skidding across the dirt. The Enyo captain screamed and flailed backward into the rest of her team. The gorilla roared in fury, shielding its partner. It bought Ariana enough time to step lightly backward and whirl her arms through the air. Energy welled in her abdomen, extending outward through her limbs.

"Dancing isn't going to help," sneered a boy, advancing. Ariana ignored him, focusing on the movements as she took another step backward. She heard the sound of metal grating against metal as the arena floor began to shake. The boy stumbled, falling to his knees. He looked up at Ariana in shock as she brought her arms down by her sides.

The ground buckled as the metal plates set above the water retracted. The gorilla howled in outrage as Enyo disappeared into the water in a tumble of limbs and screams.

Ariana dived backward, snatching up the flag as Enyo resurfaced, spluttering.

The siren blasted. They'd won, and she hadn't fired a single shot. Ariana felt no thrill at the victory.

Spence cleared the water, raising her arm in a cheer. Chris sat next to his polar bear, stroking her neck as a medic knelt beside her prostrate form. Lucy and the others surrounded the polar bear and cut Chris' pained face from sight. Ariana dropped to her knees and held out a hand to the Enyo captain. The girl frowned but took it. Ariana heaved her from the water as the others clambered out, only their pride injured.

Behind you. Ariana turned at Jericho's words, looking up to the stands.

Derek stood by the railing, eyes narrowed.

23

Induction

Derek replayed footage of the match. The floor plates should never have buckled like that. Onscreen, Ariana jumped backward, her arms rising through the air. Derek pulled up the solitary cell vids and an image of Ariana sitting cross-legged on the bed appeared. He hit fast-forward. *Ah.* He rewound, hit play, and watched as Ariana moved through her cell in an identical set of forms. He frowned, looking across at the match footage. The faintest glimmer of blue light hung above her skin.

"Derek." Fang's voice sounded across the command centre.

Startled, he turned. An air of excitement hung around Fang and he felt instantly wary.

"Vulcan wants to see us. Now." She turned on her

heel and disappeared. Derek closed the footage and grabbed his folder of statistics.

The laboratory was filled with scientists, all intent on their benches. The sequencers in the centre of the room thrummed as they processed another legion of samples. Derek registered their presence but passed through lost in thought. That blue haze made him uneasy. Ariana shouldn't have access to any amount of spirit energy, but there was no change in the implant readout from Fang. Looking up, he saw Fang enter Vulcan's office. He picked up the pace.

Derek glanced at Fang, perched on the edge of an armchair. At his desk, Vulcan chuckled.

"Mechanical malfunction, sir. The plates weren't strong enough for the combined weight," Derek lied, taking the other chair.

Vulcan shook with laughter as he watched the footage. "The look in the gorilla's eyes – it's hilarious." He froze and rewound the video, shaking his head. "Jesus."

"It won't happen again. Tech is on it as we speak." Derek had sent technicians to patch up the damage, though he doubted they'd find what had caused the plates to buckle.

"Good, good." Vulcan waved away Derek's concern. "We're several rounds in. Do we have a clearer picture of the combatant pairs?"

Derek nodded, pushing a folder across the Chief Director's desk. Vulcan's eyes lit up.

"Perses and Ares are the strongest teams in terms of brute force. They incapacitate and they do it quickly," Derek summarised.

"Excellent. The bear and lion *are* impressive." Vulcan flicked through the statistics and waved his hand dismissively. "Enyo and Eris can go. They're just taking up space."

Derek baulked, almost rising out of his chair. Surely he meant they'd be transferred out of the program? Yet the way Vulcan said *go* made the hairs on the back of his neck prickle, as if the lives of the convergers meant nothing to him. He dug his nails into the side of the chair. "Sir? Is that wise? They all show promise – they've only been bonded for several months."

Vulcan raised his gaze. "You think it presumptive of me?"

The coolness in Vulcan's gaze threw Derek off balance. "Not exactly, sir. But it is early days."

"Early days," Vulcan repeated. He put the folder down. "Eris and Enyo are out."

"Sir, if I may interrupt." Fang stood and smoothed her jacket. Derek's cheeks burned at Vulcan's easy dismissal, so like old times. He'd thought they'd moved past that. He remembered the morning he'd returned with Fang, Vulcan's face lighting up with a smile Derek had never witnessed in his year and a half as his PhD student. He'd sworn to himself that he'd do whatever it took to keep that smile directed at him, but now he wasn't so sure. For months now he'd watched Ariana being beaten up in the games, unable to do anything except record statistics. Even her slow return to strength didn't make him feel any better. *Robyn would never have done any of this*, he thought with a heavy heart. He blinked as he realised he'd missed what Fang was saying.

"You're right, sir. The bear convergent bond has proven itself exemplary. If I may take the liberty of introducing you to someone? I think it's time you met the first ever artificially induced convergent pair: a human without the convergence sequence who now has a high-functioning animal connection."

Derek reeled. As far as he was aware, no genetic work

had been authorised. All energies had been directed to the planning and monitoring of the battle games. The door opened, revealing a chestnut-coloured bear. It stomped into the room, followed by a scientist with a blissful smile. The woman ran a hand across the bear's shoulder.

Derek clutched the edges of the armchair as he thought of Robyn, of meeting Fletcher and Eva. The memory washed over his mind like a wave, disappearing with startling speed. He gaped at the woman. Not Robyn. Not Eva.

Vulcan stood slowly. "You've already started," he said, his voice a reverent whisper. He sounded even more excited than when Derek had handed over the vials of the activation dose.

Fang shrugged. "Why waste time?"

She'd planned this from the beginning, Derek realised. She'd used him to get a step ahead in Vulcan's estimation.

Vulcan stalked around the edge of his desk, stretching out a hand to the bear's jaw. The animal stiffened but didn't move.

"The lion is being sequenced as we speak." Fang moved over to the window and looked out over the lab. "Then the orca."

Vulcan watched the bear, entranced. "Why waste time, indeed." He glanced at Derek. "You're dismissed for now."

Derek gathered up his folder of carefully compiled statistics, his mind whirling. He hadn't seen this coming. He'd known Fang was unhappy relegated from the main action, but this? Of course he'd thought about the possibility of inducing convergence, but he'd never taken it further than idle musing. The major problem was stability of the transferred DNA, as was a safe carrier virus. Not to mention finding a compatible animal to treat simultaneously. Now Fang had achieved it, leaving him by the wayside. Worse, she'd thrown him from a moving vehicle.

Stewing over Fang's betrayal, he nearly bumped into Brock in the hallway. "Sorry, sir."

Brock made a face. "There's no need to call me sir." He gestured to the folder. "Game stats?"

"Yes, but –"

"Lovely. Come and have a drink." Brock opened his office door and ushered Derek inside.

Derek found himself sitting on a squashy lounge with a tumbler of whisky, his mind still in Vulcan's office. Fang's deft wrestling of Vulcan's admiration and her Nobel prize-worthy genetics. *The woman is brilliant. Unhinged maybe, but a genius.*

"Tell me about the teams. I named them, you know," Brock interrupted his thoughts.

Derek relinquished the folder and sank further into the lounge. It took a moment for him to grasp Brocks' words, his mind still on Fang. "Really?"

"Greek gods and goddesses of war. Technically, Perses is one of the titans, but that's semantics, really." Brock poured through the data. "I've been watching the recordings. Athena are really something, aren't they?"

Derek sipped his whisky. He'd avoided Brock's company. If he was being truly honest with himself, he found the idea of someone spending so much time with Robyn unnerving. As her supervisor, Brock probably knew her, truly understood her, better than he ever would. So Derek had kept his distance. Juvenile maybe, but effective.

"I guess."

Brock adjusted the top button on his cardigan. "But you must think so. You added Ariana to the fold."

Derek shrugged. "I like their strategy."

Brock nodded. "Yes, yes. Cunning ploys and gambits. The computer doesn't know what to do with them," he said, waving the folder with glee. "Ingenious."

Derek had been paying close attention to Athena. It was true their approach didn't lead to a high ranking on the leader board, but with Enyo and Eris gone, they'd be in trouble. No more cruising along in third place.

"May I borrow this?" Brock asked, looking up at Derek with raised eyebrows.

Derek didn't exactly need it now that Vulcan had a new favourite. He'd shared his data with Fang and she'd stabbed him in the back with it. "Go ahead," he said, placing the empty tumbler on the desk. Had he really drunk the entire glass? "Look, I'm sorry, but I need to get back to work."

"Of course." Brock didn't look up from the data as Derek left. "I'm always here, if you'd like to talk."

Settling in his own office down the hall, Derek wondered how he'd been burdened with Vulcan, while Robyn had Brock. Calm, quiet Brock. He banged his fist on the table. Robyn had made her choice. And he'd made his.

Now he just had to live with it.

24

Panic

"It was beyond foolish for the UN to believe the threat of an impending disaster was sufficient to keep the existence of the Planetary Emergency Committee a secret."

"Word did leak incredibly fast. Less than a week."

"Well before the ninety-day deadline."

"Panic is not a fertile ground for wise decisions, Miranda. The cardboard-toting prophets on street corners are preaching Armageddon."

"Military troops are obeying the summons to return to their home countries, only to remain on high alert. Lip service is being paid to the safe removal of nuclear weapons, nothing more."

"It's pretty clear, isn't it?"

"Exactly. In the event of the coming Earth-wide disaster, no country wants to be left unprepared for invasion. Which is precisely why it's so foolish. When this happens, traditional weapons, communication, everything will be useless. All except for –"

"Vulcan's protégés and Fang's experiments."

Through their tapped satellites and millions of computers seeded by BeyonceKnows, Kara and Kate watched the unfolding chaos with dismay. Their attempts at damage control failed to assuage the tide of opinion. Hypatia published a series of articles in support of the UN's plan, each more vocal than the last. Kara made the solar storm data freely available on the web in a bid to silence her particularly outspoken adversaries, but it did little to calm public sentiment. For them, there was no safety in data, only in the increasingly inflammatory rhetoric thrown around by their leaders. They cared about mortgages, disruptions to education and stock portfolios. They wanted to be told that their governments would protect them. The backlash against the UN intensified. Politicians the world over accused them of plotting an international takeover. Conspiracy theories bounced from server to server, only heightening the public's unease.

After a particularly gruelling morning responding to the forums, Kara sat back in her chair. She'd wanted to make a difference, unite the world against a common enemy, but if anything she'd only succeeded in bringing back old divisions. It had worked before – the Greek city states uniting to throw off the Persians, the Americans and the Soviets fighting the Nazis. Why not now? *Because people wanted an enemy they could imagine conquering*, she realised. *The sun is not a conquerable enemy.*

Kate pushed away from her computer. "We have to tell Robyn and Catherine."

Kara sighed. "I know."

"I can't believe this is what you've been doing in the studio." Robyn sat on the lounge, a stack of Hypatia's columns competing with toast crumbs on the coffee table. Kara had waited until she'd read every single one, including the journal article on the solar storm. Kate fidgeted beside her as Robyn leaned forward. "It's one thing to know it's coming, it's another to see the data. It feels ... inevitable now." Robyn shook her head, staring at the pile of papers. "You two are bloody geniuses."

"But now you see the ramifications," Kara pressed.

"So on top of figuring out how to stop Nyx, we have to worry about a war," Catherine summarised.

"Unfortunately, it seems to be a by-product of warning the public about the solar storm, which was necessary."

Catherine looked aggrieved. "I didn't mean ..."

"I know," Kara sighed. "I thought we could control the public reaction, but we were wrong." She glanced at her sister. "We're worried the convergers appearing around the world will play a role in whatever is coming."

"She's right." Sara appeared from the hallway and leaned against the wall. "You don't pump kids full of chemicals without a reason." She crossed her arms as everyone turned to her. "After I was activated, they put us – Ming and I – on this intense training regime. Circuits, sprints, you name it. There was hand-to-hand combat, too. Blood tests every day."

Monitoring the changes. Robyn closed her eyes as Sara continued.

"I think I was a trial. A practice run. They would've had Jacob there, too, except they didn't know about Poppy. We made sure of that." Sara glanced down at her hands.

Robyn doubted the MRI would have approved of Jacob's partnership with a bee. If Fang had discovered Poppy … she didn't want to think about it.

Sara met her eyes. "I'm worried about what they'll do now. If they were just getting started with me, what will they do with the convergers on that list? With Ariana?"

The room went silent. Kara and Kate exchanged glances.

"What is it?" Catherine asked.

"There's more." Kara sighed and added another file to the stack.

Adulterated flu vaccination death toll reaches five million.

Robyn picked up the newspaper article with shaky hands. "No."

Catherine paled at her side.

Robyn jumped to her feet. "No way." She pointed a trembling finger at Kara. "You kept this from me?"

Kara flinched. "There's nothing you could have done. This is Derek's doing, not yours."

Robyn shook her head. "All of these people would still be alive if I'd never tinkered with the convergence sequence."

"If *we'd* never tinkered with the sequence, you mean."

Catherine reached for Robyn's hand. "You're not solely responsible for this. Derek took an experimental genetic activator and delivered it straight to the MRI. *This is not your fault.*" Catherine bristled with anger.

"He betrayed us. I never really thought he'd do something so terrible, so unethical." Robyn's skin flared with white light.

Kara stepped backward as brightness filled the room.

"Robyn?" Fear filled Catherine's voice.

"Murderer." Robyn's voice echoed through the room as white light pulsed in a sphere from her body.

Kara ducked as the windows exploded outward. A hail of glass fell to the ground.

The light retracted in a rush, leaving Robyn heaving for breath. She looked at the destruction with wide eyes before sinking into the lounge and burying her head in her hands.

"I don't know what happened." Robyn cradled the mug Catherine had thrust at her. "I was just ... so angry, so ashamed." She sipped her tea, tasted a hint of whisky. A cool breeze pushed past the sheets pegged to the empty window frames.

"The important thing is that you're okay." Catherine joined her on the lounge, their knees brushing together.

"The mid-year solstice can't come fast enough," Robyn murmured. "There's so much I still don't know. How can our activation sequence have brought so much death and destruction when all we wanted to do was good?"

"We're still doing good. Every day. And we're going to keep fighting as long as we can." Catherine pried the mug from Robyn's hands, depositing it on the coffee table. She linked fingers with Robyn and pulled her up. "Come on. We should get you to bed. It's late."

Bed? Panic coursed through Robyn as Catherine led her down the hall to their shared room. *We kissed. Catherine likes me. Oh God, I don't know how to do this. Am I ready?* The door closed behind them and Catherine suddenly looked shy. Robyn pushed her fears away and brought her hands to Catherine's face. Leaning in felt as natural as breathing; their lips connected and a thread of energy tingled between them. Catherine gasped and broke the kiss. "Was that you?"

Robyn pulled Catherine closer and deepened the kiss. Her legs hit the edge of the bed and she toppled backward. Catherine landed on top of her, braced on her forearms, a sly grin on her face. "Move over," Catherine murmured between kisses, "if you don't mind sharing." She dropped onto the bed and pulled the blanket up to cover them both. Robyn snuggled under it, sighing as Catherine curled into her back and drew her in tight. She wanted to lie awake and savour the exquisite feeling of Catherine's heartbeat against her spine, but sleep claimed her far too quickly.

25

Aquarium

From 4000 BC to 1800 AD, the human population remained below a billion. In less than two centuries, we hit seven billion. If this exponential increase doesn't plateau out soon, it's inevitable that some other force will do it for us.

Miranda Collins, Working Notes.

In the space of a week, everything changed. Instead of group training sessions, each team had free run of the arena for three full sessions. Morning classes were reshuffled, assignments and tasks added to their tablets automatically if training clashed. Ariana began to enjoy training as the energy in her system strengthened. She laughed at Jason's jokes and listened to Sia's gossip. But mostly, she watched as Spence deftly wrought them into a unit. Simple gestures, the odd compliment on form and speed. Spence gave each of them leeway in achieving the tactical goals she set.

"If you see an opening, weigh the risks, and take it. There's no point looking over your shoulder for a thumbs up from me."

They loved her for it. Ariana found herself wondering if she could trust them for real as Athena's indifference to her crumbled.

One of the study halls was converted into a separate gym for general use, a clear indication of the MRI's priorities. Ariana spent extra time on the treadmill to bring her legs back to speed, always watching, waiting. It had to be after lights out, and there was no getting around the problem of Flint. The moment she entered the water after hours, the orca would know. Which meant Spence would know.

She got lucky one evening just before lights out. They were in the bathroom, Spence brushing her teeth at the steam-fogged mirror. Alone. Ariana double-checked the toilet stalls were empty before writing a single word on the mirror.

TUNNEL.

Spence narrowed her eyes and spat out her toothpaste, wiping her mouth on the towel hanging over her shoulder. She deliberated for a long moment before writing HATCH.

Spence fiddled with the edge of her towel and leaned in close. "I'll show you. But you need to be completely honest with me. You're different from the rest of us, aren't you?"

Ariana nodded. Inwardly, she wondered how much she could tell Spence, whether she could trust her at all.

Spence exhaled onto the mirror and wrote MIDNIGHT before rubbing the words away with her towel.

Ariana returned to the dormitory behind Spence. Girls were already in bed, a loose conversation about boys circulating the room. Ignoring the gossip, she climbed into bed, curling onto her side as the lights went out. The grumbles at the interruption dissipated. Ariana lay awake, plotting. If it was possible to get into the laboratory through the tunnel, then she should be able to get onto a computer. Send a message to Robyn and the others, maybe find evidence of the MRI's endgame. Maybe. Ariana rolled over and pulled the blanket tighter. Too many maybes. Maybe Spence was setting her up, reporting back to Derek even now.

Maybe, maybe, maybe.

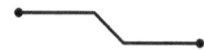

Ariana woke feeling disoriented. "Come on," Spence hissed. Ariana glanced at her wristband: 00:05.

You needed the rest. I was watching. Ariana shook off Jericho's reassurance as she noticed Spence stood in her bra and underpants. More importantly, Spence's wrists were bare.

Spence pointed to Ariana's pyjamas, motioning for her to take them off. Ariana stripped, feeling self-conscious even though they were the only two awake. Spence placed the discarded clothes back on the bed and reached for Ariana's wrist. She slid a disk between the two clasped ends and the wristband clicked open. Ariana freed her hand and the wristband snapped closed again as Spence removed the disk. Spence held a finger to her lips and beckoned Ariana toward the door.

Ariana followed, tiptoeing down the corridor and into the arena, her bare toes curling against the cold. Spence stepped out of the shadows of the stands onto the arena floor. The empty air above felt oppressive in the darkness. Mechanical echoes rose around them, making Ariana shiver.

"How'd you do that?" Ariana asked, rubbing her arms.

"Nickel-cadmium battery. Took it from one of the pool perimeter lights, figured they wouldn't notice. And they haven't."

"How long?"

"Only a few weeks. I wanted to spend more time with Flint, and to do that I had to get creative. Didn't take long to figure out the wristbands were magnetic. Then all I had to do was find a decent enough ferromagnetic material to disrupt it. That's what took the time. Plus, I had to figure out how long I could be away from the damn thing without it realising. They have an input memory of one hour. Everything just keeps ticking along, given you don't move it."

Ariana gaped at Spence. She knew the converger was smart, but damn, this was next level. If Spence routinely evaded security to visit her orca, then she obviously wasn't completely on board with the MRI's screwed-up version of a school, either. *Maybe I can really trust her*, Ariana thought, hope swelling in her chest. "Have you told anyone else?" she probed.

Spence shook her head as she squatted and grabbed a small hatch set into the floor. She grimaced as she strained to lift it. "Not worth the risk."

Ariana leaned forward to help and the hatch popped upward without a sound, revealing a dark rippling square of water.

"Why me?"

"You're different." Spence drew her arms across her chest and dropped through the opening in a perfect pencil dive.

Ariana counted to five under her breath, feeling the emptiness of the arena around her. She dropped into the water. It felt like millions of icy pinpricks against her skin. She blinked as her sight adjusted to the near-darkness. Underwater lights lightened the gloom but did little to improve visibility. Jericho clung to her shoulder. Gills flaring, Ariana spun in the water and saw Spence breast-stroking toward the end of the pool. She kicked forward and followed her into the tunnel. The walls engulfed them.

Spence stopped at a metal grille set into a panel of wide bars. Wide enough to keep out the orca, but not them. A light caught Ariana's eye as Spence slipped through. *One wall of the tunnel is made of glass*, she realised. Cupping her eyes against it, she saw a bank of computer monitors. There was no time to think about it. Spence was beckoning to her through the bars. Ariana worked her shoulders through then her hips. Flint was waiting for them. Spence hooked a hand through the orca's saddle and Ariana grabbed her outstretched arm. Flint surged through the tunnel into the aquarium. She let go of Spence's hand and kicked upward. Flicking the hair out of her eyes, Ariana breast-stroked for the edge as Spence broke the surface, heaving for breath.

"It's a long way," Spence said as she joined her. "I'm getting better, but Flint can stay underwater much longer than I can." She frowned. "But you're fine."

Ariana nodded, her mind on the lab below. She could have stayed under for days, weeks.

The laboratory was dark, the only light came from an array of machines in the centre.

Ariana pointed to the humming machines. "That's a DNA sequencer."

"How do you know that?" Spence asked, resting her chin on her forearms.

"My brother's a scientist." The words came so easily it took Ariana a second to realise the falsehood. My brother *was* a scientist. He's dead, gone.

Spence pointed at a tall metal box against the side wall. "What's that?"

"It looks like a cage," Ariana whispered, as a light flickered on above the lab.

"Shit." Spence swam to the rear of the aquarium. Ariana followed, sinking into the darkness against the wall. The orca swam in a figure of eight below them, watching. The main door swung open and Fang walked in with a brunette in a lab coat. Fang flipped a switch and a segment of the lab lit up. By Ariana's side, Spence exhaled in relief. Fang had illuminated the side of the lab closest to the door, leaving the aquarium in darkness. For now. Ariana barely registered their good fortune. As the light fell on the side wall, for a moment Ariana was transported back to Beijing, the stacked cages filled with terrified animals seared forever in her mind.

No. Not again.

Except here she couldn't liberate them. Ariana's insides clenched. She had to force down the energy rising in her limbs. Not yet, anyway.

"This is unbelievable," Spence said. Ariana blinked. Birds of prey, big cats, wolves. Drugged and docile, tongues lolling from their mouths. Except for one. The big cage shook again, its occupant edgy.

"We need regular reports on the converger bond, considering its infancy," Fang said as she opened a clipboard. The scientist walked toward the tall cage as if drawn by some invisible force. Ariana's eyes widened as a massive paw extended through the bars and tenderly grazed the woman's hand.

Fang stood by, her face impassive, as the scientist stepped backward. The bear's paw remained outstretched as she returned with a handful of electrodes, reaching into the cage to attach them to the animal.

Ariana paled. It let her.

Fang made notes. "All vitals within acceptable ranges. That's enough for now." She closed the clipboard.

The woman lingered. "Can't I – just for a moment longer," she began but withered under Fang's gaze. The scientist palmed the electrodes and stepped away from the cage. The bear huffed at the separation, jostling the bars. The entire cage rocked.

Fang and the scientist left the lab and the lights went out.

Ariana's mind reeled with possibilities. This couldn't be happening. She had wanted to know what the MRI were up to? Well, now she did.

"What the hell is that?" Spence whispered. "They've got a zoo in here. And that bear?"

Ariana shook her head. "They're using us. To make others like us."

A flicker of understanding passed across Spence's face. "You know more about this, don't you?"

Ariana closed her eyes. She needed a friend, an ally. If the MRI were already building convergent technology, she had to do something. She didn't know if she could trust Spence, but she had no choice. Fletcher and Eli weren't here.

Hunkered in the gloom at the back of the aquarium, she told Spence everything.

26

Acceleration

Spence stared at Ariana in amazement. "Can I see it?"

Ariana lifted her wet hair and felt Spence run a finger across the base of her skull, shivering at the contact.

Spence shook her head in disbelief as a hum filled the laboratory.

Ariana cocked her head. "Can you hear that?" Banks of fluorescent lights flickered on. *All of them.*

"Oh crap," Spence muttered, grabbing Ariana and sinking against the rear wall.

The doors from the student corridor flung open. Ariana heard the squeak of wheels against the floor. A team of people in blue coveralls entered the lab, each wheeling a covered gurney.

"Now what's going on?" Spence hissed. Gurney after gurney passed the aquarium.

"Don't move," Ariana whispered. With all the lights on, if one curious person looked up, they'd be spotted. She couldn't afford to lose access to the tunnel. Not now. She glanced up. There was nothing above them but roofing panels and dozens of parallel metal beams spanning the length of the laboratory. At this height in the aquarium, they were at the same level as the glassed mezzanine.

"Who are these people?" Spence whispered. "And why are they wearing hazmat suits?"

One of the gurney-bearers turned, their face covered with a mask. *Not hazmat*, Ariana realised. *Surgical scrubs. But why would they need them? What's on the gurneys?*

The first gurney disappeared through a door set into the opposite side of the laboratory, into the corridor where she'd spent weeks in a cell.

Spence and Ariana watched the procession in silence. The last gurney clipped the edge of the door and the sheet caught. Ariana stared, willing it to be a trick of the light, a symptom of her tiredness. Spence tensed beside her as a limp pallid arm drooped over the side of the gurney.

The buzzing noise stopped and the lights went out.

Ariana pulled herself out of the hatch onto the arena floor, her mind racing. Convergers. People she'd eaten with, studied with, trained with. Fought against. She shuddered, bracing herself on all fours as the adrenaline wore off. Would she feel better if it was Mikey's or Daniel's arm she'd seen? Ariana shook her head in frustration. No. The MRI wouldn't compromise their top students, their assets.

Spence pushed the cover back into place and ran her hands through her wet hair. "Those were students. Jesus."

"We need to get back. Before anyone realises we're missing." Ariana caught the manic look in Spence's eyes.

"What if they got the others?" Spence whispered.

Athena. Ariana and Spence jogged down the corridor into the bathroom. Ariana caught the towel Spence tossed her and dried off. Now she understood the underwear. No wet clothes to explain later.

The dormitory door hung open.

Spence froze in the doorway and Ariana edged around her. She stepped on a pile of blankets strewn on the floor.

They're gone. Jericho's voice echoed in her mind. Empty beds dotted the room.

Ariana stepped around the pile of bedding. Spence made to close the door behind her, but Ariana raised a hand and she desisted.

"What is it?" Spence whispered.

"Leave everything as we found it." Ariana took in the still sleeping bodies, the gentle rise and fall of their chests. *Too steady.*

"Lucy. Oh, thank God." Spence touched her hand to Lucy's forehead before bounding across the room. "Sia, too. They're still here."

Ariana dropped to her knees in front of Lucy's bed and pressed her finger to the girl's wrist. Her pulse was sluggish.

"Drugged. They've all been drugged."

Spence straightened. "Where were they taking them? The others." She rummaged under her mattress for the nickel-cadmium battery and pulled on her wristband.

"I don't know." Ariana held out her wrist for Spence to do the same.

"Do you think they're – you know – dead?"

Someone is coming.

Ariana stiffened at Jericho's warning. "Into bed. Pretend to be asleep. They're coming back."

Ariana darted across the dormitory and dived into bed, pulling up her blankets. She glanced at her wristband. Her heart rate was too high. Calming her breathing, Ariana watched the numbers dip. Slow, too slow. Panic gripped her.

Footsteps. The twist of the doorknob.

Ariana peered through her eyelashes. Three people in blue coveralls entered the room, piling the remaining blankets and sheets from the empty beds into trolleys. It took five excruciatingly long minutes before the door closed again. Ariana counted to two hundred before she dared sit up.

"What the hell is going on?" Spence whispered, eyes wild.

"I don't know." Ariana swung her legs onto the floor. "But we need to figure a way out of here."

Spence nodded. "How did they pick who stayed, and who was ... taken?"

Ariana stood, her wristband catching in her blanket. She froze as she tugged it free. Hundreds of hours of biomonitoring. The rankings board. This is what the statistics from their wristbands were being used for. It all made sense. "The battle games."

Spence was silent for a moment. "Oh my God," she breathed, examining her own wristband. "So we need to stay on top of the board to … to stay alive."

Sleep. I will keep watch. Jericho clambered off her shoulder onto the bed frame.

"We need a few hours sleep, or people will suspect we weren't here. Weren't drugged like the others. Jericho will keep a lookout. "

Spence sighed, clutching her blankets. "I believe you – everything you told me. This place isn't what I imagined. We have to look after them. Get them out of here."

Athena. She means Athena, Ariana realised.

"We will." Ariana sank back down into bed and closed her eyes, desperate for sleep to claim her, but she kept seeing the still bodies.

27

Experiment

"Vulcan's getting close, Miranda."

"He's moved much faster than I would have anticipated, I'll give you that."

"Yes. But he's hasty. He's accelerating the timeline. He wants the technology now, everything else be damned."

"The loss of twenty new converger pairs is regrettable. But is it any different to our initial testing? Losses were sustained there, too. On my command, no less."

"None of us are above blame, Miranda. And you know as well as I do that Vulcan pressed for results in Beijing, too. I'm not quibbling semantics here. Vulcan deemed them inferior and removed them from the program."

"So he's not wasting time."

"His protégés are bloodthirsty. He watches from the sidelines, enthralled by their ferocity, their willingness."

"His very own private army."

"As instructed, Fang has your folder. But I'm afraid she's already under Vulcan's sway. The man is charismatic. Someone you want to please."

"Fang will figure it out. We'll need her."

"I fear Vulcan's loyalties lie outside the program. The UN has created a powder keg by taking control. There are rumours China is courting India, consolidating its hold on the Eurasian bloc."

"And instead of an archduke we have the sun. Vulcan's a fool. We will need these children when the time comes. And not for war – for a chance at restoring the planet."

"What would you like me to do?"

"Lay low. You're my eyes and ears. For heaven's sake, don't do anything rash."

At breakfast, two tables stood empty. The covered gurneys rose in Ariana's mind. Of course. First, segregate everyone into groups. Rank them. Remove the weakest, or what the MRI *judged* to be the weakest. The remaining cliques wouldn't question the decision because it reinforced their superiority.

"Where's Enyo and Eris?" Lucy asked.

Chris jerked his head toward the rankings board, where Mikey and Daniel stood surrounded by convergers. "Didn't you see the notice? They were cut from the program. Sent back to regular school."

Lucy shook her head. "So now we're at the bottom of the ladder. Figures."

It would have been easy to slip into the dormitories and drug the exhausted convergers. Ariana wondered if someone had ticked names off a clipboard as the gurneys were loaded. It made her sick thinking about it.

Mikey broke away from his teammates. Ariana stiffened as he approached.

"Looks like things are going to start getting interesting around here."

"They weren't *interesting* enough for you before?" Ariana said.

Mikey smirked at her in a way that made Ariana want to kick him in the groin. People were missing, maybe even dead, and all he cared about was the stupid games.

Mikey leaned in close, dropping his voice to a whisper. "See you in the arena." His warm breath ghosted against her ear. Ariana shivered.

Ariana sat on her bed with her back against the wall. The dormitory was empty. Most girls had headed to the Dome or one of the study halls in the precious hour between training and dinner. Her unfinished essay on cosmology lay open on the tablet propped on her lap, but her mind was on the missing students and Mikey's threat. Did he know what was happening? She doubted Fang or Derek would have confided in him, but anything was possible.

It all made sense. Run an experiment but don't tell the subjects. The opposite approach to the operation in Beijing. Create a safe comfortable facade, like a school, then add an element of segregation by creating teams. Pit them against each other and make the battle statistics paramount. And all the while, watch. The wristbands. Gigabytes of data, all streaming somewhere, being processed, deciding who was the *best*. But the best for what exactly?

The door swung open and Spence strode in, interrupting her thoughts.

Ariana pushed her tablet to one side. "About time."

Spence plopped onto the end of her bed. "It's been driving me crazy all day. What if they're not dead? We can still save them. And what did Mikey mean when he said things were going to get interesting?" Spence rubbed her eyes with the heels of her hands. "And the bear. Jesus."

Ariana let her rant. It had taken the entire morning for her own thoughts to crystallise. The *best*: the strongest, fastest, meanest. Build convergent technology based on those attributes.

"They've started with Mikey. They've found a way to use his genes to induce a bear-human convergence." Ariana straightened. In someone *without* the convergence gene sequence. The consequences were unthinkable. Every military force would grapple for the technology. Animals would be hunted down, rounded up, forced to bond with humans. "We need to get back through the tunnel. Figure out what really happened to Eris and Enyo and get onto a computer."

Their wristbands flashed in tandem. *Dinner.*

"Tonight. I'll wake you up." Spence jumped down from the bed.

"No, it's too risky. I'll go solo this time. If anything happens, it's stupid for both of us to get caught."

Spence hesitated before nodding. "Be careful." She rummaged under her mattress and passed Ariana the battery. Ariana ran her thumb over the metal. Lights out couldn't come fast enough.

28

Spy

The great civilisations that followed Homer's Greece would have been unfathomable to that simple poet. The powers today are poised to conquer more people than have lived in the entirety of five thousand years of human civilisation. War seems to be a defining component of the human condition. Although we've progressed from spears to guns, there is always some justification for the unjustifiable. Yet in every age, there are always heroes, fighting for what is righteous, what is good. Time has a way of weaving the mythical with the factual, producing a tapestry that cannot be unwound without damaging either thread.

The temple is a case in point. I believe there is truth in those ancient mosaics, long ago lost to our collective understanding. Homer would recognise the individuals depicted on the temple walls as gods among men, and if history has taught us anything, it is that gods are not well received when they deign to join the masses.

Miranda Collins, Working Notes.

Fang lingered in her office despite having finished the carrier virus sequences for both the orca and the lion. She could tell she'd surprised Vulcan by taking the initiative. He'd immediately upped her lab access, given her control of the entire lab floor. *I should be excited, thrilled even*, Fang thought. *The first artificially induced convergence technology, all thanks to me. Miranda's legacy will live on*. Instead, there was a dull emptiness where the vindication should be. She had no-one to share it with. She wanted more than anything to share breakfast with her father, to listen to her brother talk business like the professional young man he was becoming, to see their rapt faces as she finally described the technology she was working on. Their absence felt like an illness swirling inside her.

Tired, she must be tired, that's all. Her bed in the staff wing waited. Fang glanced at her watch: 23:00. She really should sleep if she wanted to run in the morning. The treadmill was at least keeping her sane and functional. Fang rubbed her eyes as the computer whirred in its quest to match gene fragments. *A quick look at the next target first*, she decided. She reached across her desk for the stack of sequencing data, nudging the worn manila folder trapped beneath. Miranda's folder. She'd always wondered why the MRI had believed in the existence of these children with such fervour, before the scholarship scheme had hooked Eli. Before the successful test subjects, Sara and Jacob. Has Jacob paired yet? She tried to imagine an animal to suit his reserved nature and failed, bears and lions on her mind. She couldn't imagine him here.

Fang stared at the folder. She'd taken it for granted that the capability for human-animal connection existed. Miranda wielded confidence like a blade, others yielding to her will. It startled Fang to realise how little she knew about her dead supervisor. They'd never had the easy relationship she imagined Robyn and Brock having, one of tea, book recommendations and cat-sitting.

Fang glanced between the stack of sequencing data and the folder in her hand. *What the hell*. She cleared a space on her desk and tapped the edge of the folder. Photographs spilled out. A young woman wrapped in a shawl, holding a clipboard. *Miranda*, Fang realised. Dark hair and a radiant smile. She wondered what had shaped Miranda into the steel she knew. *Had known*, Fang corrected, looking past the woman. In the background, a blurred wooden ruin clung to a rock face. She moved the photograph aside, reaching for another, this one more familiar. Fang traced the watermark on the paper. Three walkers with their animals, with lines of red, blue and green tiles. She'd so readily dismissed Miranda's superstitions. Seeing Eli and Ariana decimate the laboratory in Beijing had left her grappling for an explanation, but even the shock chamber experiments had failed to provide a rational mechanism by which it was possible. She flicked through the photographs. Miranda with a small brush, kneeling over a sandy trench filled with bones. Miranda standing with her arms around a smiling man in a bamboo rice hat. The same man again, sitting in the ruin. Fang flipped the photograph over. June 21, '86 was scrawled in the upper-left corner. Frowning, she flipped them all over and arranged them linearly.

June 21, '80.

June 21, '84.

June 21, '86.

June 21, '90.

What was so special about June 21? She reached for the documents still in the folder. Working notes, she realised, skimming the first notebook. Miranda's writing style echoed her no-nonsense speech, clipped and to the point. The notes covered a decade of excavations at the ruins of a temple in northern Laos.

Frustrated, Fang threw the notes down and shoved the folder aside. What was she supposed to gather from all of this? She didn't know anything about archaeology, had never guessed Miranda had been an anthropologist. Perhaps she'd never really known her at all.

Ariana surfaced in the inky blackness of the aquarium. The orca broached the surface beside her and

Ariana stroked his nose. The lab was empty, the upper level dark. She waited a full five minutes hovering in the water before she swam to the edge, pulling herself onto the ladder and shimmying down its length. She grabbed a towel from a stack by the base of the aquarium and dried off, afterwards mopping the puddle at her feet. The orca followed her progress in the water, skimming a flipper against the glass.

She skirted around the lab, catching a glimpse of a mountain of chestnut fur as she jogged toward the corridor. Doors were strung along the hallway, each with a light above. A cold sweat gripped her as she passed her cell, the tiny white room now empty, then the shock chamber.

Here. Jericho's voice stopped her in front of a heavy-looking door set into a thick seal. Trickles of cool air emanated from the edges. A recess in the wall held a touch screen like the one on her tablet. Ariana tried the door handle, but it refused to budge. *Damn it.*

Jericho darted onto the touch screen. *It all comes down to energy, sea walker. Energy within, energy without.*

Ariana raised her arms, pushing her panic aside. *Atlantis is a part of me, wherever I go.*

Part of us, Jericho projected.

Ariana focused on the screen, willing the correct algorithm to present itself as she whirled. Blue light skittered across her body as she finished the movements, bringing her arms down by her sides.

She waited.

Blue light flared around Jericho and the screen beeped. A *thunk* sounded in the wall as the security mechanism retracted. Ariana pushed open the door, shivering as cold air swirled around her. The harsh light revealed a long row of stainless-steel hatches. She walked over to the first hatch, her heart racing. Ariana pulled the handle and the drawer slid out. She clapped a hand to her mouth in shock. The cold unseeing eyes of the Enyo captain stared up at her. Ariana slid the drawer closed, her breathing choppy. *It's a morgue.* In horror, she looked down the length of the room. *They're all dead. Every single missing converger is here.*

Ariana backed out of the room, pulling the door closed behind her. She wanted to run, to make whoever had done this pay. She took a shaky breath and leaned against the door. *I'm going to get out of here and I'm taking whoever will come with me.* She levelled her breathing and slipped up to the next level, which held a long corridor of offices. *Focus. I have to focus. There's no time to get emotional.*

Derek lay in bed staring at the ceiling. The tiny room was all he needed; a single bed, long desk, kitchenette and bathroom. It could have come straight from an IKEA showroom. It was about the same size as Ariana's cell, though with a better fit-out. He should be happy; his work on the convergence project was on a bigger scale than he'd ever dreamed. Vulcan was finally taking him seriously – there was even talk of him finishing his thesis before the year was out. He'd have his doctorate, finally be able to make his father proud after twenty-five years of mediocrity.

So why couldn't he sleep?

He didn't know any of the scientists working on the main floor, couldn't stand their deferential glances as he climbed the stairs to his office. Did they see him as the mass murderer he was? The activation vector he'd hand-delivered to Fang, that had made all of this possible, had already killed millions of innocent people. He'd known it was dangerous, but he hadn't realised *how* dangerous.

Cold sweat ran down his spine. If he'd known this would be the price of his ambition, he'd never have left Robyn and the little family in the lab outside Cobalt Valley. And Fang. Fang was up to something. Dread filled him as he thought of the inevitable casualties as Fang advanced her research.

Derek gave up on sleep, pulling on a pair of track pants and a shirt. He might as well be working instead of contemplating the ceiling. If he could just keep busy, keep his mind off Robyn and the others, he'd be fine. He pushed open the door and padded into the corridor, passing Ariana's old cell. He paused at the shock chamber for a long moment, remembering the sick fear that had gripped him when her heart had stopped, refused to keep pumping no matter how hard he tried to resuscitate her. *She nearly died on my watch. I'm sorry, Terence.*

Derek Smith. Ariana pushed past the bronze nameplate. Unlocked. So he even had a plush office. She turned on the monitor and wheeled the chair closer. A window prompted her for a password. What would Derek use?

Something straightforward? *Convergence*. Nope.

Okay, maybe where he went to school. *Duke.* Nope.

Walkers. Nope.

Ariana's fingers hovered over the keyboard. Maybe …

Robyn.

The home screen materialised. Ariana blinked at it in disbelief as Jericho scurried across her shoulders. *Hurry*, he projected. She found the internal system that listed each of the students, flicking past the names until she found her own. When she clicked on it, a new window showing the contents of her tablet opened. Ariana skimmed the long list of library titles, terrarium video feed, her half-finished assignments. Backtracking, she dumped the other student records onto her tablet alongside anything that looked remotely useful. Blueprints of the building. Employee records. She dug deeper and gave her tablet access to the security feed. *So far, so good.*

Ariana watched the progress bar blur past red into green. The transfer would take a few minutes. While she waited, Ariana rummaged around Derek's desk looking for anything else that would help her, but it was spartan. Nothing personal in the entire office. She opened the statistics program he used to compile the battle statistics, but it was too complex for her to dump on her tablet. It didn't give her anything new anyway; the rankings were on permanent display in the cafeteria. She froze as his mail app bobbed for attention. Surely he wouldn't be foolish enough to leave it open. *Right?*

Ariana held her breath as Derek's messages filled the screen. Battle game stats, internal memos. She had to remember the email address Kara had used when she contacted Terence. *Think.* She remembered Terence in her father's study, the email onscreen with the photo of Fletcher and Eva. *Ah.* She zipped the files she'd copied from the internal system and hit send. The computer pinged and returned an error message, kindly explaining that there was a firewall preventing communication with offsite servers "to ensure data security". *Shit shit shit.* Ariana leaned back in Derek's chair. She was so damn close it was almost painful. *Robyn, you have to get me the hell out of this place.* Jericho slid down Ariana's arm and coiled around her wrist. Remembering the way the spirit energy had coaxed open the morgue security mechanism, Ariana closed her eyes and held her hands over the keyboard, feeling the energy welling in her palms. *Come on.*

Robyn choked on her breakfast as energy pooled in her sternum, leaving her winded. She recognised the energy tether immediately; it was the unexpected strength of it that left her reeling.

"Robyn?" Catherine turned to her in alarm.

"It's Ariana," Robyn wheezed, getting to her feet and running toward the studio. The sea walker's energy tether pulled against her chest, and the image flashed before her eyes again: Ariana in front of a computer, Jericho free on her shoulder. Her call for help pierced through to Robyn's nerves, her veins, her very bones. She pushed the door open. "Ariana's at a computer. I think she's trying to get a message to us," Robyn explained in a breathless rush as the twins gaped at her. Pressing a hand to her sternum, she added, "and I don't think we have a huge window in which to help her. She's anxious."

With a curt nod, Kara turned back to her computer, pulling up a window of code. "They've got a firewall that makes the Great Wall of China look like a dollhouse accessory," Kara said, her fingers dancing over her keyboard. By her side, Kate ran a hand through her pink mohawk. "We've been chipping away at different sections of it for a while now. If you can't make a tunnel ..."

"Then destabilise it to the point where it'll blow over in a strong wind," Kara finished for her twin sister.

Catherine followed Robyn into the studio and reached out to take her hand. Robyn squeezed back and closed her eyes, focusing on the dizzying push and pull of Ariana's frequency. "It's Derek's computer. She's in his email somehow." Her chest ached as if someone had punched her. "How close are you to bringing it down?"

"Getting closer and closer all the time," Kate quipped, though her forehead was creased in concentration.

"Not close enough." Energy surged through Robyn's body and Catherine released her hand with a jolt. Concentrating on Ariana's energy tether, Robyn pressed her hands to Kara's computer. White light flared as she felt the energy leave her body, zinging through her fingertips as Kara's fingers danced across the keys.

The white light disappeared with a rush and Robyn took an unsteady step backward. "I've got you," Catherine murmured, propping an arm around her shoulder. Robyn leaned into her embrace, feeling the strength of Ariana's energy tether slowly fade.

For a long moment, the only sound was the twins

tapping away. Then Kate punched the air. "Oh baby. The firewall's down."

Ariana jerked her hands away from the keyboard as it zapped her. *What the hell was that?* Jericho, tethered around her wrist, was still hazy with blue light.

It felt familiar, the salamander projected. *Perhaps ... try it again.*

Hands still trembling, Ariana hit resend, waiting for the inevitable ping of doom, but it didn't come. *It's sending. Holy shit, it's actually working.* A progress bar flashed onscreen as the server processed the attached files. Ariana let out a shaky breath as the computer dinged. The transfer to her tablet was complete.

Beware. Jericho's voice caressed the edge of her mind as the progress bar inched closer. Flashlight beams appeared in the laboratory below.

"Shit," Ariana muttered under her breath. The blob of light diverged into separate beams. Six guards.

She just had to hold out a little longer.

The guards spread out; Ariana heard boots on the stairs. She glanced up at the ceiling panels. Light-weight insulation, still with the shiny foil covering. She climbed onto the desk and jumped, dislodging one of the panels.

Hurry.

Jericho leapt from her shoulder into the ceiling space. The sound of boots against the floor stopped.

Ariana swore under her breath as the attachment finally uploaded. She jabbed *send* and flicked over to the *sent* folder to delete all trace of the email. Her hands shook as she turned off the monitor and positioned herself under the open panel. Jumping up, she hooked an arm over a metal beam, her tricep burning as she swung. Hurling her other arm up and over the beam, she lifted herself clear, shoving the panel back in place just as the door opened.

"Thought I heard something, but it's clear."

Ariana crouched on the beam, her heart pounding as the flashlights swept further down the hallway. She glanced at her wristband: 02:34. If she'd had access to Derek's records earlier, she'd have known the guard rotations.

We were lucky, she projected to Jericho.

I know.

Derek stopped on the landing, shielding his eyes against the glare of the flashlight. "It's me, Derek Smith."

"Apologies. I thought I heard something up here." The guard lowered the beam. "You're up late."

Derek shrugged. "Work to do."

A door opened further down the hallway and Fang stuck out her head. "Oh, it's you. I heard voices." She emerged fully from the room, locking it behind her. "Goodnight."

"Night," Derek and the guard chorused.

Derek watched her disappear downstairs.

The guard let out a low whistle. "You're a lucky man, working with that."

Ariana gripped the beam as she listened to the exchange below. She heard the door open and Derek enter his office. The guard continued down the hallway. Ariana assessed her options. Derek's presence meant she couldn't go back the way she had entered. Her gaze landed on the metal beams spanning the ceiling. Maybe she could leapfrog across them. She stretched out a hand to the next beam, her fingers just scraping the metal.

You'll have to jump.

Great.

Ariana swung outward from the first beam, wrapping her arms around the second as she hit the metal. She landed awkwardly, driving the wind from her lungs. One of her legs missed the edge and swung uselessly. Her heart thudded in her chest as she pulled herself up, arms burning. She draped herself over the beam and regained her breath, listening for any movement beneath her. Guards moved between rows of lab benches. *Focus.* Ariana positioned herself for the next leap. This time she landed more cleanly, legs on the edge and hands secure on the top. Now that she had the movement down, it took only minutes to reach the aquarium. She dropped into the water, adrenaline coursing through her, draining her body of its reserves. She slumped against the rear wall. She'd been lucky. Ariana considered whether she'd triggered the sweep but dismissed it. Nothing had happened after last night's foray through the tunnel. She'd know for sure when she made it back to her tablet, now a gold mine of information.

Ariana submerged, kicking her way down past the orca who shadowed her to the bars in the tunnel, hiding her from the guards.

Derek ran a finger through the fine layer of white dust covering his desk. He frowned at the ceiling panels. The dust had to have come from somewhere. Stepping onto his desk, he tested each panel with the flat of his palm.

Ah. One panel lifted readily from its neighbours. Derek replaced it and wiped down his desk, removing all traces of the dust layer. Someone had entered his office – always unlocked – and had found it necessary to leave by unorthodox means.

Ariana.

He logged on to his computer and scanned his files. She'd been careful, but there was still a directory trail. Derek erased every transfer stamp with his name on it. How had she managed to enter the lab, let alone get up here? *I don't want to know*, he thought. Derek hesitated for a moment before tagging the items she'd accessed. *I don't want to know, but I'll be watching.* Rattled, he leaned back in the chair, all thought of work evaporating from his mind. The lock on the tablets meant Ariana couldn't *do* anything with the information she'd taken, so why take it in the first place? She couldn't get word out to anyone. Derek's mouth went dry. *Could she?* She'd managed to sneak into his office without raising the alarm, hadn't she? That was supposed to be impossible. There were guards and high-tech door security mechanisms between the student quarters and the laboratory, but that hadn't stopped her.

He sat bolt upright, reassessing the gravity of the files she'd chosen, thinking of Robyn's best friend, Kara, and her twin sister, Kate. Binary was their second language. If anyone could find a way to bypass the MRI's systems, it was them. A strange combination of fear and elation coursed through him as he checked the sent folder, but there was nothing out of the ordinary. He brought up his latest message to his brother, Damian, but it hit the firewall and rebounded as usual. He switched off his computer with a sigh. It had been a stupid thing to hope for.

"Oh my God, I need coffee, stat," declared Kara as she leaned back in her chair. "Do you know how hard it is to make it *look* like a firewall is still working?"

Robyn shrugged helplessly and pulled the blanket tighter around her shoulders. "I have no idea, but I'm sure it's very complex."

"Very complex," Kate scoffed. "Try mind-bendingly difficult."

Catherine returned to the studio with two steaming mugs. "Extra sugar, and actual cream," she announced. The twins beamed at her.

Ariana's message was displayed on Kate's computer alongside another window with a rapidly growing list of files. *Robyn. Here you go. Get me out of here.*

29

Plan

"Fang has to be insane," Catherine said, pushing away a thick file. Two days worth of research detritus covered every inch of the kitchen table: scrawled notes, laptops, power cords and empty mugs. Kara looked up from her pile of blueprints and technical data. Robyn was half-hidden behind a thick stack of student records and pathology results beside Catherine. Eli and Sara sat on the lounge, working their way through files on the MRI's extraction unit; Fletcher and Jacob lay sprawled at their feet going through staff records. After Robyn had lit up the earthship like a lighthouse beacon, they'd all come barging into the studio looking for answers, then demanded to help churn through the information Ariana had compiled. Everyone stopped working to listen to Catherine.

"These games … they're sick and twisted. Using them to gauge the strength of the converger pairs is highly unethical." Catherine rubbed her temples with a frown. "Not to mention Fang's convergence technology. Stripped-down virus sequences like the activation dose for specific animals would be extremely difficult, not to mention risky."

Kara reached forward for Catherine's discarded files and flicked through them. "Grizzly bear. Lion. Orca. It's likely there are more in development."

"We need to get her out of there," Robyn said, her voice soft but laced with steel. "We need to do it now."

"And we will. We just need to do it right," Kara said. Catherine stood with a sigh and busied herself in the kitchen, returning with a stack of sandwiches. Kara's stomach rumbled as she grabbed one, inhaling it without even registering the nutrition it likely contained. The convergers and walkers filled plates. Sara clapped Fletcher on the shoulder as they turned back to the lounge. "I told you she'd be fine, you *idiot*, she's tougher than all of us."

Kara nudged her sister, grabbing her laptop and making for the studio as the others returned to their work. Kara sat down and turned her sights back to the blueprints. The warehouse was a deliberately misleading exterior. The inside was partitioned into separate wings for staff and students, including an enormous golf-ball glass dome shielded by high fences at the rear.

The twins had already scoped out the surrounding industrial lots. A failed cannery, a cardboard distributor and a cotton processing plant. The other warehouses stood empty in various stages of neglect. It would be simple enough to get close to the warehouse itself; the problems arose in penetrating the security. Kara modified one of her hacked satellites to take a three-minute detour from its assigned orbit to investigate the warehouse and the hangar next to it. The photos it captured showed a steady stream of choppers and military aircraft in and out of the hangar. Kara zoomed in and saw teenagers and their animals being led into the main warehouse building.

Kara decided the hangar would be a problem.

Yet the biggest shock came when she turned to the security feeds. She'd assumed Fang was in charge, and she'd been wrong. Dead wrong. Neither Fang nor Derek were key players anymore. This Vulcan she knew nothing about. After checking him out, she discovered he was ostensibly ex-navy, discharged with a handsome payout in the nineties after a dive accident. But he also happened to collect two salaries, both from Washington, DC – one from the MRI, the other from the US Department of Defence.

"What exactly are you up to?" Kara whispered to the monitor.

"We need help with this." Kate leaned back in her chair and rubbed her eyes. "You know we do."

Aster's face bobbed on the secure comms line. The sight of the dirty kitchen and computer station behind him conjured up the cloying smell of decaying wax paper and stale grease.

"So you're Hypatia. Damn." Aster leaned back in his chair. "You've really stirred the pot, you know that? They think you're some philosopher or scientist extraordinaire."

Kate stuck her head into frame. "Are you saying we aren't?"

Kara sighed and pushed her sister away. "Yes, I'm aware. Can you help or not?"

"It's not often the unofficial leader of the free world asks for your help. Sure."

Kara laid it all out. Aster nodded to himself as he processed what needed to be done.

While she talked, Kara assessed the mould patches on the ceiling behind Aster, combining it with her memory of the loose floorboards and rat pellets. She had no doubt Aster could easily have afforded one, or both, of the apartment blocks next door. "Why haven't you moved from this dump?" she asked.

Aster grinned and pulled up a list of wi-fi networks. "And give up easy access to more than 200 individual networks from which to base my work, scot-free? No, thanks."

When Kara gave him the access codes to the computers seeded by BeyonceKnows, Aster nearly had a heart attack.

They worked alongside each other, Aster's face a perpetual frown of concentration as he worked in Canberra. Every now and then, he'd interrupt and ask for clarification on a particular blueprint, guard rotation, the metal the warehouse was made of. But mostly, they each worked in silence, their fingers launching bytes through their own private universes.

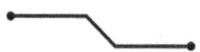

Ariana sat cross-legged on her bed, her tablet in her lap. The wealth of data on her tablet occupied every minute of her spare time outside of classes and training. She rolled her shoulders and brought up another student record. She was making good progress, about five each day. Age, home country, religion, test scores, rankings detail. The convergers came from all over the world. Lucy from India; Spence from Ireland; Jason from the Congo; Basil from Iceland; Sia from Indonesia. And that was just Athena. The MRI held a significant pool of the world's new convergers here in Bulgaria. When the public found out about their existence, would their home countries clamour for their return? Probably. By making the first move, the MRI had created a private repository of convergers. But what for exactly?

Ariana committed to memory the details of each converger pair, not knowing what information would be useful. Mikey and Daniel remained prominent in her mind. Mikey's juvenile history of breaking and entering had escalated to supermarket hold-ups before he'd been picked up by the MRI. Daniel, on the other hand, had been a straight-A student. Chess club, even. It changed how she saw them. Both of them cocky and arrogant, quick to ensure their power over their teams was absolute – Mikey because of his thirst for it, Daniel because he knew he could wield it. Both of them were drunk on power because of their rankings.

The stupid rankings. Ariana turned to the raw statistics and quickly identified an obvious flaw. The number and location of hits clouded the more important assessment of whether a converger had innate ability. Compared to Mikey and Daniel, Spence's record was poor because she didn't raise herself above her teammates. She spread the victory among all of them, which rendered each member of Athena essentially similar. But Derek had to know his data didn't reveal the whole picture. Was he intentionally shifting focus from Athena? If so, why? Ariana flicked to the security feeds, swiping through until she saw Derek. Light danced across the bank of monitors in front of him. This puzzled her until she realised the cause. The computer-filled room Derek occupied was flush against the marine tunnel linking the aquarium and the arena. Ariana pulled up the blueprints. The command centre. The hive mind behind the battle games. Even if none of the other teams registered the impact of the disappearance of two entire teams, Mikey was right. Things would change.

The battle games would change.

Ariana palmed her tablet and locked the screen as bodies joined her on her bed. Sia, Lucy, Spence. Access to the system would help, but it wasn't the most important development. Because now she had allies inside. She had Athena.

30

Camaraderie

"She's found a way to get information out."

"Ah, then she is a clever one. You kept your correspondence hard-copy as I advised?"

"Apart from our little chats on this secure line, my online presence is that of a bright-eyed boy scout. Nothing to arouse suspicion."

"I think you'll be interested in who Ariana contacted."

"Well?"

"I think we've found Hypatia."

The treadmill whirred beneath her feet. Fang wiped her face with a towel mid-stride. *Swing, step. Swing, step.* The staff gym was empty in the pre-dawn, just the way she liked it. Endorphins coursed through her system, washing away the remnants of her unsettling dream of the ruined temple. Fang shuddered. The ancient beams had flickered with energy exactly like Ariana's aura. *Get a grip*, she told herself. Her subconscious had simply drawn from a real memory of Ariana's aura to add to her dreamscape, that's all. Still, Fang couldn't completely push the dream aside. It had felt so viscerally real, like she was actually standing on the cold stone floor, palms flat against the pitted wooden supports, skin tingling with the energy crackling through the air. She wondered if Derek knew anything more about the temple and the mosaics it contained. Miranda had dedicated years to examining the ruins. She must have found *something*.

The treadmill beeped. *15 km.*

The door opened and Fang turned, legs still pumping. Derek stood in the doorway with a towel over his shoulder, as if summoned by her thoughts.

"Sorry, I didn't think anyone would be here."

Surprised, Fang said, "You run?"

Derek nodded. "Do you mind?" He motioned to the empty treadmill beside her.

"Go ahead." Fang glanced over at Derek as he fussed with the machine. He wore a thin singlet and basketball shorts. Fang couldn't help noticing that his arms were corded with muscle. She realised she'd never seen him so relaxed before. Seeing him like this, without the weight of Vulcan's gaze and away from the busy lab, made her heart flip. The phone strapped to her arm vibrated. *Oh crap.* Fang flailed as she unbalanced, almost losing her footing on the treadmill. She couldn't afford to let emotion cloud her judgement. Not now, when Vulcan was actually listening to her, when her research was pushing the boundaries of possibility. Fang slowed her treadmill to read the message. "Vulcan," she said when Derek tipped his head in inquiry.

Derek started jogging then picked up the pace beside her. "Early summons."

Fang hopped lightly to the ground and downed some water. "It's unusual."

Derek grinned. "I swear the man doesn't sleep."

Fang chuckled as she headed toward the door. She paused and looked back at Derek, loping easily at a fast clip. He looked strong, fierce even.

"Have a good run."

Derek turned and saluted her with a smile. "Thanks."

Fang settled into the armchair in Vulcan's office. She felt uneasy. The Chief Director had never called such an early meeting, yet despite the hour he looked – there was really only one word for it – pleased.

It unnerved her.

"We've had a security breach," he began.

"Sir?" Fang asked, unable to fathom how Vulcan was in a good mood if their data had been compromised. "Was anything taken?"

"Tech have only just identified a six-minute breach in the firewall that occurred a week ago. Several staff logins were active during that time, including Derek's." Vulcan's eyes were bright. "Have you ever seen Derek use his tablet in view of any of the students?"

Fang shook her head. "We've all been drilled on the security measures." It shocked her, this sudden protectiveness. When had she started caring what happened to Derek?

Vulcan raised a hand. "It's no matter. I believe the breach was undertaken by the other members of the original program."

"Catherine and Robyn?" A memory of wrestling with a bloodied Catherine flitted across her mind. Robyn remained an enigma, but a pang of regret settled on Fang's shoulders. *We should have been colleagues, not enemies.*

"Unwittingly, they've revealed their location." Vulcan was watching her closely. Did he expect her to share his excitement? Or to ruminate on the fact that without Miranda, she'd be just another unaware PhD student wrapped up in all of this?

Vulcan leaned back in his chair and abruptly changed topic. "Have you finished processing the samples from the failed subjects in cold storage?"

Fang nodded and slid over her report. She'd assumed that's why Vulcan had called the meeting in the first place. Rattled, she adjusted her jacket. The meeting had taken an unforeseen turn. Fang wondered what Vulcan planned to do with Robyn and Catherine. Would he bring them here? She thought of Derek, smiling at her from the gym door. Everything would change if they came.

Vulcan tapped a finger on it. "Excellent. And the new patents?"

"Coming along nicely, sir."

Vulcan shifted in his seat. "I've noticed you and Derek don't seek each other out."

Fang frowned. Had Vulcan just read her mind? "We

have separate directives. I fail to see how my conduct has a bearing on anything."

Vulcan steepled his fingers and brought them to his chin. "Of course not. Your output has been exceptional. The project has advanced in leaps and bounds. I can assure you that you are not under scrutiny. But perhaps you could keep an eye on Derek. Spend more time with him. If there is another firewall breach, I want to know who is responsible."

The flattery did little to disguise the threat. She read between the lines. *As long as you keep the project on track, you're an asset.* He trusted neither of them. Fang wondered if he truly trusted anyone. Keeping her face a placid mask, she said "And Robyn and Catherine?"

Vulcan smiled, his eyes cold. "They're being taken care of as we speak."

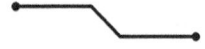

Three Blackhawks briefly touched down outside Darwin to refuel. Soldiers stretched their legs in the red dust, bickering about the long cramped trip. The lead pilot ignored them. They had a job to do, comfort be damned.

It took several hours to reach the outskirts of Cobalt Valley. The dawn light blurred into golden fingers through the smoke haze of the valley as soldiers leapt to the ground, guns up, and ran toward the earthship.

"Kitchen, clear."

"Hall, clear."

"Bedrooms, clear."

A whine began building in the air, a buzzing sound that increased in volume to a keening wail. Soldiers clapped their hands to their ears in an attempt to stifle the excruciating pain tearing through their skulls.

"Fall back!"

"Status report."

One of the soldiers noticed a small metal box on the wall, but his fingers stilled as he reached for it, blood streaming from his eyes and ears. Thuds filled the earthship as bodies hit the floor.

"Report," the lead pilot's voice sounded over the comms line. "Do a sweep."

"Nothing on the first one," replied the second pilot.

"I said, do a sweep."

"Oh, shit. We've got multiple high-frequency signatures, high grade. Hang on —"

Robyn, Eli and Fletcher stepped out from the forest, arms raised. Sara and Jacob stood behind them, followed by Sensei Mick.

"Steady now. Don't rush it," Sensei Mick cautioned. They moved through the forms together in synchrony, silhouetted in gentle light.

In the van hidden down the track, Kate and Kara tapped at their laptops. "The high freqs worked a treat," Kate murmured. "We should patent that shit."

Kara glanced over at Catherine in the driver's seat as the van cranked into life then turned back to the clearing as the Blackhawks shuddered, blades slowing. White light glinted across Robyn's skin and Eli was wreathed in red at her shoulder.

"Sir, we've lost the main gauges."

"Get them back online, and someone get the damn targets, they're right there."

"No-one's responding –"

The figures in the clearing stilled, bringing their fists together.

"Sir?" A terrible screeching sound echoed through the aircraft as metal was cleaved from metal.

Robyn watched the smoke haze engulf the

Blackhawks. The terrible crunching sound intensified. When the smoke cleared, the grass stood empty. Robyn stared at the peaceful emptiness in wonder before turning to Sensei Mick. He bowed lightly to her and each of the others in turn. "Go. I will remove all trace of their presence here." He reached out a hand to Robyn's right eye, tracing the throbbing birthmark there. "It has been an honour."

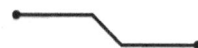

After her team of scientists had finished for the day, Fang knocked on Vulcan's door. "You wanted to see me again, Chief?"

"Come in, come in." Vulcan indicated the lounge and coffee table by the window, the real window, with the crisp edge of the mountains highlighted against the sunset.

Vulcan poured two glasses of port and gave one to her. She accepted it with a small nod.

"I've issued invitations to buyers."

"That's good news." Fang lifted her glass and clinked it with Vulcan's, wary. He seemed to lurch from placid to animated in the blink of an eye. "Is there something in particular I can assist you with?"

Vulcan nodded. Sweat beaded at his hairline as he sipped his glass. Fang wondered how much he'd already drunk. "Have you come across the demagogue styling herself as the voice of the people?"

"Hypatia." Fang sipped. She'd been following the essayist closely, her columns coming thick and fast, well researched and devastating to the governments involved. The latest was a commentary on the response to the UN's Planetary Emergency Committee, disarmingly accurate. Fang had read it earlier in the day between meetings with the floor scientists.

"I want you to know that I'm taking this solar catastrophe very seriously. Miranda warned us about it, you know."

Fang cradled her glass, frowning as she thought of the temple. *What exactly did Miranda learn from that ruin?* Her supervisor would have loved to meet the syndicate behind the moniker Hypatia.

"Fang?" Vulcan reached out with the bottle of port. Flustered, Fang accepted the top-up.

"Hypatia sees it as we do. A world carved up in the

aftermath of a global catastrophe the like of which we have never seen. But disorder is the natural order, is it not?"

Fang tipped her head. "Equilibrium is always attainable."

"I beg to differ. Homeostasis can only be reached for a moment before imbalance tips the scales."

When Fang left Vulcan's office, she was lightheaded. She rarely allowed herself to reach this point and felt uncertain of the gravity of what they'd discussed. Her mind was still on Miranda's past as an anthropologist and the secrets she'd uncovered. *And taken to her grave.*

When she returned to her office, Derek was waiting for her.

Fang collapsed in her chair. "What do you want?" She straightened the files on her desk, covering the photographs spilling from Miranda's folder.

"You set me up." Derek's affronted face was etched with familiar strain. The calm, relaxed Derek she'd glimpsed at dawn was long gone.

Fang frowned. "I did no such thing. I conducted some independent research, which turned out to be fruitful." She was glad the port hadn't made her less articulate.

Derek snorted. "Independent research." He unwound his tie and loosened his shirt, gesturing to her visitor's chair. "May I?"

She nodded, wary of his sudden politeness.

Derek sank into the armchair. "You said we would be a team," he said quietly. "When I brought you the activation dose ... and Ariana." Derek ran his hands across his face and suddenly he was the same Derek she'd joked with in the gym. Vulnerable, kind, and a potential friend.

Fang pushed Miranda's folder deeper among the stack of data files on her desk. Yet he'd betrayed his friends, abandoned them while thinking only of himself. Sudden loathing filled her. "And we were, until you left me by the wayside on your ascent up Vulcan's alimentary canal."

"Right. I see. So I did my job, and you did yours, but this is *my* fault." Derek pulled off his jacket and rolled up his shirtsleeves. "I came here to propose a truce, but I can see that instead you'd rather just berate me." He spread his palms in surrender. "Look. Neither of us will win Vulcan's popularity contest. We're pawns and nothing more. You must know that."

Fang exhaled sharply and glowered at him. "A truce, really. Fortuitous timing now that I'm in charge of the entire research operation." It irritated her that he was right, but it was even more infuriating that he thought he could barge in here and lecture her.

"None of this would have been possible without me and you know it," snapped Derek.

That hurt, the liquor allowing his words to cut deeper into her armour. The fact that Derek – mild, attractive and annoying Derek – had cracked the convergence gene sequence before her felt like a blade through her ribs. "What do you want, Derek. Speak plainly."

Derek sighed and leaned back in the chair. "I've lost the data streams for twenty students. No explanation from Vulcan. I wasn't consulted."

Fang remained impassive, though her stomach knotted. Vulcan hadn't consulted her either. The names of the Enyo and Eris convergers swirled through her mind, innocent teenagers sacrificed at the altar of knowledge on Vulcan's whim. Sure, Miranda had taken experimental risks, but she would never have authorised this. This was *murder*.

"The transfer spiel is bullshit. No transport was

organised, nothing." Derek shook his head. "Nobody will tell me the truth, but I deserve to know."

Derek looked so earnest, still clinging to some small thread of hope. Despite Derek's jabs, Fang hated to destroy it, to plunge him fully into the reality of the situation. Her pain must have shown on her face, because the truth slowly dawned in his eyes. "They've been euthanised. Vulcan's orders," Fang said, her voice soft.

Derek's shoulders sagged and he cradled his head in his hands. After a long moment he straightened. "This isn't what I signed up for."

It's not what I signed up for either, Fang thought, though she said nothing as Derek stood and began pacing. "I don't even know what his plan is, Fang. I wanted to spread the activation dose, trigger the next evolutionary leap. We've done that. What more does Vulcan want?"

Fang's heart went out to Derek as he whirled around to face her. The words left her lips before she fully registered them. "I don't know if I can really trust you."

"That makes two of us." Derek's eyes searched her own, desperate and pleading.

Fang considered her response. Derek would find out soon enough, even without her. Vulcan *had* insisted she spend more time with him. Feeling drained, she crossed the room and sank into the second visitor's chair. Her knees brushed Derek's, but he didn't pull away.

"Vulcan has a number of parties interested in the convergent technology."

"Parties," Derek repeated, frowning.

"Think, Derek. Who would benefit most from such a technology? Who has the funds?" How could he not see it? Vulcan's rhetoric rose in her mind. The wars of the future would be fought not with drones and robots but with animals. The lines on the map would be redrawn, history's deficits finally balanced. Miranda had never revealed her plan, but this made sense, crystallising into a vision Fang could support. Her legs felt shaky at the realisation. This *must* be what Miranda had wanted.

"Military." Horror flashed across Derek's face.

"Precisely." Fang crossed her legs. "Strength, power, agility – the convergers and their animals are a formidable force."

"You knew?" Derek looked aghast.

She shrugged, though her heart was racing. "In Beijing, the trials leaned heavily toward military field applications. Under Vulcan, we've taken it a step further."

This *must* be what Miranda had envisioned. *But why didn't she talk to me about it?* Fang wondered.

"So now we're creating living weapons. I thought …" Derek trailed off, eyes unfocused.

Fang leaned forward, forcing him to look at her. "What did you think?"

Derek's voice was small. "I thought we were unlocking the evolutionary leap that would change the world."

Fang straightened and pressed both hands to her temples, her head beginning to pound. "It will." *One way or another*, she thought.

31

Consequences

There were no games the following week. Ariana moved through regular training and classes with a heightened awareness. Everything was changing too quickly for it to be merely coincidence. Yesterday, their tablets were confiscated for what the teachers dubbed 'routine virus check-ups'. Ariana had hidden the files she'd copied from Derek's computer within the military history section of the extensive library, but still she sweated as her tablet was taken. On palming her returned tablet, only her original restricted access loaded. No-one singled her out and there were no consequences, so she guessed each tablet had simply been wiped and reloaded. Sloppy. But it meant the MRI had been alerted to a security breach. And, more than likely, someone else was being blamed for her activity.

The lingering tension permeated everything, kept everyone on edge. After several scuffles in the corridor, Spence split Athena into rotating units of two to train together. Each team was fully autonomous, able to make decisions without direct command from Spence. Outside of training, they used sweeping rotations to ensure no-one was left alone in the cafeteria, in training, in the Dome. Ariana always had a team with her.

Except now. Ariana sat in the warm mugginess of the Dome. Lucy was finishing a report in the study hall and Basil had begged off to fit in a treadmill session before dinner. Ariana didn't mind. They were only down the hall; Perses had scheduled training and Ares was stuck in the classroom. She lay back in the soft grass and watched the light dance through the hexagonal glass panels. She let her mind glide to the edge of the in-between.

"Spence won't talk to me about it," Ariana said.

Yves sat with his feet in the water, trousers rolled up to his knees. "It's obvious she intends to stay behind."

Ariana sighed. The projection of Yves flickered. A memory, a thread of a past life. The only person who really understood. "I know, but she's being so stubborn.

If only there was some way to get her orca out of here …" Ariana sighed. "I don't want to leave her behind. I don't want to leave anyone behind."

"Your friends will come."

"You don't know that." Ariana fingered the implant on her neck. "I can reach you, but I still can't reach the spirit world. Some part of this chip is still working."

"And Jericho can't access his spirit form," Yves added. "A dilemma."

Ariana heard the door open and sat up, expecting to see Basil.

The door closed behind Mikey with a soft *click*. His lion lurked behind him, tail twitching.

"So you talk to yourself, too. I knew you were a little cuckoo."

Ariana stood up, instantly alert. "What do you want?" She glanced up at the camera on the Dome roof. *Surely someone will see what's happening and intervene.* Yves pulled his legs from the water and shadowed her.

Mikey ambled around the Dome, peering over shrubbery and behind trees. "Nope. No bodyguards today." He whistled and the door banged open. The rest of Ares filed in. Several convergers blocked the door while the rest flanked Mikey. Animals loped out of the foliage to join them.

With sudden clarity, Ariana realised she was completely out of her depth. Jericho skittered down her arm and dropped onto the ground, disappearing into the grass.

"Normally, I'd never hit a girl, but in this case I'll make an exception."

"What's the special occasion?" Ariana's eyes skirted across the gathered convergers as fear coiled low in her stomach.

"Finals are coming up. Just found out. I don't know exactly how your little dance destroyed Enyo, but it's not going to happen again." Mikey turned with surprising speed and punched her in the gut. Ariana doubled over, stars erupting behind her eyelids.

She gasped for air as she pushed herself up. Yves tensed by her side. "You're outnumbered. You have two choices. Submit and be beaten, or go down with a fight and be beaten."

"I choose option two," Ariana muttered, raising her arms.

She struck out at her next two attackers, landing clean

blows on the sternum of one and sweeping the legs out from under the second. It only delayed the inevitable. The ring of convergers tightened. Pain lanced through her stomach as another fist hit her, then another. An elbow collided with her skull and bright light filled her vision. *I have to stay conscious, mustn't allow them to get me on the ground, or it's all over.*

Mikey came into focus. His fist connecting with her jaw was the last thing she remembered.

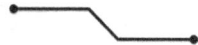

Ariana woke up with a pounding headache in a bright room. She gasped as she tried to pull herself into a sitting position. Pain exploded through her synapses. Not a cell, thank God, though the same antiseptic smell permeated everything. The room was hospital-like, with blipping machines by her head, a thin blanket over her legs.

"Don't move. Hang on." Derek stood and peered at the IV drip connected to the inside of her elbow. "Your morphine is low. Probably why you woke up."

A blanket lay sprawled over the chair behind him, a

tablet carelessly perched on top. Ariana wondered how long Derek had been waiting for her to wake up.

Ariana coughed, her throat was dry. Derek passed her a bottle of water and she took it gratefully.

"Athena made it to the Dome before Mikey could do any significant damage. You have Jericho to thank for that." Derek sent a wan smile toward the salamander curled on Ariana's chest. "He found Spence before security had been mobilised."

I'm sorry I could do no more, little one. Jericho's apology whispered across her mind.

"I should have envisaged something like this would happen when I integrated you, assigned you to Athena early." Derek sat down, moving the tablet to a low table. In the movies, the table would be filled with bright flowers from well-wishers. But this wasn't a movie.

Derek ran his hands over his face and cupped his chin. Yves shimmered into being behind him.

"He is sincere, this one." Yves crossed the room and sat at the end of Ariana's bed. "Perhaps you can trust him."

Ariana shook her head.

"Ah, it is difficult to forgive after a betrayal."

He killed my brother. I can't forgive him.

Terence knew the risks, Jericho gently reminded her. *It was his decision.*

Derek stood and folded the blanket. He hovered for a moment before handing her the tablet. *Her tablet*, she realised.

"You'll be in here for a few days. Promise me that you'll be more careful."

"I wouldn't need to be more careful if it wasn't for you," Ariana rasped.

Derek nodded and turned on his heel, disappearing down the row of empty beds.

Ariana stared at the void in his wake, still processing the pained expression on his face. It was almost as if he thought he'd never see her again.

32

Weapons

Spence and Chris were waiting for her outside the hospital wing under the watchful eye of a scientist. Spence was furious. "This should never have happened. I've already spoken to Lucy and Basil."

Ariana sighed as they fell into step on either side. She had no doubt Spence had already remonstrated with them both. "It's not their fault."

"Unacceptable," Spence said. "It's not going to happen again."

"They wouldn't let us visit you," Chris said. "I'm glad you're all right."

They passed the morgue room, where Ariana felt the whisper of cool air on her ankles, then her cell.

Chris met her eyes and Ariana nodded.

They walked faster.

The scientist led them through the lab to the student corridor. The door slid home with an electronic *beep*.

Yves materialised beside her. "Hurry, there's not much time."

Ariana stopped and turned to Spence and Chris. "Today. It's happening today."

They stared at her for a second but nodded. Chris disappeared down the corridor at a run. Spence drew Ariana into a hug. "I'm going to miss you. Take care of them for me."

When they drew apart, Spence's mouth formed a grim line.

Yves extended his arm. "Come."

Derek didn't trust Fang. He couldn't talk to Ariana without raising suspicion, had to feign indifference to conversations centred on the upcoming buyers' visit among the command centre technicians. Derek frowned at his workstation as more rumours floated over him. Next week. A fortnight. Two days' time. He didn't care anymore.

Ever since Ariana's late-night visit to his office he'd

been on tenterhooks waiting for Vulcan to pounce, but nothing had happened. Vulcan must have discovered Ariana's intrusion, or evidence of the copied files, to have instigated the mandatory tablet reboot. He could only hope he'd removed all trace of her activity quickly enough. No-one had questioned him yet. He was going crazy trying to stay one step ahead of Fang and Vulcan and keep Ariana safe.

The conversation around him crescendoed. Derek looked up from his computer feeling shaken.

"Sir?" A technician bobbed by his side, waggling his tablet. "We've just received word. The buyers are coming today. We're to prepare the field immediately."

Derek took the tablet and skimmed Vulcan's orders. A field for maximum engagement between two forces. He felt an immediate pang of fear for Ariana.

Fang sat at her desk, Miranda's notebooks sprawled in front of her. Would Miranda support Vulcan's plan to create living weapons? Unease settled in her stomach as she flicked through the old photographs. Or would she be horrified to learn of the direction the MRI had taken? With Vulcan as Chief Director, the convergers would be tools in whatever global conflict erupted next. Whichever country was positioned to utilise their unique capabilities would come out on top. Military forces around the globe would pay a ransom for their own genetically enhanced human-animal armies. The sickly sweet taste of port rose in the back of her throat as she remembered her conversation with Vulcan. *Disorder is the natural order.* With the devastation wrought by the solar storm, the world would be left reeling, pent-up hostilities bubbling over with no means to retaliate. Without power, without functioning ammunition, modern weapons would be useless.

All except Vulcan's gene technology and his converger protégés.

Her phone rang and Vulcan's gravelly voice filled her ear. "I need you in the laboratory to greet our buyers."

Fang jumped in her seat. "Of course, sir. On my way."

Today. It's happening today. The beginning of a global rebalancing of power. Fang swallowed thickly, pushing aside Miranda's notebooks. She froze upon entering the lab as fragmented groups turned to face her. Starched collars with glinting medallions. Faded khakis with assault weapons. Hard men in dark suits.

Did Miranda really want these people to hold this sort of power?

Robyn watched the stars through the airplane window, going over the last week of frenzied preparation in her mind. Now she just felt drained and empty. She leaned back against the plush seat and wrestled with the sickening emptiness as she thought of the blackhawks that had attacked the farm, the bodies, the blood smeared throughout the earthship. *It was a home, a sanctuary, and now ... My parents are going to kill me.* Unbidden, a grim smile rose to her lips.

They'd taken off at midnight from a rural airfield several hours north of the earthship. She hadn't asked how the twins set up the private plane. More favours from their burgeoning network. Hypatia wielded real power. Robyn jerked in her seat as yet another shriek of triumph echoed from several rows down where Kara and Kate sat hunched over their laptops. Next to her, Catherine didn't look up from the volumes of MRI data, just squeezed Robyn's hand. She squeezed back.

"Probably found out Fang has an extremely painful hernia resisting treatment," Sara offered from across the aisle where she sat with her legs across two extra seats.

Eli sighed behind her. He tossed a lightweight vest over the seat. "Try this on."

Sara rolled her eyes but strapped the armour on and moved her torso to test the fit. "Not bad."

The MRI wouldn't be expecting a rescue mission now. Ariana's information had allowed them to plan an assault. Weak points in the building infrastructure, delivery times, guard rotations. The MRI files contained everything down to student dietary requirements. Even with the twins' assurances, fear filled Robyn. *I have to keep it together. Everyone is depending on me.*

Catherine closed her folder. "Hey, why don't you let me keep going through these? You should try to get some sleep." Catherine raised her voice, gazing at Sara. "We should *all* try to get some sleep."

Fletcher's frequency was already dulled. Robyn peered around the edge of her seat to see him slumped against Eva on the floor at the back of the plane. The pilot had nearly passed out when the bear had boarded.

Sleep. Soon, they'd be touching down in Sofia,

Bulgaria. Robyn closed her eyes and listened to Catherine's pen scratching on paper as she replayed the plan in her mind.

It has to work.

33

Attack

Two distinct life forms inhabit the millions of environmental niches provided by our planet, each governed by an artefact from the initial coupling of cells clambering from the primordial cauldron. Plants, those miraculous oxygen-generating machines that terraformed Earth, are dependent entirely on chloroplasts. The growth and spread of animals would not have been possible without mitochondria. We consider it symbiosis or mutualism, but what if we are simply hosts and the line drifts toward commensalism, or even parasitism?

Brock Williams, Working Notes.

Cold sweat trickled down Ariana's spine as she waited for the siren. She assessed the arena in front of her. A steep wall of rock led to a raised plateau surrounded by rivulets of open water. *Nowhere to hide,* she thought.

"Today's battle will emulate a real engagement with an enemy. You are authorised to use deadly force to complete your mission." The speaker crackled and for a moment there was stunned silence. It didn't last long. Cheers and whoops rose from the Perses end of the field, and Ariana's stomach plummeted. *Daniel won't hesitate to tear us apart. This is exactly what they've been building to – make us want to hurt each other, to kill.* She glanced up at the stands where she knew Mikey would be glowering at her, angry to be devoid of the chance to freely attack her, but the bright lights blurred her vision. Behind her, Athena didn't flinch. They knew the plan.

The siren sounded and Spence shot forward, leading the others to the water. Ariana didn't look back. She charged alongside Chris up the incline to the plateau, reaching the top just as Perses began straggling over the edge.

Daniel stepped forward, alone, his eyes wary. *Good,* thought Ariana. *Let him think this is a trap. The longer he lingers, the more time Spence has to get the others clear.*

"Listen, you don't need to do this." Ariana pointed to the glassed box. "We're a commodity to them. Just technology, not real people."

Daniel's bear began advancing. Chris' polar bear, Iki, mirrored its movements.

"I think you're afraid to lose. To die." Daniel began moving in a wide arc toward Chris.

Derek stared at the screen as Vulcan's voice came over his earpiece, narrating for the benefit of the buyers, all ensconced in the private box above the arena.

"Two of nature's top predators. The grizzly and the polar bear. Well matched for strength and agility. You're about to witness a clash of titans, a privilege few have shared. Either bear would make an excellent addition to a military assemblage."

Ariana would be torn apart, completely defenceless without her energy aura. Derek strode through the command centre. *I have to find the receiver, have to give her a chance. I won't stand by while she dies in front of me.*

Fang sat on a stool at her lab bench, frozen. *No.* Vulcan had played her, told her what she wanted to hear, steered her research. Miranda would never have used the power of convergence to make a quick buck, to enable terrorism and war. Her supervisor was a force to be reckoned with, but she followed the science, not the money. Vulcan had *outsmarted* her. The lights above flickered and shook. She took a deep breath and assessed the reagents within her reach. *I am Fang Fisher, and goddamn it, I'm the one heading this project, no matter who sits in the cushy office.*

In the arena, the grizzly bear pounced, knocking Iki onto her side. The polar bear's roar momentarily deafened Ariana. The plateau shook under the force of the combined impact. Iki pushed the other bear away with her back legs, shaking her neck as she regained her footing. The two predators growled before rushing together, colliding in a whirlwind of sheer strength. Convergers grabbed at each other to stay upright.

Now's my chance. Ariana exhaled and brought her arms upward, moving rapidly through the poses she'd practised in her cell. Energy surged through her system, looping back on itself, filling her limbs with power.

Rock heaved, followed by the snap of metal, as the facade of the plateau cleft in two. The rift widened as

Ariana skipped away. Perses fell back with a cry, leaving Daniel and his grizzly exposed on one side with Ariana and Chris.

Daniel launched forward, pinning Chris to the ground. Ariana's vision blurred and she panicked, blinking rapidly, willing her eyesight to clear. She took a shaky breath as it did; slowly, too slowly. The implant in her neck burned.

Chris turned and slid on his knees before pulling Daniel over his shoulder and pinning his arm behind his back. Daniel's face hit the dirt, hard. The two rampaging bears danced around them. Iki and the grizzly clashed and pulled apart, swiping heavy claws at each other.

Panting, Ariana dropped her arms, the energy dissipating. Daniel bucked under Chris' hold, kicking Chris in the ribs and rolling away as Chris' grip loosened. Ariana staggered forward, brushing her mind across Iki's. The polar bear's movements seemed to slow down. Chris and Daniel edged toward each other, fists raised. Ariana moved through them, reaching out to touch Iki's crimson-stained flank. The last remnants of energy spooled through her hand and rushed into the bear's body, the chip searing her skin once more.

On her shoulder, Jericho uttered one word. *Move.*

The fight rushed back to full speed as she dived sideways. The bloodied polar bear surged forward, barging into the grizzly's side. Its claws scraped through the dirt, but Iki had too much momentum. She drove into the grizzly, sending it flying off the plateau. The bear flailed in empty air for a long second before hurtling down to the ground. A sickening *thud* echoed around the arena.

"No." Daniel slid down the incline, showering the fallen bear in dust. Ariana dropped onto her knees, drained and shivery. She glanced up at the stands, but they were empty. Dread curled in her stomach.

"We have to get out of here, now." Ariana registered the shocked faces of the remainder of Perses as Chris pulled her up, his breathing laboured. A bloody gash ran across his chest.

"Look what we have here."

Ariana turned at the voice, resting an arm on Chris' shoulder for support. Mikey stood with Ares at his back.

Ariana straightened. "Let us through," she said, hoping Spence had managed to get the others clear.

The convergers behind Mikey spread out to circle Ariana, Chris and Iki. She swallowed, trying to overcome her fear.

"I think I'll stay to finish what Daniel started," Mikey said.

Ariana firmed her stance, desperately pushing her awareness to the in-between, but the lion was too fast. She screamed as claws raked across her torso. Blood soaked through her ripped bodysuit and a dizzying lightness descended on her alongside the certainty that she was about to die. Mikey pulled a taser gun from his holster.

Boom.

The entire field rocked. Ariana clutched her stomach, her breathing shallow, expecting the sizzling pain of electricity at any moment.

Boom.

One of the Ares convergers fell as the plateau fragmented again, his screams cut off as he hit the ground.

Ariana didn't have time to figure out what was happening. For at that moment, a huge section of the roof gave way, fracturing the remnants of the plateau and sending her flying into space.

34

Laying On of Hands

There has never been perfect equilibrium on Earth. A plant grows strong and tall, distinguishing itself from its sisters only to provide better access to a grazing herbivore. The plant adapts. Sharp leaves, poison. The herbivore, too, adapts. Specialist enzymes to break down the serrated cellulose structures, keener eyesight to distinguish dangerous from safe. Likewise, animals grow and evolve based on their interactions with each other. Humankind learned to carve stone, make tools, hunt; then realised they could subdue the ground through agriculture, keep their meat happily living in pens. With less time devoted to pure survival, they created script and language, machines to do their bidding – from the simple wheel to the computer. All the while hosting their own tiny living relics of the dawn of time.

We don't truly understand their origins. Only recently have we unravelled the shifting micro biomes within our own bodies. We acknowledge the role of the myriad bacteria within our digestive systems, yet fail to observe our own position as part of the Earth's microflora. Mitochondria have for so long been a part of us that we dismiss their very existence. Of course, we consider ourselves the apex of the evolutionary chain, but no doubt dandelions share this very same delusion. We are quick to take phenomena we don't truly understand for granted; we slap on labels with abandon and deem the world mapped for posterity.

Brock Williams, Working Notes.

Inside the command centre, Derek watched in disbelief as a spiderweb of cracks raced along the reinforced glass. The orca had *rammed* the wall. He caught a flash of movement as the orca disappeared down the tunnel toward the arena, a small figure clinging to its back.

Spencer.

The cracks spread, merging into an almost living network.

Derek took a step backward. "Out, everyone out!"

The other operators looked up in confusion as he scrambled toward the door, his focus on the terrifying splinters in the glass that thickened as he watched.

With a sickening crack, the glass imploded under the pressure of twenty tonnes of water, which spewed into the room with incredible force. Screams filled the air as Derek reached the door and raced out onto the field, water surging past him.

He froze as he realised what had caught the operators' attention. Light streamed into the arena through a gaping hole in the roof. Intruders slid down ropes onto the now flooded arena floor, blazing with familiar light.

And standing there, water up to her knees, was Robyn.

Kara stepped into the reception area with Sara and Jacob on her heels. A breeze wafted through the smashed windows, and glass crunched underneath her boots as she strode onto the mezzanine level. Scientists milled in an anxious cluster below, surrounded by a bedraggled group of convergers. The whole building lurched. Machines crashed to the floor and the glass walls of the mezzanine smashed to the ground. The screams of the scientists followed Kara as she found the office she wanted at the end of the hall and set to work. Sara took the stairs four at a time, swinging a pair of boltcutters in front of her. The three wet convergers looked up at her warily.

"Athena?" Sara asked.

Jacob hacked at the locks on the animal cages with his own boltcutters. Doors sprung open and terrified animals escaped, scurrying toward the open air.

The group nodded.

"You'll want to be coming with us then."

Robyn sloshed toward Ariana's body, the walker's frequency muted despite their proximity. *No.* Ariana lay face down, a ring of blood diffusing through the water.

Robyn sank to her knees, lifting Ariana into her arms. Ariana's frequency strengthened as Robyn pushed energy into her body. *Alive. She's alive.*

Ariana jerked and gasped for air. "Robyn," she exhaled. "It's you."

"I'm here. We're all here."

Ariana wheezed. Moans rose around the arena as a line of convergers began to form up among the rubble.

"We don't have long." Ariana coughed up blood. "The soldiers will be here any minute."

Red light filled the arena as Una morphed into her spirit form with a wave of sound. Eli raced forward, Fletcher behind him. Robyn felt the answering pull of energy in her spine.

Electricity arced through the air and Eva collided with a snarling lion. Blue sparks ricocheted from Eva's neck as a boy plunged a taser into her shoulder. Fletcher launched himself at the boy's back, grabbing him in a chokehold from behind.

"Watch out, Fletcher," Ariana spluttered.

Mikey managed to maintain contact with Eva for several long seconds before Fletcher pulled him away.

Mikey used his free arm to elbow Fletcher savagely in the ribs, ducking out from under his grip. Eva swiped at the lion as it lunged onto her back, dropping into the water in an attempt to dislodge it.

Ariana stiffened and Robyn restrained her.

"I have to help."

Robyn looked properly at the wound in Ariana's stomach, grimacing at the torn flesh. She needed a hospital, emergency surgery – there was no way she could go back out there. Energy coiled in Robyn's spine and her hands lifted of their own accord, pressing deep into Ariana's wounds. Ariana screwed up her face in pain.

Screams rose around them. *Concentrate. I have to concentrate.* Robyn closed her eyes as energy welled in her hands, trickling through her fingers into Ariana's wounds. She'd never funnelled so much energy before, had never felt the zinging, almost burning sensation of it leaving her body like this.

Ariana screamed as her flesh reknit itself. Robyn opened her eyes to see a rib click into place. The skin under her hands began to ripple with movement, angry red gashes closing, skin marbling back to pink.

Ariana went limp.

Robyn pulled her hands away, the breath heaving out of her. "Ariana."

Water lapped against Ariana's hair, spreading it into a halo. Robyn shook the walker's shoulders as tears welled in her eyes.

"Ariana, come on, you can do this." Robyn stared at the bloody handprints she left on Ariana's bodysuit. "Please."

Ariana convulsed and sat bolt upright. She clutched at her stomach in shock and took a series of deep breaths. "How'd you do that?" She stood clumsily then straightened, testing her mobility.

Robyn spluttered in relief. "I'm not sure. How do you feel?"

"Better." Ariana stretched her neck. "Much better."

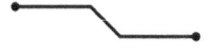

Blue light tingled along Ariana's arms as she felt the oppressive weight of the implant completely disappear. Jericho spiralled upward in his spirit form as she dipped into the in-between. The arena had reached an unstable equilibrium as the water settled. Every few seconds the metal plates screeched and the floor pitched. Ariana scrambled between floating chunks of debris toward the centre where Eli and Fletcher held off Ares and Perses.

Taser blasts hit Eli's red sphere and rebounded, sending sparks high into the air. Only the faintest rippling of green coated Fletcher's limbs as he grappled with Mikey. Ariana grimaced as Fletcher's body jerked under another taser blast. She ran, surging through the water, pushing beams and metal from her path as she tapped fully into the stream of spirit energy. It filled her limbs with new power.

Three more members of Ares joined Mikey. Fletcher convulsed under the added current, falling to his knees with a cry.

Blue light erupted from Ariana's body, cascading over Fletcher and sweeping up his attackers. They flew backward with a bone-jarring thud. One of the boys wailed, his body hopelessly twisted on a piece of jagged metal. Ariana dropped to Fletcher's side. "You came."

Fletcher managed a weak grin. "You bet."

Duck. Ariana swerved in response to Jericho's warning as a taser shot sizzled past her ear.

Mikey was streaked in dirt, his hair sopping wet. He flicked it out of his eyes as he raised his taser again. "So you can glow, too. Cute little nightlight."

Jericho swirled downward around Ariana's torso and Mikey took a step backward, eyes wide.

Boom.

Ariana swung her arms out for balance as a section of metal plates exploded upward near Eli. A sleek black nose pushed through the gap, sending four convergers flying through the air.

Spence.

Bodies hit the broken floor with a series of bone-wrenching *cracks*, screams cut off instantly.

Mikey sent a disgusted look over his shoulder before returning his attention to Ariana. His eyes lifted to gaze above her, but Ariana ignored him. She launched herself forward, knocking Mikey into the shallow water. Jericho unwound from his orbit around her body to rake his claws across the lion's back. Blood spilled into the murky water as Ariana grappled with Mikey. She kneed him in the chest, hard enough to dislodge the taser, which she kicked away.

Mikey spluttered as he breached the surface, and

Ariana did something she'd been dying to do. She punched Mikey square in the face, shattering his nose with a *crunch*. His body went limp.

"Ariana." She turned at Robyn's yell, registering the sound of boots on metal. The stands were filled with soldiers in dark fatigues. They held rifles against their shoulders.

Ariana glanced down at dozens of red dots on her body. Rifles trained directly at her.

35

Sacrifice

Catherine ran across the roof at a low crouch, the laser cutter strapped to her shoulder swinging against her spine. The gaping circular hole in the warehouse roof exuded screams and eerie metallic scraping noises, but she ignored them. She clicked in her harness and rappelled off the side of the building, heart hammering. *One. Two. Three. Ignore the fear, concentrate on the slide of the rope, feet on the wall. Bounce, drop, bounce, drop.*

Her feet hit the ground and she disengaged the rope. Pulling the laser cutter over her shoulder, she scurried around the side of the warehouse. Discordant sounds floated down from the arena. She shuddered as she stopped in front of the hangar. The laser blazed through the metal door like a knife through butter. Inside, helicopter blades glinted in the low light opposite a line of camouflaged all-terrain vehicles.

Catherine ran through the centre, slapping Kara's device under the hull of a chopper in the middle of the warehouse. It lodged with a dull *thunk*. Catherine cast one final glance at the hangar before she turned to pelt back outside.

Two battered vehicles sat outside an empty warehouse two lots down. Catherine skidded to a stop by the first van. Both bore the logos of a local cleaning company, on loan from more of the twins' benefactors.

Kate adjusted her ear bud as another plume of dust rose from the warehouse. "Sis?"

Catherine heard the response in her own link. "First wave coming out now. Hold tight for the others."

A crackle of static filled her ear as a knot of teenagers and their animals led by Sara and Jacob burst from the shattered frontage onto the bitumen. Catherine recognised them immediately from the student records. She waved her arms and they changed direction.

The static resolved into a burst of gunfire. Without thinking, Catherine sprinted toward the exposed convergers, screaming "Get down!" It was only when she reached them that she realised they weren't under fire. The sound had come from Robyn's link. She skidded to a stop as Robyn's voice came over the line, faint and breathless.

"No. No no no."

Terror gripped Catherine, scrambled her brain. She raced into the quaking building as Kate yelled behind her.

Ariana tensed as the bullets zinged around her, pushing her aura outward to encapsulate Fletcher and Eva. Eli raced over to add his red energy shield to hers. Spence was nowhere to be seen; Ariana hoped she'd dived in time.

The barrage was relentless. Bullets ricocheted from the energy field and soldiers fell as their own bullets rebounded.

"Any ideas?" Eli called over the noise.

Ariana closed her eyes and pushed through, feeling her limbs absorb more energy. She funnelled it into her aura, spreading it outward around them.

Eli watched its progress, nodded, and soon his own shield matched Ariana's.

"You can get there, too – the in-between!" Ariana shouted over the noise.

Eli nodded, his face pained.

The light crept toward the stands, inch by blazing inch. The soldiers took a wary step backward, but there was nowhere to go.

"Now," Ariana yelled, pushing the energy field further, straining with every inch.

A shockwave erupted from the combined auras, throwing the guards backward. Bodies fell at odd angles across the seats, sliding to the floor in a crumpled heap. Ariana's arms dropped as her aura sucked back toward her. Jericho tumbled out of the sky onto her shoulder, once more the little salamander. Ariana fell to her knees. Down the field, Eli too heaved for breath, Una on his forearm. A faint tongue of red light dissipated from his skin. He met her eyes with a sober shake of his head. *That's it. We're done.*

"Ariana, watch out." Fletcher staggered to his feet. Eva lumbered toward Ariana as she spun. Too late.

Crack.

The rifle shot seemed to echo in the air. Eva froze before tipping forward. Her green eyes met Ariana's as she crashed to the floor. Blood blossomed from the bear's chest.

Fletcher tilted forward, eyes rolling into the back of his head. Ariana watched him fall, frozen in terror.

"No. No no no," Robyn whispered.

A deep hum filled the arena.

"Everyone, down!" Robyn screamed as she dived for the ground. The hum built to a high-pitched whine, followed by a series of loud popping sounds. The arena shook.

Catherine.

When Robyn looked up, the shooter had disappeared, the private box empty.

But it was too late. Eva was gone.

Fletcher's frequency dipped dangerously low. Robyn scuttled through debris to pull him up by his armpits.

"Fletcher, can you hear me? You stay with us." Robyn shook the limp body.

Eli sank down beside her, lifting Fletcher over his shoulder. "We have to go."

"No way. Robyn can save Eva. You just healed me!" Ariana pleaded. "You have to at least try."

Robyn pressed both hands into the bear's shoulder, willing the energy in her spine to come, but felt nothing. "There's no energy for me to bolster. I can't bring anyone back from the dead."

Robyn stared at Eva's still body, at the blood-matted fur, remembering the nights she'd spent nestled against the bear's comforting heartbeat. A steady drumbeat now silenced. Exhaustion swelled in her chest, tears prickling at her eyelids. This was never supposed to happen. But she had to focus. If they didn't move now, they'd all be dead. She had to keep going. *For Terence. For Eva.*

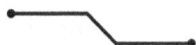

Derek ran through the laboratory, mercifully empty. Animal shrieks echoed from the walls and scientists pushed through the staff corridor in a frenzy. He ignored them, taking the stairs three at a time. Fang's office was locked. He stepped back a few paces and rammed it. The lock buckled. He stood in the doorway for a moment, eyes raking the files towering over the desk, unsure where to start. There was no sign of the receiver, but he was sure Fang must have it.

Sequencing targets. Lists scrawled in Fang's neat handwriting. He pushed over a stack of blood results and a worn manila folder slid out. Derek thumbed a photograph, frowning as a thread of recognition flared in his mind. He emptied the folder. More photographs. He splayed them out on the desk. Not the woman – he had no idea who she was – but the man who frequented the background of each shot. There. Derek pulled up a photograph of the man standing with his arm around the woman, both smiling into the sun, eyes creased into narrow slits.

The man in the bamboo rice hat was Brock. Much younger, but definitely Brock.

"Derek. What are you doing in here?"

He slid a stack of papers over the photographs, heart pounding, before turning to Fang. "I was making sure our files were safe."

Fang pointed to the door. "So the door was broken down *before* you came in."

Derek bristled. "We're overrun with intruders, or haven't you noticed?"

Fang joined him at the desk and Derek felt a sharp pain in his neck. His vision blurred. "Brock," he slurred. "In the photo."

"I'm sorry, Derek."

He hit the floor, darkness engulfing him.

Robyn burst into the laboratory, fire in her veins. She wanted to hurt someone, to make them pay for what had happened to Eva. She wanted that someone to be Fang.

She froze instantly. A man stood waiting for her in the middle of the room, holding a gun to Catherine's head.

"Look. Here she is now," the man said, wrenching Catherine's arms further behind her back. Catherine grimaced in pain. "We haven't officially met. Vulcan."

Robyn's anger evaporated. *Not Catherine.*

"And you, walker. I don't know how you managed to override your little collar, but playtime's over." Vulcan raised a metal receiver at Ariana and clicked.

Nothing happened.

The Chief Director frowned and jabbed the button again. Still nothing. He shoved the receiver into his pocket.

"A shame." Vulcan turned his attention away from Ariana and back to Robyn. "There's no need for this display. You're all part of the same program. You, Derek, Fang, and the lovely Catherine here. Terence's loss was regrettable."

Ariana stiffened. Robyn held out an arm to calm her, sending her a pleading glance.

"Speaking of which, where is Derek?" Robyn swept her gaze across the laboratory, half-terrified and half hoping to see him.

"He's busy." Vulcan patted the pocket where he'd stowed the receiver. "Quite an aptitude for the games, that one."

Robyn stepped forward. "You're right. We are all part of your program."

Vulcan tipped his head, obviously wary.

"The convergers, too. So why kill them?"

Vulcan smiled. "The boy you call the earth walker? I did you a favour. You and me both."

Robyn clenched her fists, feeling energy thrum through her limbs. "There's a fundamental difference between us."

"And what is that?" Vulcan's eyebrows raised in amusement.

"This."

The lights went out. The humming of the remaining machines died; the ventilating fans chugged to a stop.

In the semi-darkness, a shot rang out.

No. Robyn ran forward, colliding with Vulcan, but he was already falling backward, eyes blank.

A hypodermic syringe stuck out of his neck. A wide-eyed Asian woman stepped backward as his body slumped to the ground.

Robyn froze. "Fang?"

The woman recovered her composure quickly. "You need to run."

There was a man ten paces behind her. It was Brock.

Fang slit the bonds around Catherine's wrists as Brock stepped closer.

"Don't you dare touch her." Robyn felt a rush of air as a sucking sound filled the lab.

"The aquarium." Ariana exhaled behind her. "Vulcan shot the aquarium."

The sucking sound stopped, replaced by a terrifying splintering.

The glass wall exploded.

Water rushed out with terrifying speed. Robyn barely had time to pull Catherine toward her before the cascade enveloped them. She caught a flicker of red light from the corner of her eye as Eli encapsulated Fletcher and Ariana in his energy aura. The last thing she felt before the deluge smashed her into a laboratory bench was relief.

Relief that they would survive this, even if she didn't.

36

Escape

In Vulcan's office, a stunned Kara watched the aquarium explode. The mezzanine shook but held as the water collided with its support beams. Robyn and Catherine disappeared under the deluge. Dark water ravaged the laboratory, a living, seething wall. The aquarium emptied with brutal force and in less than a minute, the laboratory fell silent. Kara dropped to her knees and peered into the dark water, willing her friends to reappear. *Please*, she thought. *Please, they can't be dead.*

The water sloshed against the walls, its surface unbroken, deadly.

Kara brought her fist down hard against the floor, choking on a sob.

A flicker of red pierced the gloom, brightening as it reached the surface.

Kara inched closer to the edge. *Please.*

The red sphere of Eli's aura rose to the level of the mezzanine, hovering alongside Vulcan's office before moving inside the jagged remnants of the viewing window. Eli collapsed onto the floor and the light disappeared. Ariana clutched Fletcher to her chest, her breathing ragged. "Robyn, she –"

Kara raised a hand and Ariana stopped talking.

White light glowed beneath the murky water.

Robyn came to in the mezzanine corridor, Catherine squeezing her hand. Brock and Fang hacked up water next to her. Her entire body felt battered and stiff. She turned her head, and she and her supervisor stared at each other for a long moment.

Kara ran down the hallway, stopping abruptly as she noticed Brock. "Robyn, we have to get out of here."

Brock pushed himself to his knees. "Go. There are more soldiers on their way. I know it's likely you won't believe me, but our interests are aligned."

Catherine stared at Fang for a long moment before reaching toward her in a clumsy handshake. "I can't believe I'm saying this, but – thank you."

Fang pulled her forward. Robyn didn't register the gun in her hand until it was too late.

Catherine gasped as the steel connected with her back.

"Fang, think about what you're doing. Miranda and I never wanted this." Brock held up both hands as he knelt on the sodden floor. A heavy crash sounded from the laboratory below, reverberating through the warehouse. The floor shuddered beneath them.

"Listen to me, Fang. Miranda is alive," Brock continued.

Fang snorted with derision and pulled Catherine closer, wedging the gun against her spine. "Liar. She's dead. Now Vulcan's dead, too. No-one's going to use my technology against me."

"Please," Robyn whispered. "Not her."

Fang tilted her head and assessed Robyn. "So Derek was right. There *is* something going on between you two." She adjusted the bud in her ear. "I'll have backup in less than two minutes. Clever trick that little electromagnetic pulse in the hangar. But not all our birds were in the roost. Some of them were supposedly taking care of you, but I see that obviously didn't go to plan."

Fang's words sounded distorted, as if she were speaking underwater. Robyn only had eyes for the rigidness of Catherine's body, the tamped-down fear in her eyes.

"You can take Ariana. She's of no use to me. But I think an exchange is in order, don't you?"

Brock stood, still holding up his hands. "You don't understand what's going on here, Fang."

"Please. Enough of the condescending bullshit." Fang tipped her head, listening to her ear bud. "Sixty seconds."

"Go." Catherine's eyes met Robyn's.

"I'm not leaving you," Robyn pleaded. As she stepped forward, Fang pushed the gun further into Catherine's back.

"You have to go, Robyn. Please." Tears slid down Catherine's cheeks. "I'm not afraid."

Brock rushed forward and Fang coolly levelled the gun at him, gripping Catherine's waist with her free hand. A flower of blood blossomed on Brock's chest. He fell wordlessly to the ground.

Robyn stood frozen in confusion, barely registering Kara's grip on her arm as her friend pulled her down the corridor. Robyn stared at Catherine the whole way. Catherine held her chin high as Fang stood behind her, watching them leave.

Outside, sound rushed toward Robyn as if the warehouse had been a vacuum, a nightmare. The clear sky hummed above them. Robyn stared at it for a moment, uncomprehending. Kara shook her.

Kate revved the first van. "Let's go, let's go! Incoming air support, not friendly."

Kara leapt into the second van. Robyn dived into the back with the walkers and the vehicles peeled onto the bitumen.

Catherine, Fang's prisoner. Brock, maybe on her side, but dead. Her mind reeled, the walkers' frequency tethers making her nauseous.

Ariana held Fletcher's limp body in her lap, both of them streaked with blood. "Help him," she pleaded.

As Robyn knelt beside them, Ariana relinquished her grip. Robyn pressed her palms on his chest, willing the energy to come. Fletcher's frequency tugged on her mind, a weak thread.

She felt the push-and-pull sensation as her body

connected to his. Energy zinged through her fingertips. Colour returned to Fletcher's cheeks and his chest rose and fell steadily under her hands.

"Why isn't he waking up?" Ariana cried.

When Robyn pulled away, Fletcher's frequency felt more stable, though she felt shaky and weak. "I don't know. He's lost a part of himself. He may need more time to heal."

Ariana squeezed Fletcher's hand, tears streaking her cheeks. "He saved me. It should have been me."

No. It should have been me, Robyn thought. Me. Me. Me.

37

Bry

"I admit, I thought Vulcan would discover the fake receiver earlier. But the walker played her part well. She never raised suspicions she had partial access to her energy source."

"Ariana thought Derek was responsible. She and Vulcan both."

"When all the while you held the keys to her salvation. A shame you're no longer my inside man. I do apologise. I never expected Fang to shoot you."

"I admit it stung. I thought we were becoming friends. I knew it would only be a matter of time before Robyn and the others came. A bulletproof vest is only cumbersome until the day it saves your life."

"You're sure Vulcan won't remember your

involvement in the laboratory?"

"He didn't see me. It's a miracle he survived. He didn't look to be in good shape when I left. He lost the leg up to the knee."

"The boy survived, too, despite Vulcan's best efforts."

"If your theory is correct, killing him would have achieved nothing in the long run. By removing the bear, you separate him from his energy source. He's a walker in name only, able to communicate with terrestrial animals, yes, but not able to cross over."

"Perhaps it would have been kinder to kill him, after all. Unless, of course, it's all entwined with your cosmic deadline."

"Please. We don't have time for this."

"I know, I know. Your solstice. How many have we spent together already?"

"Not enough, clearly."

Two helicopters awaited them in the Serbian mountains. Robyn sat in the first helicopter to take off, a medical blanket wrapped around her torso. She watched the scenery change without really processing it. Her mind felt fragmented, as if she were losing a part of herself. She had no memory of saving Catherine from the deluge. One moment she was prepared to die, the next she was on the upper floor, her body humming with energy. None of it made sense. If Fang hadn't incapacitated Vulcan, he could have killed Catherine. When the white light had crept from her limbs, it had surrounded both Brock and Fang as well, saving them. Had she chosen to save them or did the energy act of its own accord?

And now Fang has Catherine.

Robyn closed her eyes. Her entire body ached and she longed for the oblivion of sleep. She was starting to drift off when her phone rang. It took several shrill beeps for her to realise what was causing the noise. Robyn scrambled for her mobile and jolted upright when she saw the caller ID. "Mum?"

"Darling. The chopper landed right on the ship and all of a sudden, your father and I are VIPs needing to be transported to an unspecified location. Can you please explain what is going on? The pilot won't tell us a thing."

Robyn glanced at Kara where she sat propped against Ariana. Kara nodded.

"I'll explain everything later, I promise. The chopper

is taking you somewhere safe. Please trust me."

Her own chopper flew low over a stretch of pine forest laced with mist. On the phone, her mother sighed. "Of course we trust you, Ro."

When Robyn disconnected, she finally slumped into sleep.

Kara woke her as the chopper touched down in a field, churning the grass into a violent sea. "We're here."

They trudged toward the stone farmhouse as the choppers lifted off, buffeting the small group with air. Ariana and Eli carried Fletcher between them. Polytunnels rose from the field behind the fairytale farmhouse. Garden beds greeted them as they followed the gravel path to the door.

"It's beautiful," murmured Kara.

"It's empty," clarified Ariana in a cold voice. She pushed open the door and helped Eli carry Fletcher inside.

A sweet musty smell assaulted Robyn as she entered a spacious kitchen. The twins sank into carved wooden chairs at the kitchen table.

"Not quite empty." A tall, lean man emerged from

the hallway. His white hair and beard, together with thick-rimmed glasses, made him look like an eccentric professor. Robyn immediately saw the resemblance.

"Dad!" Ariana ran into the kitchen and was enveloped in a bone-crushing hug. Her shoulders shook as she cried into his shoulder. Bry looked up, his eyes searching. He must have seen the truth in Robyn's gaze, because he gripped Ariana harder.

"I'm so sorry I wasn't here. You shouldn't have had to bear this alone."

"I saw the auroras and headed home. I've been worried sick ever since I found the farmhouse empty," Bry said over his shoulder as he led them into his study. Convergers slumped across the lounges, asleep after triage and a hasty meal. Fletcher lay on Ariana's bed upstairs, still unresponsive. Robyn swallowed past the lump in her throat as she followed Ariana into the impressive ode to polished wood. Bookcases bulged with musty leather-bound books. Bry muttered under his breath as he relocated several shining crystals and chunky fossils before spreading a graph over his desk.

"Over the last thousand years, solar activity levels have been steadily dropping. This is a carbon-14 dated record of solar activity from 1000 AD to the present." The graph showed a series of low dips before a mammoth rise. Bry jabbed at the dips. "Wolf Minimum, 1280 – 1350 AD; Sporer Minimum, 1450 – 1550 AD; Maunder Minimum, 1645 – 1715 AD; Dalton Minimum, 1790 – 1820 AD. A consistent lull in solar activity right up until the last century."

From where Bry's finger landed, the graph teetered upward at an alarming rate. "Solar activity has been rising dramatically since around 1900. We're due for a big solar event any year, any day now. So when you say there's a solar storm coming, I can't help but believe you."

Bry pushed his glasses up his nose as he straightened. "Unfortunately, we can't stop the sun from 'singing', as you called it." He glanced out the window at the falling twilight. "I'm not sure anyone can."

38

HAARP

Over the last several millennia, the delicate push and pull of the evolutionary dance has shifted. Human greed has set us against the planet herself, draining her of her dark blood to power increasingly complex machines; felling her lungs; contaminating her seas and damming her rivers. Philosophers argue over the depths of this human failing, this inherent darkness.

We are swirling masses of energy and we will return to the air, land and sea upon our demise. We are affected by the energy around us, the cosmic rays passing through our flesh every new day. The vacuum, the darkness lodged within us, has borne many names throughout our short and tremulous history. The ancient Greeks first named it Nyx: the primordial, shifting entity associated with the terrors of the night. There is a fine line between what we consider 'history' and what we deem 'myth'. All the stories are rooted in truth.

But who will believe such an assertion? Yet the temple certainly instructs such a conclusion, depicting an intimate relationship between human and animal that exceeds our understanding of molecular jugglery. Spirits, beings of pure energy, exist. The temple shows us beings from the three major biomes: land, air, sea. We call them Gaia, Notos and Atlantis, respectively. The temple shows unique individuals able to channel energy, to communicate with members of each individual biome. A miraculous feat by modern standards, but perhaps not uncommon in our collective 'mythology' of stories recorded across the globe.

But where there is good, there is also evil. The temple warns of the dark force, Nyx. I've found it foolish to ignore the lessons of history.

Miranda Collins, Working Notes.

Fang clutched a medical carrier spewing liquid nitrogen. Bloodied water lapped against the debris of the laboratory. The destroyed command centre provided a slanting view into what remained of the arena where the orca's carcass lay surrounded by limp forms in dark fatigues.

Two soldiers waded through the slick water toward her. "It's time to go."

Fang nodded. The momentum lay with the living, not the dead.

Outside, three helicopters idled on the bitumen. Fang held the styrofoam carrier to her chest, her experimental convergence viruses safe inside. Convergers and the surviving scientific staff already filled two choppers. Fang shielded her eyes against the swirling grit as they took to the air.

When the dust settled, she noticed Derek. He stood

alone, uncertainty plastered on his features. "Fang? What happened?"

My attempt at a coup failed, she thought, *only no-one knows it even happened.* Vulcan hadn't died. With that much propofol in his system, he should have keeled over instantly. She'd chosen the compound for its rapidity of action and short half-life, which made it almost undetectable. Maybe she'd have been better off pumping him full of drain cleaner. It was too late now. Bizarrely, the propofol had slowed down his body processes enough to allow him to survive the crushing debris, and later, the amputation. She'd been more careful with Derek's dose. Just enough to knock him out and fuzz his memory.

"Robyn and the other walkers. They took Ariana," Fang said as she joined him. A medic appeared at her side with blankets. Fang shook her head but motioned to Derek. He stood soaked to the skin. Derek cloaked himself in the dry warmth with murmured thanks.

"What happens now?"

A soldier waved impatiently at them and Fang stepped forward. "I don't know."

They were the last to leave.

The helicopter thrummed with sound, the rotors

sending vibrations through her chest as it ascended. Derek curled up on the seats beside her and slept. As the clouds enveloped them, Fang watched the ruined warehouse disappear into the distance.

She didn't recognise the soldiers sitting across from her, although they wore the dark fatigues of the MRI extraction unit. Fang held the medical carrier on her lap, listening to Derek's even breathing. Part of her mind registered the succession of scenery through the window, but it felt alien, unreal.

They'd lost a significant amount of data before the backup generators had kicked in and tech salvaged the operating system. None of her important work had been lost – a small miracle, all things considered.

But still, she'd failed. Vulcan remained in charge of the MRI. Would any of these soldiers have listened to her in his stead? Fang wondered how far Vulcan's reach extended, how far ahead he'd planned. He'd obviously had a contingency plan in place if the base in Bulgaria was threatened.

Stupid, so stupid. Even if my plan had worked, it wouldn't have made a difference.

They passed over snow-covered mountains deep into

thick forest. Fang shook herself out of her reverie as the helicopter descended, touching down onto a blustery runway where a line of soldiers awaited them.

"Where are we?"

One of the soldiers raised his eyes. "Alaska. You're at HAARP, ma'am."

Alaska. US soil. Fang stared at the enormous array of antennae as they walked toward the building. *What the hell?* She paused to examine the system, some sort of complex radio frequency transmitter.

"Keep it moving," one of the soldiers barked.

Fang frowned as she fell back in step with the flanking soldiers. *HAARP.* She'd heard that name before, at a conference while she was still at university. The High-Frequency Active Auroral Research Program. Home to a high-frequency radio array capable of stimulating the ionosphere, the layer of charged particles where solar radiation met the Earth's atmosphere. It was the only one of its kind, supposedly shut down years ago due to lack of funding. It looked pretty damn operational to Fang.

39

Expansion

"Fang. It's good to see you again."

Fang turned from her laboratory bench at the familiar voices. She shook the hands offered to her, puzzled. *Weaving and Deckker, here?*

"I wanted to offer my congratulations personally. It seems Miranda's confidence in your abilities was well-placed. You've certainly exceeded all expectations with your carrier viruses," Deckker said. "The project is well ahead of schedule because of your efforts."

Fang didn't reply immediately, her mind churning. She'd assumed the other directors had been integrated into the clerical structure of the MRI, with Terence gone and Catherine missing. Only now Catherine was no longer missing. Was that why Deckker was here? But how did that explain Weaving's presence?

"What brings you here?" Fang asked.

Weaving cleared her throat. "You. We had to accelerate our procedures." She glanced at her watch. "Ours should be here now, as a matter of fact. I wanted you to be the first to meet them. And Derek, of course."

Curious, Fang abandoned her workbench and followed them. Heads turned around the laboratory, but Fang ignored them. Her research scientists had work to do. Derek joined them in the corridor with a nod. It felt like more than two weeks since Robyn had attacked the base in Bulgaria. The research wing here was huge, humming with technical machines and scientists, but there were more soldiers than Fang had ever seen. They were everywhere: in the cafeteria, running drills outside, standing at attention in the hallways. Fang tried to ignore the glint of cold metal as she passed another gauntlet of soldiers in the main hallway.

Helicopters idled on the runway, rotors thrumming. Fang shielded her eyes against the glare as they stepped outside. The parade ground in front of them was filled with teenagers and animals, all wearing dark bodysuits. Hundreds of them.

Vulcan stood stiffly, reliant on a stout cane. He

nodded at them before turning to face the assembly before him.

"How?" Fang managed, mouth agape.

Deckker smiled and clapped his hands. "You didn't think Bulgaria was our only operation, did you?"

"Oh my God," Derek murmured, his face stricken.

Fang stared at the convergers standing to attention. They wore their dark bodysuits, only now the coloured stripes were gone. Their animals stood silent beside them. A girl sat propped in a wheelchair among them. *Spencer*, Fang realised. *She survived.*

Vulcan addressed the group. "You've all performed extremely well. You've proven yourself capable, resourceful fighters. It's time to begin the next stage of your training."

Fang remained silent as the convergers saluted. Vulcan's voice droned on. Derek flinched beside her. Eventually, Vulcan tapped his cane in dismissal and Fang blinked, focusing again on the parade ground. The convergers saluted and turned. In the sunlight, dozens of implant chips winked back at her.

Catherine sat on a narrow cot. Sounds echoed

down the corridor. The clank of boots, doors opening and slamming. Snippets of murmured conversations. How many days had it been? Five? Eight? She assessed her injuries again. Bruised ribs, but not broken. She grimaced as she pressed her side. The gash along her leg had been treated. It still stunk of iodine. The only clothes they could find for her were a pair of faded dark fatigues. She'd twisted the waistband so they stayed up, but she still felt ludicrous in them.

She rolled over and lay on her side. She hated the memory of the gun pressed against her back, Fang's easy manipulation of her. She'd frozen, unable, unwilling, to move. Afraid to die, no matter what she had whispered to Robyn. Catherine wiped the tears spilling from her eyes. *No.* Ariana had survived in this same situation, found a way to overthrow her captors, figured out what they were up to.

For the third day in a row, no-one came with food. Things were going to get a lot worse before they improved. She had to sell them a story, any story, while protecting their research. *I won't let Robyn down. Not now, not ever.* Catherine curled up on her side and slept. She would need what strength she could gather.

Down the hall, Derek lay in bed unable to sleep. His memory of the attack was blurry, a mishmash of sounds and images. He remembered the jolt of elation and fear at seeing Robyn and the other walkers blitzing into the arena. But he'd left, looking for something. The receiver. He frowned at the ceiling. Had he found it? No. But somehow Ariana had escaped anyway. So what had he been doing? He remembered going to Fang's office, moving files, looking for the receiver. He'd found something else, something important. The half-memory niggled at his brain. Derek sighed and reached for the pills on the nightstand. The on-base psychiatrist had prescribed them, calling it a mild case of post-traumatic stress. He took two, dry-swallowed, and waited for the welcome embrace of oblivion.

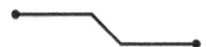

Kara rewound the footage, watched it again. And again. The pixellated video was seared into her mind, but she still couldn't believe it. Kate had collated the offerings of a dozen cameras seeded by BeyonceKnows into one video, smoothing out the jumpy transitions. Kara had

had to pause the video twice to throw up before she finished. *I'm one of the first people to know*, she thought and clicked play again.

Onscreen, a group of teenagers with a retinue of animals ran toward the Capitol Building in Washington, DC. The group burst inside, killing the guards outside the room where the NATO conference was being held. Not with guns, but with tooth and claw. Blood sprayed high along the walls, flecking the camera screen with gore. Kara flinched as she had for each of her viewings. What came next was even worse. The group coolly entered the conference room and sealed the door shut.

The Netherlands delegate stood to speak. "My fellow delegates, in the face of the global crisis, the existence of our organisation of nations is entirely prescient. For decades it has guided the West through calamity, providing stability even in dark times. I have every faith that NATO will continue in this role for another century or more."

The British delegate interrupted, raising gasps from the assembly at his audacity. "I disagree with your optimistic view. The UN's move to seize power is reminiscent of Hitler's proposed dictatorship, the very reason we formed such a coalition in the first place. Even now, by our obeisance, the UN attempts to take part of our joint military for itself. I, for one, will not stand idly by –"

All heads turned as the doors blew open. Twelve teenagers strode in, animals by their sides.

Mikey felt the collective outrage at being interrupted turn to all-out fear. He saw it on their faces, the abrupt switch. He enjoyed it, that control. People were so predictable. Prod them here, listen to them scream. His lion growled by his side, the menacing sound filling the now quiet room. The convergers spread out, easily surrounding the cowering people. There were few heroes in real life.

Still the man standing spoke. British, Mikey recognised the accent. "Terrorism will not be tolerated here. This is a peaceful meeting of nations."

Mikey opened and closed his right hand. At his signal, Daniel and his new bear launched themselves at the delegate, disembowelling him in one rapid strike. The man collapsed to the ground, his frenzied shrieks tipping the balance in the room. Mikey raised both hands as the delegate continued to wail, clutching his intestines like thick sausages.

The screams began in earnest.

Kara watched it through. Bodies lay draped over desks at odd angles; blood smeared across the wood, pooling into the carpet. Even the flags lined up behind the main desk were speckled with red.

The image was powerful. Even more powerful when it served as the backdrop of every major news report that followed.

Kara couldn't take it anymore. She retched into a bucket.

40

Fall

To: Hypatia

From: secgeneral@un.org

Re: advice

The brewing conflict has undermined our global authority. It is not yet common knowledge, but I have no doubt the media will know of the dissolution of the Security Council in less than six hours. How can a governing body exist when its members are at each other's throats? I lay it out clearly for you here, because I believe you campaign for the good of humanity. If I am wrong, well, I doubt my office will hold much meaning in the months to come.

No organisation has claimed responsibility for the NATO massacre. NATO itself has utterly collapsed. The smaller European nations have dropped UN membership and instead are playing a waiting game. The Shanghai Cooperation Organisation (SCO), NATO's Eurasian counterpart, has reconvened its planned meeting, drawing the suspicion of Western commentators. I feel you know more about those responsible than I do. But I digress. China is cementing the SCO together, signing non-aggression pacts with both Russia and India, no doubt planning to divide the smaller nations in their way among them. In only days, they are likely to control most of the Eurasian landmass between them, and more than half the world's population. I can only hope you have a better plan than I did. So this is both a warning and a handing on of the baton. Good luck.

Kara stared at the email from the Secretary-General. Every now and then, she'd longed to be able to tell someone what was happening in her life. Sitting in a lecture theatre, finishing a report for a client while the lecturer droned on about a concept she'd mastered months ago. She was already richer than all of her fellow students combined; and no matter how successful they became or how many 100-hour weeks they worked, they'd never catch up to her. But now, sitting in Bry's study, the feeling gnawed at her again. A personal letter from the UN Secretary-General. But to sing and dance would be to unravel everything she had worked for. The world wasn't ready to know who Hypatia was. Maybe they'd never be. The content of the letter grounded her. She and Kate had a lot of work to do.

"Big project we've taken on," Kate said, returning with two mugs and a plate of sandwiches balanced on top. She deposited them and sat down. Kara grabbed one.

"The biggest," Kara concurred through her mouthful.

Robyn sat on the stoop, peering into the darkness. Ariana was upstairs with Fletcher and Bry was organising food for them all. She closed her eyes, feeling the connection to Eli, Ariana and Fletcher. Fletcher was alive but still unconscious. *He has to wake up soon, he just has to.*

The door swung open and Robyn flinched, still immersed in the frequency tethers.

"Feeding time," Bry said. "I can't cook like my wife or son, but it's edible."

"I'm not hungry."

Bry sat next to her and crossed his arms. "You saved my daughter, and for that I'll be forever grateful. She's all I have left in this world."

Robyn drew her knees to her chest. *A lot of good I am, leading everyone into danger at every turn*, she thought.

"You have to be bold sometimes, willing to take risks. Danger finds you in the end anyway, so you might as well step out to greet it. That's what Terence did, and I'm proud of him for that. I'm proud he protected his sister and all these other children. I'm proud he met you." Bry stood and surveyed the darkening horizon. "Come inside. You need to keep your strength up."

He's right. Robyn stood and followed him inside, nodding at the new faces. She sat at the table between Eli and Sara, who surprised her by taking her hands. All around the table convergers linked hands, creating a closed circle.

"We want you to know that we're with you," Sara said.

"Always," Eli added.

Energy skittered across Robyn's spine, and the convergers gasped as it zinged around the circle. The light flickered above them. Robyn released Eli and Sara's hands.

Eli caught her gaze. "The mid-year solstice – it's tomorrow."

Robyn's heart hammered. *Finally.*

41

Solstice

"The UN has discounted any claim to the NATO massacre, instead pointing the blame squarely on the shoulders of the SCO."

"Who have been suspiciously quiet, may I add, Miranda."

"The breakdown of NATO serves both their interests. But you and I know who is truly the mastermind of the attack."

"Vulcan."

"By destroying confidence in the leading coalition of Western nations, he breaks any semblance of union. Each for themselves, as they say."

"But the attack took place on US soil; the US delegate also perished in the massacre."

"Wouldn't want to draw attention after all that

work now, would he?"

"So in a single foul swoop he's removed both NATO and the UN as major players. I don't necessarily welcome a Russian tzar or Chinese emperor, you know."

"Better brush up on your languages."

"It's sick and twisted. Using those children as weapons should be condemned."

"But the opposite will happen now. Each country, freed of any middling league of nations-style pandering, will scoop up its convergers the moment they know of their existence. The redrawing of the map will be brutal."

Fletcher jerked in the darkness. Tiny pinpricks of light appeared around him. He pushed himself upright, his heart hammering in his chest.

"Ariana? Eli? Anybody." His voice echoed into the blackness.

He heard a nicker and turned. A horse coalesced from the dark, its black flanks shimmering under the gentle lights. Fletcher took a step backward and the horse followed. He closed his eyes, attempting to drift his consciousness together with the animal, but he couldn't hear her thoughts. He paused. There was a niggling worry in the back of his mind. *Eva.* She wasn't here, but she must be close by. She wouldn't leave him.

The horse stopped and watched him. Fletcher flexed his fist, examined his fingers one by one. This felt real, looked real, but it wasn't the spirit world.

"Stay away from me." Fletcher said, stumbling away from the horse. But just as he felt he had put some distance between them, he found himself back in the same spot. "What the hell is going on?"

"A way forward," said a female voice. A girl appeared, rubbing the horse's neck. She wore a simple tunic and riding pants. A leather headband held back her long blonde hair.

She looked familiar. Even the strange perpetual darkness began to feel normal. Fletcher's heart leapt as he realised why. "You're the last walker of the earth, aren't you? This is the in-between."

The mysterious girl smiled. "I've been trying to reach you for months. My name is Ana. It's nice to finally meet you, young walker."

"Where are we exactly?" The darkness around him felt infinite.

"A place between your world and the spirit world," Ana said. Fletcher squirmed under her intense gaze. "You have been through much for someone so young. I can see the fractured pieces. You are not whole." She reached out to him. He tried not to flinch as she traced her hand along his face. She pulled back, a slight frown on her face. "And now you have lost your animal guide, Eva."

No. Eva wasn't gone, he was simply dreaming. None of this was real. But then he remembered the echo of the gunshot, Eva's wail as she fell to the ground, the fading glimmer of green light. And the blood, so much blood.

"No." He said it aloud this time, surprised to hear the hoarseness of his voice.

"It's my fault," Ana said, her eyes clouded. Green light flickered on her skin. "It's my fault your aura is weak. Unknowingly, I did a terrible thing as earth walker."

Fletcher screwed his eyes shut to stop the threatening tears. "You freed Nyx."

Ana sighed. "Yes. It cost my life, and that of my guide, to set it right. At least, I believed it to be so. But our efforts were not as strong as the original bonds put in place by the spirits Gaia, Notos and Atlantis. Nyx found a way out. It's my fault Gaia became tainted. Nyx has spread like an infection through the earth spirit. Through you."

Fletcher gasped as pain erupted in his chest.

"And only you can make it right." Ana's voice faded to nothing and the glimmering lights disappeared. Darkness gathered him in. He screwed his eyes shut in a vain attempt to stop the nausea rising in his stomach.

When he opened his eyes, he felt sick and dizzy.

Ariana hovered over him. "Fletcher. You were crying out." She drew him into a hug. "I've missed you so much. I'm glad you're all right."

Her tears felt like firebrands on his skin. *It should be me saying that to you, not the other way around.* This is all wrong. Ariana leaned down and pressed her lips against his. He tasted her tears. *I don't deserve this, I don't deserve anything.*

Fletcher pushed Ariana away, throwing the blanket aside. He stumbled to his feet. *Eva's gone and there's no way to make it right.* Ariana yelled at him to stop, to come back, to *talk* to her, but the pain drove him onward. *I have to get out.*

Robyn sat in the overgrown field by the farmhouse, wind whipping her hair as she tried to slow her breathing. If none of this had ever happened, Bry would still have a son, Ariana a brother. Catherine would be safe. Derek wouldn't hate her. But maybe the MRI would have found Fletcher and Ariana as well as Eli. Hundreds of teenagers around the world with the convergence sequence would have been rounded up, experimented on. She knew it wasn't a matter of balancing either option on some sort of moral scale, but she couldn't help it. *Have I made the right choices?*

Dawn light brushed her shoulders, caressing the stone walls of the farmhouse behind her. Could she really make any difference to what was happening? There had been far too much sacrifice already. She couldn't sleep knowing Catherine was in Fang's hands, couldn't help imagining torture she could do nothing to stop. Catherine, battered and bloodied, finally breaking, revealing the walkers' secrets. How long would she herself last in the exact same situation?

Robyn sighed. She'd been looking forward to this

date for weeks, but now she longed for more time. The mid-year solstice. Energy welled in her spine, zinging through her body. She closed her eyes and let the familiar wrenching sensation take over.

The temple loomed high above her. Robyn ascended slowly, uncertain of what she would find at the top. The stone felt cool and polished under her bare feet and the temple doors sprang open at her touch. An orange-robed man sat in the centre, facing the circular mosaic surrounding the three walker figures. Robyn bowed low as she stepped inside, her heart pounding. This was it. Answers, she needed answers. She crossed the floor and sank to her knees behind the figure, who chanted softly in a language she did not understand.

"Liro, I come seeking your guidance."

The man turned and Robyn gasped. "Lenti?"

But no, not quite. The face was older, contoured with wrinkles.

The man smiled. "It is good to meet you. Properly, this time."

Nobody followed him. Fletcher wiped his face on his sleeve as he shuffled downstairs, through the kitchen and out to the open field. His whole body ached. Robyn sat unmoving surrounded by wildflowers, no doubt already in the spirit world. Fletcher froze. Without Eva, was the spirit world even open to him? He forced himself across the field and clambered over the low stone wall separating it from the next field. Projecting his consciousness, hundreds of voices came into focus. Rabbits in their dens, foxes on the prowl, tiny grubs and worms mining their territories for nutrients. But when he tried to slip into the spirit world, nothing happened. Fletcher leaned against the stone wall, pushing back tears.

Liro sat with his hands clasped in his lap. "I tried to leave a messenger in my stead. I only partially succeeded. I saved the last novitiate monk of our order, a boy named Lenti. No doubt you have many questions, but perhaps it is best if you allow me to tell my story."

42

Liro's Story

This temple has long served as a meeting place for those few gifted with the ability to bridge our two worlds. It has stood for thousands of years, straddling a meridian common to both the physical and spirit world. Our history is largely preserved here in these stones. We kept records of each walker as they arose, though our records are far from complete. We do not know much of the original generations of walkers; their names have been lost to history. The stories tell us that in the times before, there was no separation between worlds – they merged seamlessly, bringing harmony to the Earth. Humans and animals lived together peacefully, able to communicate with the gifts of the spirit realm. For each human there existed an animal partner; someone able to understand their thoughts and wishes, hopes and dreams. The world was whole. Humans roamed and foraged, slept in simple shelters with their animal companions. Spirits wove their beings into the natural world: the sea, the air, the earth.

But then humans began banding together, forming insular groups. They wandered ever further and diversified, recognising their brethren now as outsiders, strangers. Following some evil hunger for power and dominion, bloody, drawn-out war followed.

The spirits who had found homes here were deeply ashamed; they had thought humans to be good, pure beings, worthy of the gifts of the spirit realm. They remonstrated with humanity, sending great floods, storms and earthquakes to stem the fighting. For a time, it worked. The bands retreated to their remote lands, but their innate distrust of the outsiders remained. A shadow fell across the Earth; a dark spirit crept into the hearts of animals and humankind alike. The spirits feared the newcomer – a fiendish rogue present at the time of the universe's conception, older than time itself. She had already cloaked more than one planet, suffocating it of life, before the lust for power among humans drew her to Earth.

The spirit's name was Nyx. Stories of her would live on, perpetuated by the Greeks and their fascination for the dark cruelty of the unknown heavens, but mostly she would be forgotten by all, except us, the order of monks devoted to the walkers. But I am getting ahead of myself.

Nyx stoked the embers of battle lust, and soon humans and their animals were again at war, razing forests for weapons, butchering the animals of fallen human warriors for food.

The earth, air and sea spirits – for they were now irretrievably linked to our world – plotted to overthrow Nyx. Meanwhile, Nyx grew tired of her human playthings, longing once again to bring calamity to distant worlds. This new world, our Earth, was close to a strong young sun whose song was building. Nyx decided to use its power to retract her claws from her playthings and drift back into the cosmos. As the sun crescendoed, the earth, air and sea spirits banded together to fight Nyx, for the consequences of her plan would be deadly to all life on Earth. They pitted their powers against the great evil, sending Earth into a period of great turmoil. Using the power of the singing sun, the spirits drove

Nyx from her human and animal puppets and entombed her deep within the Earth.

But Nyx fought hard, using the power of the sun to cleave the two worlds apart. When the sun song faded, the spirit world and physical world were separated, with Nyx deep underground, trapped by the forces within the Earth's core. Humankind woke up as if from a long slumber, the gifts of the spirit world stripped from their grasp. They remembered their previous abilities as nonsensical dreams, for how could they communicate with the dumb animals around them? The spirits watched sadly – for in saving humanity they had stripped them of their essence, their link to the Earth. They wept for many years until three were born with gifts far surpassing the spirits' comprehension: the walkers. Tears of despair turned to tears of joy. Seeing the miracle as a chance for redemption, they forged their own beings with the new walkers, equipping these humans with powers beyond any human reckoning and the ability to travel between both worlds. They hoped that in time, the walkers would be able to do what they alone could not – bring the two worlds back together and restore harmony.

Years passed. The walkers were reincarnated more and

more infrequently until their lineages slowed to a trickle. All the while, the spirits watched as humans continued to fight among themselves and raid their surroundings for weapons, tools, fuel and food.

By the time I was born, hundreds of walkers had already left our plane of existence. Alongside each walker, a guide was summoned, taking residence in the temple for the course of their life. The energies here allowed each guide passage to and from the spirit world, from which they could commune with their walker. All was well for many thousands of years. Though the walkers became rarer, they still brought balance.

I was left at the temple stairs as an infant because of my unusual birthmark, though a guide had not been known for generations. The order of monks I had joined became intrinsically linked to the energies of the temple. I grew up among the elders of the temple, learning the lineages and the songs of old. I had many brothers, a home, and thus, a family. The temple provided everything I could ever need. Many of my brothers despaired of a walker arising in their lifetime and left the order to become farmers or to marry.

Yet one did come.

The year was 1275. I was sixteen when I became a guide to the earth walker Ana, a headstrong fifteen-year-old from Iceland. I added her story to the stones, meeting with her in the spirit realm every day. She was born into a world of troubles. The northern continents faced murderous winters that destroyed farming land and villages alike. I felt her life force as if she were a part of my very being. The years passed; we grew up together. When she told me she had found a way to commune directly with the earth spirit, in a realm between the physical and spirit world, I was overjoyed. Naively, I imagined a future in which humankind understood their brethren and their links to the ground at their feet, the sky above them, the seas that buoyed them.

Ana did indeed reach the earth spirit, who warned her too late of Nyx's slow escape from the Earth's core to the surface. This dark, heinous being was once again let loose on the world. I felt Ana's energy aura change, the goodness replaced by evil. I knew the stories, knew I could not allow Nyx to spread her influence among humanity again.

Ana fought Nyx as the spirit took control of her energies, travelling through the snow with her partner animal, a horse named Inga, to a fearsome volcano. The air and sea spirits could only watch in agony – being tied to the human reincarnation cycle meant they had no means to aid Ana. I meditated long and hard in the spirit world, willing to find a solution apart from the one Ana and I had discussed. But I could find no other way.

Astride Inga, Ana plunged headlong into the volcano, once again returning Nyx to the earth. I felt the loss of her – my truest friend and confidant – as an almost mortal blow. On my knees in the temple, I felt the inky spread of darkness rise from the ground and penetrate the walls. It felt like living death, sucking the oxygen from the air.

My birthmark ignited with the familiar light of crossing between the worlds and, in my anger and despair, I reached for the spirit world only to breach some strange and foreign energy. I let it fill me, and white light expanded outward to encapsulate the dark spirit. It struck me that I would not survive such a feat, yet it only filled me with more conviction – to join Ana was all I wanted. Perhaps Nyx sensed it; somehow the white light overtook it, sending it spiralling back into the ground.

That was my last day on this earth. We managed to re-entomb Nyx but only with our sacrifice. The worlds beyond have their own charm, for in them I am once again by Ana's side.

I have watched through the intervening centuries, hoping beyond hope that our sacrifice was not in vain. When all three walkers emerged and you were called, I felt the stirrings of real hope. For you are the true guide, Robyn. Perhaps now is the time the spirits long awaited, the time to restore harmony and the gifts of the spirit world. Yet in my observations, I must also issue a warning. Despite all of this, Nyx has retained a connection to the earth spirit. This connection has grown ever stronger as humans persist in their exploration of the earth, pumping dark oil from the depths, mining for minerals and leached elements. Nyx is an inescapable part of Fletcher, an infection of the earth spirit.

Over the centuries before Fletcher was called, Earth has been ravaged like never before. Humans have spread like a plague across all continents, destroying countless species of plant and animal in their hurry to build their towering resource-hungry cities. The divide between human and animal has never been wider.

Which brings me to the present. I have meditated long and hard. To restore both spirit and physical realms to the same plane requires the presence of all three walkers. We were lucky to have battled Nyx when the sun song was at its lowest point for thousands of years. Now the song is building, as is Nyx's strength. The sun's power will peak on the next solstice. But I fear that by then Nyx will have already extended her reach to the other walkers.

If Nyx succeeds, she will not fail in her quest to destroy all life on Earth, leaving us to join the cold dead planets dotted throughout this galaxy and beyond.

43

Laos

Light glinted across the swirling mosaics as Robyn stared at Liro in the aftermath of his tale. Tears pricked her eyelids. *It's true. I really am the guide.* She squeezed her eyes shut, momentarily dizzy from a combination of fear and wonder. She swallowed thickly as she processed Liro's warning. "No. Not Fletcher."

Liro nodded. "I'm afraid so. I know you think of him as a brother, so this will be hard for you."

"I won't kill him. You said it yourself. The problem will continue. The next earth walker, the one after that." Robyn jumped to her feet and began pacing the temple. She stopped in front of the circular mosaic around the three walkers. Fletcher, Eli, Ariana. It was easy for Liro to condemn Fletcher, having only ever known him as the mosaic figure on the wall. Except – he hadn't. He let

Ana die and he loved her. Robyn dropped her hand and clenched it by her side.

Liro rose and walked toward her, his hands behind his back.

"I brought you here to tell you the truth, though it hurts. When I first showed you the temple, you were drawn to one figure in particular, weren't you."

Robyn remembered. "The horse, Inga."

"Yes. Because I am a part of you and the image stirred a memory. You felt the darkness in her even then."

Robyn said nothing. She *had* felt it, although she hadn't understood it then. "But Eva is gone."

Liro shook his head. "It is a unique phenomenon among joined human and animal pairs for one to live without the other. If the human partner should die, then the animal dies also. But the reverse is not true." Liro traced the circular mosaic. "Of course, you are right. Fletcher's death is at best a short-term solution. But it may be the best we have. Like Ana and I before you, we do not have much time. The next solstice is less than six months away. If Nyx gains complete control of Fletcher before that time, the planet is doomed."

Robyn thought of Fletcher's moodiness, his retreat

into himself. What if it hadn't been hormones and aggression but Nyx slowly taking over? She shuddered. "He's just a kid. He shouldn't have to die."

"Ana did not deserve her fate either. Yet surely the sacrifice of one is a just trade for the survival of the many."

Robyn thought of the millions of people who had already died because of her, of the now-dead convergers snapped up by the MRI. Every death was one too many. "There has to be another way. You said it yourself. This could be our chance to reunite the spirit and physical worlds. We need Fletcher for that."

"Only if he can overcome the spirit paralysis within himself can all three walkers join in breaking the veil between the worlds. I speak plainly because you must be prepared." Liro glanced at the golden ceiling, which was beginning to fade. "The day is ending. I must bid you farewell. Remember what I have said."

Liro stepped backward to the centre of the temple and sat in the circular beam of light falling through the aperture in the ceiling. As Robyn watched, the light contracted.

"I bid you good luck."

White light rippled around Liro as the sunlight

disappeared. Robyn's feet left the ground and the familiar wrenching sensation gripped her.

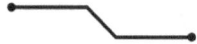

Fletcher lay on his back in the long grass feeling sick to his stomach. *My fault. It's all my fault.* He reached out a hand to stroke Eva's fur but froze as he remembered. *I'm alone now.*

A stone clattered down the wall and he jerked upright. Ariana climbed over the top and jumped down beside him. Jericho snaked over her collarbone.

Fletcher held out a hand. "Stay away from me. I'm dangerous, I'm diseased, I'm … I'm useless."

Ariana moved closer. "No, you're not. You're strong and brave, and kind. Eva, too." Tears streaked her cheeks.

Fletcher stopped. Ariana sat beside him. He rested his head on her shoulder and she drew him in tight.

"You're not alone," Ariana whispered into his hair.

"Robyn?"

Fletcher pulled away from Ariana's shoulder and hurriedly wiped his face on his shirt. Kara climbed the wall, eyes wild. "Have you seen Robyn?"

Ariana shook her head. Kara stood on the wall and cupped her mouth with her hands. "Robyn!"

"What is it?" Ariana asked.

"She's missing. Robyn is gone."

"But she was right there – in the field." Fletcher straightened and joined Kara on the wall, but only wildflowers danced in the breeze.

For a moment, Robyn sat with her eyes closed. She'd wanted to know how to stop Nyx. Now she did. When she opened her eyes, she frowned in confusion. The ruins of a wooden temple rose around her, missing walls admitting a spectacular view of terraced hillsides and bustling roads. At the front of the temple was a faded section of familiar mosaics.

This was the temple, not in the spirit realm, but in the physical world. *Her* world.

"Where am I?" she whispered.

"Laos," answered an unfamiliar voice.

Robyn whirled around. A woman in linen pants and a colourful shawl lowered her sunglasses.

"I've been waiting to meet you for some time, Robyn. I think we have a lot to discuss." The woman stepped forward, hand extended. "Allow me to introduce myself. My name is Miranda."

About the Author

Marita Smith is a freelance editor and gourmet mushroom grower based on the South Coast of NSW. She has a PhB (Hons) in Science from the Australian National University and considers chemistry a language in its own right. She spent several years as a paleobiogeochemist, splitting her time between Australia and the Netherlands, before travelling through Europe to work on small farms. The first story she can remember writing involved being able to speak to her donkey, Mindy.

@ @maritasmithauthor

maritasmithauthor

www.maritasmithauthor.com

www.ingramcontent.com/pod-product-compliance
Lightning Source LLC
Chambersburg PA
CBHW050109120726
47904CB00004B/1278